THE HOUND AND THE FALCON TRILOGY

VOLUME II

THE GOLDEN HORN

THE HOUND AND THE FALCON

BY

JUDITH TARR

VOLUME I: THE ISLE OF GLASS

VOLUME II: THE GOLDEN HORN

VOLUME III: THE HOUNDS OF GOD (February 1986)

Published by Bluejay Books

THE HOUND AND THE FALCON TRILOGY

VOLUME II

THE GOLDEN HORN

By

JUDITH TARR

A BLUEJAY INTERNATIONAL EDITION

A Bluejay Book, published by arrangement with the Author.

Book design by Joann Hill

Manufactured in the United States of America

First Bluejay Printing: August 1985

Library of Congress Cataloging in Publication Data

Tarr, Judith.
The golden horn.

(The Hound and the falcon trilogy ; v. 2)
I. Title. II. Series: Tarr, Judith. Hound and the falcon trilogy ; v. 2.
PS3570.A655G64 1985 813'.54 85-15741
ISBN 0-312-94190-0

For my parents

O City, City, jewel of all cities, famed in tales throughout the world, leader of faith, guide of orthodoxy, protector of learning, abode of all good! Thou hast drunk to the dregs the cup of the anger of the Lord, and hast been visited with fire fiercer than that which in ancient days descended upon the Five Cities. . . .

—Nicetas Choniates

. . . And therefore I have sailed the seas and come
To the holy city of Byzantium.

—W. B. Yeats

1

Rain and sun and thirty years' neglect had faded the tiles of the courtyard and softened the curves of the marble dolphin in the center. But the fountain played still, though half choked with weeds and leaves and verdigris. The pilgrim sat on its rim, letting her veil fall, here where there was none but her companion to see her face. She was very pale, her gold-bronze eyes enormous, staring at the fall of water without truly seeing it.

"Thea," the other said softly. When she did not respond, he knelt by her and took her hand. "Althea. Was it wise to come back?"

She blinked and shook herself. "What? Wise? That's a virtue neither of us has much of. Are you still determined to watch the Frankish armies overrun Byzantium?"

"Are you still determined to stay here and be reminded over and over again of what time can do to the rest of the world?"

"Aren't both our follies actually the same thing?"

He bowed his head. His hat's broad brim hid his face; she

took it off, uncovering his hair. It was thick and long and very pale, silver-gilt like the eyes he raised to her, just touched with gold. "Do you know," she said, "if I'd left here even a season later than I did, I would have been caught in the plague."

"Would it have made any difference?"

"Who knows?" She spoke easily, lightly, as if it did not matter. "I promised you a bath and a good supper and a soft bed, and the best company east of Anglia. Will you forgive me if all I can offer you is a roof over your head?"

"You know there's nothing to forgive."

"Such a good Christian Brother." She rose. "Shall we sample the hospitality of House Damaskenos?"

The fountain gave them water to bathe in, and Thea's wallet yielded an ample supper. They settled for the night in a wide cool room where the painted walls retained much of their splendor: a wild garden full of fierce golden beasts.

"I did that," Thea said, sitting in a corner, clasping her knees. "Miklos wanted lions, and I gave him lions, eight of them, one for each of his birthdays. He was delighted, though not everyone else was. Father used to test people here. He'd ask them what they thought of the painting, and if they said it was outrageous, he knew they were honest."

The other smiled. "Do you remember the lion of Saint Mark? Poor bedraggled creature, shut up in a cage for people to stare at. I like your lions better."

"They're not very good ones. I wasn't a very good painter. It was easier to become a lion, though it upset people if they caught me at it."

"Only upset them?"

Upon her mantle lay a great tawny lioness with Thea's eyes. He regarded her in neither surprise nor fear. And, as she returned to her own shape: "I'm of your own kind," he said. "And I know you."

"Do you?" asked Thea.

"I know you shouldn't stay here. Let's go to Constantinople. Now. Tonight."

"Why? The house is empty and so are our purses. We can

stay here for a while, rest, tell a white lie or two; and when we're well ready, go to the City in proper style."

"With nothing but bare floors to sleep on, and no bread but beggars' bread, and the chance of being stoned as witches."

"Food and furniture are easy enough to come by."

"And the other, Thea? What of that?"

She sat on her heels near him. "What of it? Are you afraid, little Brother?"

"Someone is bound to remember your face."

She shook her hair away from it. "And if someone does? Althea Damaskena ran away thirty years ago. She's an old woman now. And how old am I?"

"Ancient. Newborn." He leaned toward her, not quite touching her. "Thea, no good will come of it if we stay here. I know that."

"As you know you have to go to the City?"

He nodded.

"So," she said calmly, "you go and watch the spectacle. I'll stay and be one."

"I haven't been with you for so long to leave you now."

"I thought it was I who'd been with you through no choice of yours. Now you can be free. I'm back where I came from; you can go on with no one to threaten your holy purity. Think of it, Brother Alfred of Saint Ruan's Abbey. Or should I call you Abbot Alfred? You would have been that if the Brothers had had their way. Now you can go back to it."

"No." His voice was barely audible. "I asked for my vows to be dissolved, and they were. I'm neither monk nor priest nor abbot. I'm only Alf." He drew a breath. It helped the pain, a little. "I won't let you face this alone. You went to the stake for me; should I do any less?"

"Little Brother," she said, "I knew exactly what I was doing. And I had, and have, no scruples at all about using witchery. You do all you can to make yourself human. You won't even shape-change as I did to fly away from the fire."

"I can't."

"You could if you would. But it's too uncanny. Who ever

heard of a man, or even a saint, who could be any living thing he wanted to be?"

"That's not my gift. But I can do what a friend must do. A kinsman. A brother."

"You don't look anything like Miklos." She traced the shape of his face with a light finger and let it continue down his cheek to his jaw, along the line of his neck to his shoulder. "I wish Father could have met you. He admired genuine innocence. It was the last thing a merchant could want, he said, but it was the first requisite of a saint."

"A saint must also be human. Not—what I am. Whatever I am."

"Changeling. Enchanter. Elf-wight. Demon, daimon, one of the Jann. Pilgrim from Anglia, healer in the hospital of Saint Luke beside the Holy Sepulcher, traveler to the Queen of Cities. And a very handsome—young—man." Her arms circled his neck. "Do you love me, Alf?"

He was as stiff as a stone, and as still, but no stone had ever burned as he burned. "Yes," he answered, "I love you. As a sister."

"I've been that to you, haven't I? Once I started to care enough about you to respect your vows, even Brother Alfred, famous for his chastity, couldn't rebuke me. And I've held to it. Five years now, Alf. There are people who'd say I was lying if they knew how long I'd traveled with you, lusty wench that I am, and never came closer than you'd allow. And you with a face like an angel and a body to drive a woman mad."

Only her arms touched him, but he felt the rest of her as if she had pressed close. Her face, tilted upward, was painfully beautiful, her voice low and piercingly sweet. "Your vows are gone. No need now to be poor or chaste or obedient. You can be the man you were meant to be. Swift and strong and fair, and as alien to a monk's meekness as a hunting leopard." Her arms tightened. They were body to body now with only threadbare linen between; their hearts hammered just out of rhythm.

With a sound between a gasp and a sob, he broke free. His robe lay draped over a broken bench; he lifted it with shaking hands. Once it had been the habit of a monk of Saint Jerome. He drew it on with fumbling haste. It felt heavy, constricting, damp from its rough washing in the fountain.

Thea knelt where he had left her. There was no anger in her. Not yet. Only shock, and a deep, tearing pain.

In a low dead voice she said, "You poor, innocent, pious priest."

He said nothing.

She rose slowly. "Go to the City. Sing in the angels' choir in Hagia Sophia, and wait on emperors, and be as pure as your saintly heart desires. The wild witch-woman won't trouble you anymore."

"Thea—" he began, but she paid him no heed.

"She'll leave you alone. Her family is dead; she can run off again and find another victim. One who knows what a man is for."

"Althea." This time she did not silence him. He went on steadily, "You expected to find your kin alive and well and not much older than they were when you left them. You've found only an empty house and a market tale; and it's struck you at last what price we pay for what we are. Beauty and strength and great power; life without age or sickness or death. And with it the reckoning: to love what must die."

"Or what must not," she said through clenched teeth, "and what will not give love in return."

"You're bitter. The house you loved is empty. The humans you loved are dead."

"The man I loved is a preaching priest." Her eyes blazed upon him, green as a cat's. "If God is just, Brother Alfred of Saint Ruan's, He will damn every one of you who ever cursed the love He made for man and woman. That is the sin, little monk. That is the horror which feeds the fires of Hell."

"Is it love, Thea? Or is it grief and anger turned to desire?"

"If that were all it was, would I be flinging myself at you, knowing what you are?" She stopped and shook her head. "But no; you're used to that. Everyone stares, gasps, and falls at your feet. And you step over them in pious disdain and walk on undefiled. Saint Alfred of Ynys Witrin, saved from burning by an angel, rapt up to Heaven before the eyes of his King. Who was just as besotted with you as I am, and just as incapable of understanding why."

"You aren't—"

"Don't tell lies, little Brother. Just look at me. Once on a time I was the Lady Althea of the Court of Rhiyana, renowned for her beauty, her valor, and her pride, and proud not least of her strength of will. Nothing frightened me; I could laugh at Death himself if he came too close to me. As for priests with their lice-ridden robes and their shaven crowns, what were they? Mumbling fools, as lecherous as any under the cant and the chanting. Then I saw you. There you lay by the fire under the trees, with your vows upon you like chains of silk and steel. But under them, fire and magic, asleep but easy enough, thought I, to wake. *You* were never meant for a monk, you who could promise so much with a glance or a smile or a turn of your shoulder." She hunched her own, then flung them back. "The rest pretended to be chaste. There was no pretense in you. I learned it soon enough, but by then it was too late for me. I was bound. When I tried to escape, I couldn't. When you fled your vows and your strangeness, I followed. All the long way to Jerusalem, through all the places between. Leagues. Years. Now as a woman, now as a hound, now as a falcon—and never as your lover."

Mutely he reached for her with healing in his hands. She eluded him to stand with her back to the wall, the center of her pride of lions. "Oh, no, Alf. No witcheries. Only stand and tell me the truth. Do you love me?"

"As a sister," he answered again.

Her eyes were all green, her white teeth bared, her face more cat than woman. "Sister!" she spat. "I am no man's sister. I am no man's kin. They are all dead. *Dead!*"

Again he tried to touch her, to heal her. Claws raked his hand. He snatched it back. A cat crouched by the wall, ears flat to its head, tail lashing its sides. Its mind was a fierce cat-hiss. *I have no kin. I have no friend. I walk alone.*

"Thea." He was almost weeping. "Thea, beloved—"

Her tail stilled save for its restless tip. *Beloved?* She flexed her claws. *Your soul is a cold cloister full of chanting and incense. Love to you is but a word, a spell to keep the mad witch quiet. And mad I was to follow you so far for so little. That is ended. I encumber you no longer. I encumber no one. I love no one. I want no one.*

"Althea—"

She arched her back and spat and sprang up to the window ledge. The cat-shape blurred and melted; a falcon spread its wings, glaring at him with a mad golden eye. Even as he cried out, it took wing into the night.

2

The Lady Sophia Chrysolora yawned and wished that there were a better way for a lady to travel. This jolting carriage was worse than a ship in a storm, and hotter than a smithy in summer. Her maid dabbed at her brow with a scented cloth; she pushed it away irritably. Her mounted guards looked hot and discontented, but at least they had the wind on their faces.

She settled a little less uncomfortably on the cushions. So close to noon the road was less crowded than it had been earlier although thronged still, little disturbed it seemed by the invaders in the city across the Bosporus.

Once again she brought out her husband's letter, although she knew it by heart. The City was quiet, the children well; she was not to worry, she could remain in Nicaea until her mother was recovered, surely the Latins would be gone by then. Irene had written a poem in the pastoral mode, which was enclosed; Anna had had a touch of fever but was well again and teaching her pony to jump in the garden; and Nikki had outgrown another set of clothes. Sophia smiled at that last with a touch of sadness and let her veil fall a moment to fan her streaming face.

The walls and towers of Chalcedon had begun to rise before her. The countryside, never rich, now seemed more barren than ever, all dun and dust with no gentling touch of green. The Franks' mark, she thought darkly, straining to look ahead. The land's rising hid the sea and the City on the other side. The changes would be greater the closer she came to it, and in the City itself the greatest change of all. Latin barbarians would be swarming everywhere, with two new emperors on the throne and a wide swath of the City leveled by fire. Their own house was safe, Bardas had written, although others nearby had been all but destroyed.

She wished she had wings to fly to see, or at least that she could ride like one of the imperial messengers, racing swiftly into Constantinople. But she was a lady, and a lady sat in hard-won patience with her veil modestly concealing her face and her hands folded in her lap.

The mules slowed from a trot to a walk and then to a halt. A laden wagon had stopped short some distance ahead; the oxen would not advance for all the driver's whipping and cursing. Opposite them milled a mounted company, the riders struggling with their horses. There seemed to be a space between, filled with something terrible.

Without thinking Sophia gathered up her skirts and stepped down from the carriage. Her maid's protests passed unheard. She walked calmly past the startled faces of her guards, one or two of whom had the presence of mind to dismount and follow her, and threaded her way through a herd of sheep, milling and bleating, and a cluster of pilgrims doing much the same, and a group of mounted Turks who stared and murmured as she walked by. The curses were clear now, and inventive.

The wagon reeked of onions. She skirted it and paused. In the road lay the cause of it all: a huddled shape, no more than a bundle of rags. As she stared it stirred, resolving into a huddled form, a long narrow body in a pilgrim's mantle rent and torn and covered with dust. Ignoring the sudden silence as farmer and riders stopped to gape at her, she knelt beside the fallen man. Carefully she turned him onto his back.

She caught her breath. His face was horribly burned and blistered as if he had stood in a fire. Yet his brows and lashes remained intact, very white against the livid skin.

His lips moved. They were cracked and bleeding, his voice no more than a whisper, breathing words she could not understand. "Hush," she commanded him as if he had been one of her children. Her eyes flashed to the men on horseback. "You, sirs. Your water flasks, if you please."

She received them, and promptly. She poured a little into the pilgrim and soaked her veil to bathe the terrible face. In doing it she had to loosen his mantle; the skin under it was the whitest she had ever seen, and smooth, no old man's. Nor was there any age in the hands which tried to fend off her own: long hands, burned not as badly as his face but beginning to blister. One bore deep parallel scratches like the marks of claws.

He could not lie in the road in that merciless sun. She beckoned to the guards who had followed her; they raised him in spite of his feeble struggles. As she led them to the carriage, horses and oxen started forward docilely; the traffic of the empire began to flow again.

The keeper of the best inn in Chalcedon received the travelers with becoming courtesy and sent at once for a doctor. Servants, meanwhile, ministered to milady and her escort and most especially to her guest who had been taken ill upon the road; undressed him and bathed him in cool water from the well, and laid him in bed covered with a sheet. His face seemed all the more terrible against his white smooth body, that in his robe had looked light and slender, even frail. But under it he had proved panther-lean, smooth-muscled, surprisingly broad in the shoulder.

And very young. Little more than a boy, Sophia thought as she sat beside him waiting for the doctor. His hair, water-darkened, was not white as she had thought, but palest gold.

Yet he was no child. His hat lay in her lap, brushed clean; its band was a braid of palm fronds, mark of the greatest of all pilgrimages, the journey to Jerusalem. And she had seen a terrible thing when the servants lifted him. His back was a sight more tormented even than his face, a mass of ridged and twisted scars, white with age.

She laid his hat aside and took up his wallet. It was very worn, patched here and there, like all he owned. It held very little. No money, no food. A water flask, empty. A book as worn as the wallet but beautiful within, illuminated with gold and silver and myriad colors, written in Latin letters. A small wooden crucifix, exquisitely carved, the suffering Christ so real that he seemed almost to breathe. A heavy ring of silver and moonstone wrought in intricate fashion. And a folded parchment with seals which, with a belated stab of conscience, she did not pause to examine. That was all.

She folded each treasure away again. Penniless Latin pilgrims were common enough, and sun-sickness their eternal companion. But she had never seen one so young or so pale or so badly burned.

The doctor arrived as she sat wondering: a stately Arab, very grave and very learned, escorted by a boy with a box of medicines. He frowned when Sophia revealed her knowledge of the patient's condition, frowned more deeply when it became apparent that she knew neither his name nor his nation, and scowled blackly at the sufferer himself, who had begun to stir and murmur. Grimly he bent to his examination.

At length he straightened. His eyes were cold.

"Can anything be done?" Sophia asked of him.

"You may summon a priest."

Her breath caught. "He's dying?"

The man's thin lips tightened. "He will not die."

"Then why—"

"To be rid of him." He bowed stiffly, conveying with eloquence his opinion of a woman who traveled about without husband or kinsman to ward her, and who took up from the roadside such a creature as this. "By your leave, madam . . ."

"You do not have it!" She startled herself with her own sharpness. "This boy is ill. Can you treat him or can you not?"

She had angered him, but she had also touched his pride. "I can heal him. But I am bound only to the care of men. This—" he made a sign over the pilgrim, as if to avert some evil "—can better be dealt with by a man of God."

"I shall see to that. You," she said coldly, "may do your office."

For a moment she thought that he would leave. But he bowed even more stiffly than before, and did as she bade.

When he had gone, Sophia left her chair to stand over the pilgrim. His face was salved and lightly bandaged; his breathing seemed to have eased. He did not look evil.

She slipped the carven crucifix from his wallet and crossed herself with it. Half in apprehension, half in defiance, she laid it on his breast. After an interminable moment he stirred. His groping hand found the cross, closed over it. He sighed a little and lay still.

Sophia remained with him. They brought her supper there; she ate only enough to quiet hunger and set the rest aside.

Perhaps she dozed. She was stiff and her head ached, and something had changed. She glanced about, puzzled. It was dark, the lamps lit, but that was not the strangeness.

From amid the bandages his eyes watched her. Great calm eyes the color of silver-gilt.

She smiled. "Good evening," she said. "How do you feel?"

"Foolish." His Greek was accented but excellent. "You're most kind to me, my lady."

"Sophia Chrysolora."

"Alfred of Saint Ruan's in Anglia."

"You've come a long way, Alfred of—Saint Ruan's?"

"Alf." His eyes took in the room. "And this?"

"The Inn of Saint Christopher in Chalcedon."

"Ah." It was a sigh. "Then I'm deeply in your debt."

"It's nothing," she said. "I shouldn't be tiring you with talking."

He shook his head slightly. "I want to talk. I don't remember much. How did I come here?"

"I found you in the road." There was water in a jar by the bed; she supported his head and helped him to drink. "Are you hungry?"

"No. Thank you." He lay back. His hands explored the bandages, fumbling with them. Before she could stop him, he had them off.

It was not a pleasant sight. He must have seen it in her face, for his hand half lifted as if to cover it. But he did not complete the gesture. "The air will heal it," he said, "if you can bear to look."

"I can bear it. It's only . . . the doctor . . ."

"He knows his trade, I'm sure, and he concocts an excellent salve. But his wrappings will strangle me and do my skin no good at all."

She looked at him: the young man's body, the flayed mask, the bright eyes which seemed to know so much. Under the swollen and blistered skin, she thought his features might be very fine. "You know a little of healing?" she asked.

"A little," he admitted. "I worked in Saint Luke's hospital in Jerusalem."

"Then you know a good deal more than a little."

He shrugged, one-sided. "It didn't keep me from making a fool of myself." He inspected his hands, raw and red as they were, and on one palm the deep scratches. His eyes flinched; he closed them. Yet his words were quiet. "You must be very tired with caring for such a great idiot as I am, and you an utter stranger. Please don't let me keep you from your rest."

"I don't mind," she said. "I have a daughter who's not so very much younger than you. She'll be fourteen next month."

There was no way to read his face. "I'm . . . somewhat . . . older than that. Is she living in the City?"

"With the rest of my family. My husband would find you interesting; he's His Imperial Majesty's Overseer of the Hospitals."

"Is he a doctor?"

She smiled. "Bardas? No, only a bureaucrat. He sees to it that the doctors have places to work and people to work on and the wherewithal for both."

Was that an answering smile? "A most essential personage."

He did not seem weary, but she rose briskly, smoothing her skirts. "I've been keeping you awake. Would you sleep better if I left?"

"If I knew that you yourself would sleep."

This, she reflected as she left him, was a very pleasant young man. Clever certainly, and old for his years. But no demon's get. The doctor was a superstitious fool.

When she looked in later, he lay deep in sleep, his cross on the pillow next to his cheek. She withdrew softly and went to her own bed.

Sophia was up with the sun, but she found Alf awake before her. Up, in fact, and dressed in his rags that the servants had cleaned and mended as much as they might, and eating with good appetite. In the morning light his face seemed much better, the swelling subsided, the blisters broken or fading. His smile was recognizable as such, as he rose and bowed and offered her his cup. "Will you eat with me? There's enough for two."

For a moment she could do no more than stare. At last she managed a smile and sat where she had sat in the night. "You seem to have mended very quickly," she said.

He paused in filling a plate for her. "Sometimes a hurt can look worse than it is. And you cared for me well and promptly. So you see, I've learned a much-needed lesson and am only a little the worse for it."

"A lesson?"

"About walking unprotected in the sun. About Greek charity. And," he added, setting the plate before her and lowering his eyes, "about my own vanity. If my face were my fortune, I'd have lost it yesterday."

"You'll get it back," she assured him.

His smile turned wry, but he only said, "Please eat. I've had all I need."

She discovered that she was hungry. Between bites she said, "I've arranged for you to stay here until you've recovered. The innkeeper has orders not to let you go without a doctor's approval, and to tend you like a prince."

He seemed taken aback. "Lady . . . you're most generous. But I can't accept so great a gift."

She waved that away. "Call it my debt to God and man."

"You've paid that in full already." He stood close to her, so that she had to tilt her head back to see his face. As if he sensed her discomfort, he dropped to one knee, setting his head lower than hers. "My lady, I'm most grateful for what you've done. I'll pray for you if you'll accept the prayers of a Latin heretic. But I can't take your gift."

She looked hard at him. He moved with striking grace, but he was not quite steady; his breath came a shade too rapidly. And there was his face. "You're not as well as you pretend."

"I'm well enough to travel."

"I don't think so." She regarded him sternly. "You were dangerously ill when I found you. You're shaking now though you think you can hide it. Go back to bed."

He sat on his heels. "I'm sorry, my lady. I can't."

If he had been one of her offspring, she would have fetched him a sharp slap to teach him sense. "You are a stubborn boy. Must I call my men to put you to bed by force?"

"It wouldn't be very wise," he said.

"Arrogant too."

His head bowed. "I'm sorry. But I have to go to the City."

"Why? Are you one of the Crusaders?"

"God forbid!" His vehemence startled her; he went on more quietly, "I'm as filthy a Latin as any. But not . . . of that kind. No; I want to see the City and learn from its wise men and worship in its holy places. While there is time. There's so little left. So very little."

She shivered though the morning was already hot. His eyes were wide and luminous, the color of water poured out in the sun, his voice soft and rather sad. "Understand," he said. "Those are not monsters camped across the Horn, but men like any others. Most of them think they've only paused on their way to free the Holy Sepulcher. They can't see what must happen now they've come so far into such hostile country, led on by a foolish prince's promises. Both greed and honor will have their due. And then—" He stopped. Perhaps, at last, he had seen her fear.

"And then?" she asked through a dry throat.

He turned away, fists clenched at his sides. "Nothing. Nothing. I've been listening to too many doomsayers."

Her voice came hard and harsh. "You *are* mad. And you're coming with me. We'll be sailing well before noon; we'll be sheltered from the sun; and you can rest a little. And when we come to the City—have you a place to stay?"

"I'll find one."

"The lilies of the field . . ." she murmured. "You need a keeper, do you know that? You'll stay with us."

He faced her. "What will people say?"

"That I'm as much a fool as ever."

"And your husband?"

"Precisely the same."

"But I can't—"

"Do you object to the hospitality of the perfidious Greeks?"

She was half jesting. But only half. He spread his hands. "I could be a thief, or—or a murderer. I could slay you all in your beds and make off with everything you own."

"I'll take my chances."

"Oh, Lady!" He seemed caught between laughter and tears. "The doctor was right, you know. You'd do well to be rid of me."

"Are you a demon?"

He shook his head. "But—"

"So," Sophia said brusquely. "I've things to see to. I'll send for you when it's time to leave."

3

The sun danced and blazed upon the blue waters of the Bosporus; a brisk wind filled the sail, lightening the oarsmen's work, carrying the barge toward the Golden Horn. Under a striped canopy on the deck the passengers sat at their ease, even the guards relaxed in their vigilance.

Alf had been docile enough when they left Chalcedon, lying quietly on the pallet Sophia had ordered spread for him in the deepest shade. But as they drew nearer to the City he grew restless, until at last he rose and settled his hat firmly upon his head and stood like a hound at gaze, his face toward the wonder across the water. Slowly, as if drawn by the hand, he moved to the rail. He stood full in the sun, though with his back to it.

Sophia sighed and came to his side. "Don't you think—" she began.

He seemed not to have heard. "Look," he said, his voice soft with wonder. *"Look!"*

All the splendor of Byzantium spread before them: the long stretch of the sea walls set with towers, guarding the Queen of

Cities; and within their compass rank on rank of roofs and domes and pinnacles. Gold glittered upon them, crosses bristled atop them, greenery cooled the spaces between, rising up and up to the summit of the promontory that was Constantinople. There on its prow shone the dome of Hagia Sophia with its lesser domes about it like planets about the moon, rising above the gardens of the Acropolis, crowning the Sacred Palace with all its satellites.

"The walls of Paris on the banks of the Seine," Alf murmured. "The citadel of Saint Mark on the breast of the sea; Rome herself in her crumbling splendor; Alexander's city at the mouth of the Nile; Cairo of the Saracens; Jerusalem, Damascus, Ephesus; Antioch and holy Nicaea: I've seen them all. But never—never in all my wanderings—never such a wonder as this."

Yet it was a wonder touched with death. The ship had turned now, sailing past the Mangana, striking for the narrow mouth of the Horn. A city spread over its farther shore, once rich, now much battered, guarded by a charred and broken tower.

"Galata," the ship's captain said, coming up beside them. "All that shore is infested with Franks, though they've camped farther up in the fields beyond the wall. Most of the ships you see there are theirs."

Sophia's hands clenched on the rail.

The captain spat. "They broke the chain. Clear across the Horn it went, from Galata to Acropolis Point, thick as a man's arm and strong enough to hold back a fleet. But they broke it. Hacked at the end on Galata shore and sent their biggest war galley against the middle with wind and oar to drive her, and snapped it like a rotten string."

"Couldn't our own fleet do anything?" demanded Sophia.

The man laughed, a harsh bark. "Our Emperor that was, bless his sacred head, called up the fleet, sure enough. Only trouble was, there wasn't any. A couple of barnacle-ridden scows was all he had. The rest of it was in the Lord Admiral's pocket. The cursed Franks sailed right over them."

"And then?" she asked. "What then?"

"Well," said the captain, "then everybody decided to do some fighting. The Frankish horseboys headed northward to the bridge past Blachernae. Saint Mark's lads took the sea side. Between them they flattened a good part of the palace up there before the real fight began. The Franks got a drubbing, but the traders got the Petrion and set it afire. Burned down everything from Blachernae hill to Euergetes' cloister, and as deep in as the Deuteron on the other side of the Middle Way."

"What of our people? Where were they?"

He shrugged. "They fought. Drove off the Franks, thanks mainly to the Varangians. But the Emperor turned tail and bolted. The mob dragged old Isaac Angelos out of his hole and put the crown back on his head, and the Franks brought in the young pup Alexios and crowned *him,* and now there's two Emperors, father and son, as pretty as you please, with the Franks pulling the boy's puppet-strings and the old man roaming about looking for his poor lost eyes."

"If I had been Emperor," Sophia said fiercely, "this would never have happened. The shame of it! All the power of the empire laid low by a mere handful."

The captain shrugged again. "It's fate, some people say. Fate and sheer gall. The traders' leader, what do they call him, the Doge; he's ninety-five if he's a day, blind as a bat, and there he was in the lead ship, giving his men what for when they wouldn't let him off first. They sat he fights better, blind as he is, than most young sprouts with two good eyes."

"He ought to." It was one of the passengers, a wine merchant from Chios. "I've heard that he masterminded the whole affair for revenge, because his city had been slighted when the Emperor was handing out favors."

"If that were all it was," the captain said, "he'd have stayed home and pulled strings. The way I've heard it, he was in the City twenty years ago when the mob burned down the Latin Quarter, and he was blinded then by the Emperor's orders. Now he's making us pay for it in every way he knows how."

"With Frankish help at least, that's certain. They're barbarian fools, but when they're up on those monstrous horses of theirs in all their armor, they're impossible to face. A troop of them, I heard once, could break down the walls of Babylon if they were minded to try."

"If the Emperor hadn't been a coward, they'd never have got into the City. They were in terror of Greek fire and of the Varangians' axes."

"But not in such terror that they turned and fled." Sophia glared at a galley moored among a hundred lesser vessels near the sands of Galata, its sides hung with bright shields, its lion banner snapping in the breeze; and turned to glare even more terribly at the walls which loomed out of the sea. "The City could have held forever if there had been men to hold her."

The men shifted uneasily. After a little the captain said, "You should have been a man, Lady."

"Such a man as sold my city to the Latins?" She tossed her head. "I'm better off as a woman. At least my sex can claim some excuse for cowardice." She stalked to her seat under the canopy, to cool slowly and to begin to regret her show of temper.

Alf remained by the rail, unconscious of aught but the sight before him. The wind had borne the barge into the teeming heart of the empire. Warehouses clustered all along the shore, thrusting wharves into the Golden Horn; steep slopes rose beyond to the white ridge of the Middle Way, clothed in roofs as a mountain is clothed in trees. Even from so far he could hear and smell the City: a ceaseless roar like the roar of the northern sea; a manifold reek of men and beasts, flowers, spices, salt brine and offal, with an undertone of smoke and blood. At the far end of the strait he could see the battered walls and beyond them great gaps in the roofs and towers, or charred remnants thrusting blackly toward the sky.

He hardly noticed when Sophia spoke to him until she tugged sharply at his sleeve. "Come. Up. Into my litter."

With an effort he brought himself into focus. A litter stood on the pier, its bearers waiting patiently. None of the many officials standing about, inspecting cargo, peering at lists, interrogating passengers, seemed at all interested in him, although one bowed to his companion. "Come," she repeated. "It's all been seen to. Get in."

He looked down at the woman. She was small even for an easterner; her head came barely to his shoulder. "I'll walk," he said.

"You'll do no such thing. Get in."

"But—"

"Get in!"

She was small, but she had a giant's strength of will. He smiled his wry smile, bowed and obeyed. She settled opposite him. With a smooth concerted motion the bearers raised the litter to their shoulders and paced forward. The escort fell into place about it with Sophia's maid trudging sullenly behind.

The house of Bardas Akestas stood at the higher end of a narrow twisting street in the shadow of the Church of the Holy Apostles, a bleak forbidding wall broken only by a grating or two and a gate of gilded iron. Even as the bearers paused before it, the gate burst open, releasing a flood of people.

There were, Alf realized afterward, less than half a dozen in all: three children of various sizes and sexes, an elderly porter, and a mountainous woman with a voice as deep as a man's. They overwhelmed the arrivals with shouts and cries, sweeping them into a sunlit courtyard. The light was dazzling after the high-walled dimness of the street, the children's joy dizzyingly loud. Alf made himself invisible in his corner of the litter and waited for his head to stop reeling.

"Come now," a new voice said over the uproar, deep and quiet. "What is all this?"

At once there was silence. The speaker came forward, a short broad man in a gray gown. The servants stepped back; the children leaped to attention. Sophia stepped from the litter, smoothed her skirts, and said, "Good day, Bardas."

"Sophia." He was as unruffled as she. "How was your journey?"

"Bearable," she replied.

The smaller of the two girl-children wriggled with impatience. "Father," she burst out at last. "Mother's home. *Mother's home!*"

Sophia swayed under a new assault. Over the children's heads she smiled at her husband; he nodded back briskly, but there was a smile in his eyes.

The elder girl had greeted her mother with a warm embrace, but dignity forbade her to join in the others' exuberance. While Nikki clung tightly to his mother's skirts and Anna babbled whole months' worth of happenings in one breathless rush, she stood aloof, trying to imitate her father's lofty calm. Her eyes were taking it all in, litter, bearers, and escort; the servants coming from everywhere to greet their mistress; plump Katya the maid deep in colloquy with the towering nurse; and if that was not she sitting in the litter, then—

"Mother," she said suddenly, "who is this?"

Sophia nodded in response to Anna's flood of news, lifted Nikki in her arms, and turned toward the litter. Its occupant emerged slowly and somewhat unsteadily: a tall thin figure in pilgrim's dress, with a terribly ravaged face and clear pale eyes gazing out of it. Irene forgot her dignity and loosed a little shriek; Nikki hid his face in his mother's shoulder.

"My guest," said Sophia. "Alfred of Saint Ruan's in Anglia, who has come up from Jerusalem to see our City."

They all stared, save Bardas who bowed and said, "Be welcome to House Akestas."

Alf returned the bow with grace and precision; straightened and swayed. Several of the servants sprang to his aid. Gently but firmly they bore him into the cool shade of the house.

4

Anna opened the door as quietly as she could and peered around it. The room was dim and cool and smelled of the roses that grew up over the window from the garden outside. There was no one there except the stranger in the bed.

He seemed to be asleep. She edged into the room, her bare feet silent on the carpet that had come from Persia, and tiptoed to the bed. Her heart was hammering. But curiosity was stronger than fear, even fear of her father's reprimand.

She looked at the pilgrim's face. It glistened with the salve the servants had spread on it over a patchwork of purple and scarlet.

His eyes opened in the midst of it and stared at her. She almost turned and ran. But they were very quiet eyes, and very kind, and that was a smile on the blistered and bleeding lips. She winced to see it. "Does it hurt?" she asked.

"No more than it ought."

She liked his voice. It made her think of one of the bells in church, the deep clear one that rang on holy days. "Then it must hurt a great deal," she said, "because it looks horrible."

"It will heal." He sat up. He was wearing a linen tunic; it was too wide, a little in the shoulders, much more in the middle. "I'm glad you came to visit me. I'm not nearly as ill as everyone seems to think."

His eyes invited her; she perched on the edge of the bed. "I'm not supposed to be here. I just wanted to look at you without everybody pushing and shoving."

"Why?" he asked.

She shrugged and looked at her feet. "I don't know. I guess because I've never seen a Latin up close before."

"Do I disappoint you?"

"A little. You're so clean. And you speak Greek. And you're not wearing a mail-shirt. Don't you own one?"

He shook his head. "I'm only a poor pilgrim. Armor is for knights."

"You aren't a knight?"

"Oh, no. I was a monk before I was a pilgrim. Never a knight."

"Oh." She was disappointed. "You're hardly a barbarian at all."

He laughed. His laugh was even better than his voice, like a ripple of low notes on a harp. "But surely," he said, "I look like one."

"You won't when it heals. The statues on the Middle Way have noses just like yours. Are you handsome under the burns?"

He would not answer, except to shrug a little.

"Mother says you are. Irene wants you to be. Irene is thirteen and getting silly. She's always looking at this boy or that, and sighing, and quoting poetry."

"That seems silly to you?"

"Well, isn't it? She tells me to wait. Three more years and I'll know what she's feeling." She shuddered. "I hope not."

"Maybe you'll escape it. I did for a long time."

"Well. You're a man. Men are slower, Mother says." She

looked at him, narrowing her eyes until he blurred. "Do you quote poetry at girls?"

"Not . . . quite." He sighed. "I haven't got that far yet. Maybe I never will. It was only one woman, you see. I lost her."

"Because you burned your face?"

"It's the other way about. She went away, and I stopped caring what happened to me."

"Irene should hear you. She'd write a poem." Anna brought her eyes back into focus. He had stood up and gone to the window. His tunic was too short as well as too wide. It showed a great deal of him; she observed it with interest. "Why did the woman go away?"

He spoke mostly to the roses and partly to her. "She'd just learned that all her kin were dead. I couldn't comfort her as . . . as she wanted. We quarreled. She left. I left soon after. That was all. Life is like that. Love is like that, I suppose."

"I wouldn't know," she said. "But I'm sorry she left."

"Thank you," he said, turning back. He had plucked a rose; he gave it to her. She buried her nose in it.

When she looked up, Nikki was standing just inside the door with his thumb in his mouth and his big eyes fixed on Alf.

Alf stood very still. Anna opened her mouth to say something, and shut it again. Nikki hesitated. After a long while he left his place by the door and inched toward Alf, sidling, stopping, never taking his eyes from the other's face.

Very slowly Alf sank to one knee. Nikki stopped as if about to bolt; Alf was still; he edged forward again. Alf hardly breathed. Once more Nikki stopped. His hand crept out. It halted just short of Alf's face. Drew back a little. Darted out, a quick, frightened touch. It must have hurt; Alf's eyes winced. But he did not flinch away, even by a hairsbreadth.

More boldly now, Nikki explored him with hands and eyes, nose and tongue. He knelt patiently even when Nikki pulled his hair. He did not try to say anything, except with his eyes.

Suddenly Nikki froze. His eyes were wide, his mouth open slightly. Alf had not moved. Nikki made a small hoarse sound.

All at once he flung himself at Alf, clinging as he had clung to Sophia. Alf held him and patted him and looked at Anna over the tousled dark head.

She stared back. "He likes you. He doesn't like anybody except Mother."

"And you," said Alf, "and Irene, and your father."

"Sometimes. He can't talk, you know, though he's almost five. It's because he can't hear; God closed his ears before he was born. We're all sinners, Uncle Demetrios says, and he's our punishment. I almost hit Uncle Demetrios once for saying that. Father gave me a tanning, but afterward I heard him say that I had more sense in one eyelash than Uncle Demetrios had in his whole head."

"I think I would agree." Alf sat on the floor with Nikki in his lap. "There's no sin in your brother. Only God's will, for His own reasons; who are we to ask what they are?"

"That's what Mother says."

"Your mother is a very wise woman."

"She has to live up to her name, doesn't she?"

"And you try to live up to her."

"I don't do very well. She's a great lady; I, says my nurse, am a perfect hellion. Someday I'd like to forget I'm a girl and travel about and see all the things I've heard about in tales."

"Maybe you will."

"You have, haven't you? Did you walk all the way from Anglia?"

"Sometimes I rode. Sometimes I went by sea."

"Where? When? What was it like? Tell me!"

Her eagerness made him smile. He sat on the bed; she sat beside him, and he began to talk. He was better than any storyteller in the bazaar; she forgot time and duties and even old terrors in listening to him.

The light in the window had shifted visibly westward when Alf paused. Anna waited for him to go on, but his eyes were fixed on the doorway.

She turned to look, and paled. A dreaded presence loomed

there. "Anna Chrysolora!" thundered her nurse. "What did your father tell you about intruding on our guest?"

Alf rose with Nikki in his arms. "But, madam, she was not—"

"You, my boy, were told to rest; and look at you." Corinna drew herself up to her full height. She was somewhat taller than he and thrice as broad. She planted a fist on each massive hip and glowered at them all. "Just look at you. What the master will say, I don't like to think. Anna, Nikephoros, come here." They came, even Nikki, dragging their feet. Alf stood alone and defenseless in his ill-fitting tunic.

"To bed with you," Corinna commanded. Her tone would have done justice to a sergeant-at-arms. He went meekly, to suffer the indignity of her tucking him firmly in. "There now. You stay put until you're given leave to get up. Do you understand?"

He nodded.

"Good." She swept up the children and bore them away, leaving him alone, half stunned, and beginning to shake with uncontrollable mirth.

5

The dome of Holy Wisdom hung weightless in the air, held to earth by columns of light. Beneath the dome and among the pillars swirled a sea of people, overlaid with a manifold mist of incense, perfume, and humanity, eddying here and there as a priest or a potentate swept by.

At this hour between services, most of those in Hagia Sophia were pilgrims and sightseers. Hawkers of relics moved brazenly among them, offering for sale splinters of the True Cross, threads from the Virgin's robe, and bits of bone and hair from the bodies of innumerable saints. The few Latins in the throng were fair prey for these, wide-eyed barbarians that they were, and ignorant of Greek besides.

One walked alone, a clear target: a burly young man, cleaner and better kempt than most, gazing about with a child's pure wonder. Under the great dome where Christ the King sat on his throne, he stood with his head thrown back in rapture.

"Twigs from Saint Bacchus' vine, Saint Andrew's fingernails, a lock of the Magdalen's hair—cheap, holy Father, cheap at the price!"

The man was like a buzzing fly, barely noticed at first but maddening in his persistence. His victim tumbled headlong from heaven into the world's mire, and crouched there stunned.

"Relics, holy relics, more precious than gold. Filings from Saint Peter's chains—a chip from Simon Stylites' column—"

The lion in repose is a great, slow-seeming, indolent beast. But aroused, he is terrible. The young Latin woke all at once to a roar of Greek, both fluent and scathing.

When his tormentor had fled, taking his wares and his ragged *langue d'oeil*, the young man stood a moment shaking with fury. Slowly his tension eased. His face regained its amiable, slightly foolish expression; he sighed and shrugged. The house of light had turned to mere stone, and no force of will could change it back again.

That was the way of the world. And since heaven was denied him, he focused upon earth: the ebb and flow of people through the wide space, the flow of light and line about and above them. He began to walk slowly, aimlessly, as a sightseer will. His size won him easy passage; his race and his priestly tonsure won him hard looks and hostile gestures and once a muttered curse.

Beneath one of the four lesser domes, under a haloed angel, he paused again. These easterners were small people; he, tall even for a Norman, could see easily over their heads. But not far from him stood a Greek quite as tall as himself though considerably less broad. He could see no face, only a long body robed in silver-gray, and a gray hat beneath which he glimpsed long white-fair hair.

The Greek shifted slightly, tilting his head back as if to gaze at the ornamented ceiling. Even from behind he seemed rapt yet not solemn, glowing with awe and wonder and heartfelt delight.

The watcher drew a slow breath. That turn of the head—that lift of the shoulder—surely he was dreaming or wishing, as he had dreamed and wished for so long, and seen what he longed to see in every tall pale stranger. And yet—

"Alf?" he wondered aloud. "Brother Alfred?"

The other turned with swift, feline grace. A fair strange face, a flash of silver eyes, a sudden brilliant smile. "Jehan de Sevigny!" Even the voice was the same, and the touch, the hands much stronger than they looked, holding him fast.

He knew he was grinning like an idiot; paradoxically, his eyes had blurred with tears. "Brother Alf. I never thought—how did you—I thought you were in Jerusalem!"

"I was." Alf drew him away from the jostling crowd into the quiet of a side chapel. Jehan's eyes cleared; he looked hard, drinking him in, incredulous still. But—"God in heaven! what ever did you do to your face?"

Alf raised a hand to it. "I did battle with the sun," he replied, "and he won."

"I'll wager he did." Jehan scowled formidably at his old friend and teacher. "Have you been in agony ever since you left Anglia?"

"Only this once," Alf said.

"But—"

"I have my defenses, as you well know. A few days ago I forgot them. Foolish, and dangerous besides, but in the end it led to good fortune. I'm a guest now in the City, and I'm most well tended."

"You look it," Jehan admitted. "Except for your face."

"Another day or two and you'd never have noticed anything at all."

"Oh, I would have." Jehan took him in again and felt his grin return, wider than ever. "Brother Alf. Brother Alf. It's so good to see you!"

"And you." Alf measured him with an admiring eye. "You've grown."

"I'm as tall as you now."

"But wide enough for three of me. I see they knighted you."

"Last year. Bishop Aylmer did it before I left for the Crusade. He made me a priest, too. Might as well get it all done at once, he said."

Alf smiled, remembering the dark grim-faced bishop who

had accepted an elf-priest with no reservations at all. "Is he well?"

"Well enough, though he's gone a bit gray. Grief, I think. We were with my lord Richard when he died." Jehan spoke quietly, but his eyes were dark with old sorrow. "Magnificent fool that he was, to take an arrow in the vitals fighting for a treasure that wasn't there. As soon as he realized that he wasn't going to get up from his bed, he told us to stay well out of brother John's way and sent us to Rome to bring Anglia's greetings to the new Pope. We've been serving Innocent ever since. A great man, that. Young too, for a Pope, and a bit more of a politician than a priest ought to be. Though I should talk, when I've been squire to Anglia's infamous Chancellor."

"Infamous only in the new King's eyes. Is it true that John has weeded out all of Richard's old friends?"

"Most of them. The last I heard, Father was in Rhiyana visiting Mother's family. Purely for courtesy, you understand. But it's been a long visit. Years long."

"Like yours in Rome."

Jehan nodded. "We were in Rhiyana ourselves for a while. The King sent you his love. Now how did he know I'd be seeing you?"

"Witchery, of course."

"Of course," Jehan said with a crooked smile. "His court is even more wonderful than legend makes it. All those Fair Folk . . . there's magic everywhere and a wonder at every turning, and Gwydion on his throne above it all, looking not a day over twenty-two. He told me he'd been cured of errantries, at least until he could think of a better one than peacemaking between Gwynedd and Anglia."

"And, I trust, until he was cured of the wounds he took on that venture."

"Well. His leg had knit by then and he'd lost his limp. His hand was taking longer. He could use it, but only just; it was stiff, and twisted a little. So, he'd say when people looked at it, at least he still had it, thanks to a witch-priest from Anglia; and he was learning to be a right-handed man. His brother would scowl whenever he said that, and thunder would rumble away somewhere. They're twins, you know, as like to look at as two peas. But Prince Aidan is as wild as his brother is quiet. Only Gwydion and that splendid Afreet princess Aidan brought out of Alamut can even begin to control him."

"Is he as wonderful a warrior as you thought he was?"

"Wonderful? More than wonderful! I followed him about like an overgrown pup; he condescended to teach me a little now and then. I've never seen a better swordsman. But do you know what he said? He was nothing; I should have seen his brother. Imagine; modesty, in the Flame-bearer."

Alf smiled.

Jehan smote his hands together. "What are we doing, talking about somebody you don't even know? Tell me about yourself!"

"Tell me first how you came to be here."

"They were preaching a Crusade; my head was full of grand ideas; I begged and I threatened, and Bishop Aylmer sent me to the Pope, and the Pope let me go with his legate." Jehan paused for breath. "Now, Brother Alf, stop evading and tell me. Why did you come here? How did you manage to get yourself up as a Greek gentleman? Where's Thea?"

"I came to see the City," Alf answered. "I'm dressed as a Greek because it was a Greek who took me in after my clash with the sun, and the servants burned my old clothes. They weren't even fit for rags, it seemed, although they covered me well enough."

He was keeping a tight rein on his vanity, Jehan could see. But he knew how very well he looked. "And Thea? Is she here?"

"No," Alf said, "she isn't here."

Something in his voice brought Jehan about sharply. "What's wrong? She hasn't—she's not dead, is she?"

Alf laughed more in pain than in mirth. "Thea? Dear God, no! She was with me until a few days ago. She was the best of companions, too, whatever shape she chose. A hound most often. In Jerusalem when I worked in the hospital, she used to sit at my feet and laugh in her mind when people petted her and admired her beauty. Sometimes she'd put on a gown and be herself and walk about the city. She marveled at it, though she pretended to be cool and worldly-wise, that she was there in the holiest place in the world."

The other gripped his arm. "What happened? Where is she now?"

"I don't know. We . . . disagreed. She went away. I've searched, but I can't find her. She doesn't want me to."

Jehan was young and a priest, but he was neither a child nor an innocent; and he had been as close to Alf as a brother. He read the quiet voice and the expressionless face, yet he offered no pity. "She'll come back."

"Will she?" Alf asked, but calmly. "In some things we were never well matched. I only wish . . . I would be more at ease if I knew where she was."

"Is that what you've been telling yourself when you want to cry?"

"I never cry."

"You should. It would do you good."

Alf shook his head slightly. "Come, explore the City with me. And after, if there's time, you can meet my hosts." His smile was no more than half forced. "I wasn't even to leave my room for a day or two yet. But I escaped this morning and left a message to assure my benefactors that I hadn't abandoned them. Maybe, if I come back with a friend—a very old and very dear friend who also happens to be very large—they'll be inclined to forgive me."

"Will they welcome a Latin?"

"They'll be mildly disappointed. Like me, you know what hot water is for, and you speak Greek. And you aren't wearing your armor."

"My squire's cleaning it, poor lad. Should I go back and get it?"

Alf laughed and shook his head, and led the other away.

Jehan was not, after all, a disappointment. Pound for pound and inch for inch, he was as close a match for Corinna as any man could be; when he promised to show Anna his armor, she clapped her hands with delight. But she was far from content. She watched him warily all the while he set himself to charm the household. Nikki, she noticed with satisfaction, eyed him in deep distrust. But everyone else seemed completely smitten.

"He's not at all handsome," Irene whispered to her, "but he has beautiful eyes. I love blue eyes. And his voice. I wonder if he can sing?"

Anna glared at her, but she was too far gone to notice. Could no one even see? He was sitting side by side with Alf. Every now and then he touched his friend lightly, familiarly; or Alf would lay an arm about his shoulders, holding him in a brief half-embrace. They were like brothers long parted, not quite believing yet that they had met again.

Her throat felt tight. This was a man from Alf's own country. He talked about Anglia, and about a king named Richard whom people called Lionheart and whom they both had loved; he talked about Rome and Saint Mark's citadel and the Latin princes camped across the Horn; and when he smiled, Alf would smile back, as proud as a cat with its lone kitten. Then, when Jehan had begun to think of leaving, he said it. "Alf, why don't you come with me? There's always a place among us for a good man."

"What would I do?" Alf asked, not in protest but as if he truly wanted to know. "I'm neither knight nor priest."

"You've been a clerk and a healer and a king's squire. Any of those, even the last, we've dire need of. And . . ." Jehan hesitated, suddenly shy. "I . . . I'd like it very much if you could be with me."

Anna held her breath. Irene, she noticed, had caught on at last; she was looking stricken. Mother looked merely interested, watching their faces as they talked.

Alf was tempted. She could see it. He wanted to see his own people again and to live with his friend.

"I'll come," he said. Jehan began to grin; Anna gathered to fling herself at one of them, she was not sure which. But Alf was not done. "I'll come," he repeated, "to visit you. For a little while. But not today I'm in trouble enough as it is for being out when I should have been in bed."

Jehan's face fell. Anna hurtled into Alf's lap, though Nikki was there already, and hugged the breath out of him. He smiled. "You see why I have to stay."

Slowly Jehan nodded, battling a sudden, fierce, and irrational jealousy. "I see," he said a shade coldly. With an effort he returned Alf's smile. "I'm singing Mass in camp on the Sabbath. Will you come and hear me?"

"Gladly," Alf answered. Jehan had risen from his seat; he rose likewise, setting Anna on her feet. But Nikki's arms had locked about his neck. He was still so the last Jehan saw of him, standing in the gateway with the dark-eyed child in his arms and the rest of the household a blur behind.

6

"Now, mind you," Bardas said as the litter bore the two of them through the crowds of the Middle Way, "Master Dionysios is the best physician in the City, and he knows it. He'll give you this one day's trial; if you can satisfy him, he'll put you to work. It might be menial labor, boy, be warned of that. I'm only His Majesty's overseer, not Saint Luke himself, to tell Master Dionysios what to do with you once he has you."

Alf watched as a troop of Varangians swung past, fair-haired giants in scarlet and gold with great axes on their shoulders. One or two, younger than the rest, looked very much like Jehan. "I don't mind servants' work. I did it in Saint Ruan's and in Jerusalem."

"You'll do it for Dionysios. A rare thing, Dionysios: a doctor who can look after his own hospital. He works his people like slaves, from the brat who sweeps the kitchen all the way to the senior surgeon—and himself harder than any."

"I think I shall admire him."

"Or hate him," Bardas said.

* * *

Master Dionysios took Alf's measure with the air of an officer inspecting a raw recruit. "This," he snarled at Bardas, "is your prodigy of medical erudition?"

Bardas bore his wrath with unruffled calm. "This is Alfred."

Dionysios circled Alf slowly, lip curled. "You. Boy. What do you know?"

"Little," Alf answered, "but of that, enough."

The Master had come round to face Alf again. "So. You fancy yourself clever. Let me see your hands." He examined them, turning them in fastidious, surgeon's fingers. "Soft as a girl's. Have you been cut, boy?"

Alf's lips tightened. "No, sir," he replied levelly, "I have not."

"Pity. You'd please the women." Abruptly Dionysios turned his back on him. "Come with me.

"We tend anyone who can be treated," Dionysios said as they walked, "and some who can't, but who have nowhere else to die in peace. Poor, most of them. Filthy. Are you afraid of dirt, boy?"

Alf shook his head.

"Well then," the Master said, pausing in a doorway. In the room beyond, many ragged figures sat on benches against the wall or squatted on the floor. At the far end a man in healer's blue, aided by a student in brown, examined a particularly scabrous specimen. The air reeked of disease and of unwashed humanity.

Alf followed the other, picking his way among the waiting bodies. The eyes which watched him pass were bright and scornful or dull and hostile or, once, languidly wanton; hands plucked at his robe, feeling of its fine fabric, inching toward the purse at his belt.

The blue-clad physician did not pause as his Master approached, although the student looked up in apprehension. "Thomas," said Dionysios, "rest yourself. This young gentleman will finish for you."

It said much for Dionysios' discipline that the man stepped back at once, without protest, although he regarded Alf in open and cheerful curiosity. Alf took his place quietly, well aware of the eyes upon him. But he had stood so, been watched so, more often than he could remember; and the first time, when he was truly the boy he looked, Master Dionysios had been drowsing at his mother's breast. He drew a breath to steady himself, and bent to the task.

"Well?" Bardas asked as Alf settled in the litter.

Alf regarded him for a moment, hardly seeing him. "You weren't there?" His gaze cleared; he shook himself. "Of course. You had other things to do. Did I see you leave?"

"As I recall," said Bardas, "you were lancing a boil and arguing with Master Dionysios: Was it God's will for a healer to quiet pain with wine or poppy, rather than to let the patient bear it unaided?"

"We weren't arguing. We were considering possibilities." Alf lay back against the cushions. "I'm to come back tomorrow."

"So you satisfied him."

"Not really. My name, says he, will not do at all. Since the Greek of 'Alf' is 'Theo,' then Theo I shall be; half a Greek name is infinitely preferable to the whole of a Saxon one. Moreover, we disagree on several crucial points. Bleeding, for instance. It's useless, I think, and often dangerous. I'm an abomination, Master Dionysios has decided: a twofold heretic, religious and medical. But I know which end of a lancet is which, and I have light hands. He'll suffer me to keep you quiet."

Bardas folded his hands over his ample stomach and allowed himself a brief smile. "You'll do. I don't suppose he mentioned payment."

"Of course not. I'm to wear a blue gown. Do I have one?"

"You will. You'll also have a salary."

Alf's eyes widened in shock. "Money? For healing?"

"This is Constantinople, lad."

"But—"

Bardas' raised hand cut him off. "No, boy. No Western scruples. If Dionysios has taken you on, by law he has to pay you according to your rank. Master physician, I should think, since he wants you to wear blue. Students wear brown and pay him; assistants get servants' wages. In one stroke you've become a man of substance."

"I don't want to be—"

"Boy," said Bardas, "this isn't your monastery. You do your healing. I'll look after your money."

"You can keep it. I owe it to you for all you've done for me."

"I'll keep it. Until you need it."

Alf framed a further protest; paused; closed his mouth. They rode on in silence.

Anna and Nikki were at the gate with the air of people who had waited a very long while. Even before the litter had stopped, Nikki was in it, pummeling Alf with his fists, moaning in a strange strangled voice. His face was red and furious, wet with tears.

Alf let Nikki's anger run its course until he suffered Alf's touch and let himself be held, though struggling still, fierce in his wrath.

"He's been here all day," Anna was saying, "crying and yelling and hitting the gate. He hit Corinna when she tried to take him away. He hit me. He even hit Mother."

Nikki quieted slowly, enough to sit in Alf's lap, fists clenched on his knees. Alf took the small scarlet face in his hands, smoothing away the tears of rage. Very quietly he said, "I told you that I would come back. I will always come back. Always, Nikephoros."

Nikki's black eyes were angry still. He raised a fist as if to strike again.

Alf caught it and unfolded it. "I promise, Nikki."

For yet a while he clung to his outrage. But Alf smiled, and he plunged forward, burrowing into the limp and bloodstained robe.

There was a silence. Bardas cleared his throat. "Where's your mother, Anna?"

"In the garden," Anna replied, "with the lady who came a little while ago."

"A friend? Lady Phoebe? Aunt Theodora?"

"Oh, no. We've never met her before. She came to see Alf."

He froze in the act of rising; swayed under Nikki's weight; drew himself erect by force of will.

Anna babbled on. "Her name is Althea. She comes from Petreia. She's been to the West and to Jerusalem. Her tales are as good as Alf's. Better, because she puts him in them and doesn't try to make him look modest. Did you really save your Abbot's life, Alf? And kill a man with his own sword?"

All color had drained from his face. "Yes," he said in a harsher voice than they had ever heard from him, "I killed a man. In the chapel of my abbey. The Abbot died, but not before he'd sent me to Jerusalem."

"They call you a saint in Anglia, she said. Are you really—"

"Anna." Bardas spoke softly, but she stopped short. "Go and tell the ladies that we'll be with them shortly. Alf will bathe and change first."

Alf shook his head. "I'll go directly."

"Don't be a fool," Bardas said. "Put the boy down and let him walk like a man, and go to your bath."

In the coolest corner of the garden where an almond tree shaded a small stony waterfall, Bardas and the ladies had settled with sweets and wine. Alf came to them scrubbed clean, wearing his best coat over a tunic of fine linen no paler than his face.

Thea sat with her back to the tree trunk, demure in a plain gown, her pilgrim's mantle laid aside in the heat; she had braided her hair and coiled it about her head and covered it with a light veil. She looked very young.

As he approached, she rose with her own inimitable grace, smiling as if there had been no quarrel between them at all. "Little Brother! How well you look."

"And you." He took her hands like one in a dream. "I'm . . . very glad to see you."

"No more so than I. You've been ill, my lady tells me; and Jehan in the camp."

"You've seen him?"

"He told me where to find you. I'd meant to stay in Petreia, but there was nothing there for me after all except a ghost or two. So I came to the City. I met Jehan as he was coming back from here." *And spent the night with him,* she added in her mind. *Everyone was fiercely jealous. Such a lovely white hound, I was.*

Alf smiled without thinking, and remembered at last to let go her hands. Both Bardas and Sophia were drawing alarming conclusions. The blood rose to scald his cheeks; he sat down too quickly in the chair she had left, refusing to meet her bright relentless stare. She stood between him and the sun and said, "It's a fine haven you've come to, little Brother. I'm delighted to see you so well looked after."

"It's generally agreed that I need a keeper." The fire had fled as quickly as it came. He had her hand again, God help him, and her mockery upon him like a lash of cold rain. "Have you unveiled all my black past yet? Murder, sorcery, heresy, and plain lust—have I forgotten anything?"

"As a matter of fact you have. The worst of all: burying your brilliance in a monastery for longer than I care to think, and hiding it with humility forever after."

"A failing you certainly are free of."

She laughed. "Certainly! I know what you're worth. As does the heir of House Akestas. How is he now?"

Her concern was genuine, and it eased his tension. "He's asleep in my bed."

A good place to be. Mercifully she did not say it aloud. She sat at his feet; he looked down at the smooth bronze braids, knotted his hands in his lap and forced himself to be calm. This was her revenge, this utter ease with its implications that even Anna could read. But he would not make it any sweeter than he could help. He accepted the wine a servant offered, and sipped it, hardly tasting its spiced sweetness, listening to the flow of conversation and saying very little. It tormented him to have her here so close after what they both had said and done and thought. Yet when she glanced up at him, he found himself smiling like the veriest, most besotted of fools.

Far too soon she rose again, saying words that meant nothing but that she must go. "No, no," Sophia said, "there's no need. We have ample room, and a friend of Alfred's is more than welcome."

"Even when you know—" He had said that; he bit back the rest. They knew nothing that mattered. Yet they knew everything, down below reason where the great choices were made.

"Hospitality is sacred here," said Bardas. "You know that, Lady; you're one of us. Honor us by honoring it. Stay with us."

It would be best if they both went far away, from the Akestas and from each other. But when Thea nodded and bowed and acquiesced, his heart turned traitor and began to sing.

7

From the Latin shore Constantinople seemed vast beyond imagining, vast and marred.

"That's a good stretch of palace wall we've taken down," said Thibaut de Langliers, peering under his hand, "and a company of our men inside to keep an eye on the Emperors."

Jehan leaned back against the tent pole and sighed, replete with good solid fare after a Mass well sung. "I don't envy anyone who has to live in that wasps' nest."

Another of the young knights regarded him with surprise. "Why, they've been made very welcome. Fed well, too. Better than we, and we're faring like princes."

"Now we are. Wait till the crisis comes. Do you think we'll get what we've been promised? Supplies for the voyage to Jerusalem, and two hundred thousand marks in gold; ten thousand Greek troops for a year and five hundred more committed to the Holy Land for life, and the union of our churches besides. Will we get all that? Will the Devil turn Christian?"

"Provisions you will have," Alf said, "for a while. The rest is a fool's dream."

Even Jehan turned to stare at him. He had been all but voiceless throughout the Mass and the meal after, sitting in the shadow of the tent with Thea in hound-shape seeming to drowse at his feet. He met the stares with wide clear eyes, and toyed absently with Thea's ears. "A young pretender promised you the world to win back his empire. Now he has what he aimed for, and it's considerably less than he thought it was. He can feed you for a time, pay to keep your fleet, but no more. If I had taken the cross, and were wise enough, I'd take what he could give and leave before another week had passed."

"And what of honor?" demanded the youngest knight.

"Honor is not the same as wisdom."

The boy leaped to his feet. "Are you calling me a fool?"

Thea raised her head from her paws; Jehan braced himself for a battle. But Alf sat back unruffled. "Did I say anything of the sort? Come, Messire Aimery. Won't you concede that the wise course is not always the honorable one?"

"That's true enough," said Jehan a shade quickly. "Look at the Greeks. Any knight worth his spurs would settle his troubles the honorable way, in the lists; but a Greek will think and ponder and negotiate and intrigue, and get what he's after without a fight."

"Greeks and priests." Aimery had subsided into his seat again. "You excepted, of course."

"There are those who say I shouldn't exist: a priest who carries a sword. And uses it too."

"And what of Saint Michael?" Alf asked.

"Well. He's an archangel."

"He does provide a precedent."

"That's our usual argument. But when God and knight's honor demand different things, it presents a dilemma."

Alf nodded slowly. "What does one do when God seems to be on both sides of the battle? When Christian attacks Christian and each wears the cross of the Crusade—what then?"

"One loses all one's illusions," Jehan answered him grimly. "We took Zara; have you heard that?"

"I've heard."

"They were Christians; they'd taken the cross. But they'd rebelled against Saint Mark, and it was part of our price of passage that we defend the Republic's interests. The Pope was livid. And yet he didn't make more than a token protest. I was appalled. How could all that was high and holy be so besmirched? Christians slaughtered Christians; Crusaders killed Crusaders—for what? Money and provisions to take the Holy Sepulcher. Would Christ want it to be saved by such horrors as we are?"

"Perhaps it's not to be saved by anyone." Alf examined his laced fingers, seeing a pattern there, clear for his reading. "I've had strange thoughts of late. What arrogant creatures men are, to presume that they know God's will. And priests are more arrogant than any, for they not only purport to know but presume to execute the commands of divine Providence. Yet, is it Providence or their own desires? If God places the Holy Land in the Saracens' hands, perhaps after all He wants it to be so?"

"That's heresy," Aimery muttered.

"It is; and I was a priest once. I'm no fit company for God's knights."

"Is that why you're not a priest now?"

Jehan drew a sharp breath. Alf smiled and shook his head. "No. I was raised in an abbey and took vows there. But I found that I couldn't be the sort of priest I wanted to be. I asked that my vows be dissolved. It was easy enough in the end. There's a law, you see, that a man raised by monks must not take full vows before his twenty-fifth year. I was much younger than that. So, a stroke of the papal pen, and suddenly I was a layman. My mind marked the occasion by conceiving half a dozen heresies."

"That's not so," Jehan said hotly, "and you know it. Here, finish off the wine and stop trying to frighten these poor boys."

"Oh, no," said a new voice, "I find him fascinating."

They started to their feet. The newcomer stood with hands on hips: a pleasant-faced young man in clothes as rich as a prince's. Although they were of Greek cut and fabric, from round-cut head to spurred heel he was indisputably a Latin. He regarded Alf with a steady brown stare, head cocked slightly to one side, lips quirked. "In dress a Greek; in accent a Latin; in name, if I'm not mistaken, a Saxon. You're an interesting man, Master Alfred."

The young knights had gone pale. Even Jehan seemed nonplussed. But Alf returned the other's gaze with perfect calm. "It seems I'm known among the high ones, my lord."

"How not, when your priestly friend has described you so lovingly, and told us that you were to be honoring our camp with your presence? You have a clear eye for all our weaknesses."

"And for your strength."

"What may that be?"

"Courage," Alf answered, "to face so great a city with so few."

"Perhaps, after all, God is on our side."

"He may be. Who am I to say?"

The young lord smiled. "Who indeed? Who is anyone, when it comes to that? Come with me, wise master. There's a man I'd have you meet."

Alf bowed his head. As he followed the brown-eyed lord, Jehan fell in behind, a solid presence, and with him the quicksilver that was Thea. Her amusement danced in his brain. *Another conquest! And a lofty one too. There aren't many men who'd bandy words with Messire Henry of Flanders.*

I'm old in insolence, he responded coolly, without pausing in his stride.

In the center of the tent city stood a great pavilion, all imperial purple with the lion of Saint Mark worked upon it. Under its canopy in sweltering shade a number of men sat over wine. Yet Alf saw first not faces, but a cloud of clashing wills. Two men leaned toward one another, one young and one not so young; although they smiled, the tension between them was solid enough to touch.

"So, my lord Boniface," the younger man said, "you would ride away to Thrace with young Prince Popinjay and leave the City to its own devices."

The other's smile neither wavered nor softened. "Why not? Someone should be with him to pull his puppet-strings. Or are you unsure enough of our position here to be afraid to leave it?"

"I fear nothing at all. But I see an empire with its young emperor abroad doing battle with the usurper he cast down, and in the palace naught but an eyeless dodderer. A fruit ripe for our plucking."

"Might not the empire do the same with us?" asked the man who sat between them. He glowed darkly, dressed in the same imperial splendor as the pavilion; on his head was a crown, but it was fashioned of cloth and marked with a white cross. He was old, bent and shriveled with age, the skin deep-folded over the strong bones of his face. The eyes which burned under heavy brows burned upon nothingness, for he was blind. Yet when he spoke his voice was deep and firm, gathering all these proud rebellious lords into the palm of his hand.

Alf moved forward, caught by the brilliance of the soul which flamed behind the useless eyes. "A blind emperor," he said; "a blind Doge. But one is a dotard, and one is stronger than any paladin."

The black eyes flicked toward him; the crowned head cocked. "A stranger? Has a spy come to overhear our counsels?"

"A sage, Messer Enrico," Henry answered, "a pilgrim from Anglia who has settled among the Greeks. I found him corrupting our youth with the aid of my lord Cardinal's secretary."

The Doge beckoned. "Here, pilgrim. Come over where I can see you." His hard dry fingers explored Alf's face, swift and impersonal, a stranger's scrutiny. "A boy," the old man muttered, "and pretty as a girl. Yet, a sage, says milord Henry, who has a legion of faults, the worst of which is his inability to lie. Who can read me this riddle?"

Henry sat beside the young lord. So close, they were as like as brothers can be, though Count Baudouin frowned at this interruption and Henry smiled, saying, "What can be simpler?

In Anglia, prophecies come from the mouths of babes, and fatherless boys foretell the fates of kingdoms. This pilgrim has seen all our future, and sat in judgment upon us."

"And the verdict?"

Alf drew a breath. They watched him narrowly, all of them, the greater and the lesser, skeptical, credulous, annoyed, afraid. That was Jehan's fear for him, that he had betrayed all his secret.

But he had never had any fear to spare for princes, nor even for commoner kings crowned with linen. Calmly he said, "If you intend to fulfill your vow and take the Holy Sepulcher, you had best do it now, or none of you will ever see Jerusalem."

"Is it our death you foretell?"

"Yours," Alf answered, "or this city's."

"How do you know all this?"

"I use my eyes and my wits, and I listen to all the wind brings. I'm not as young as I look and sound, Messer Enrico Dandolo."

Suddenly someone laughed. Marquis Boniface grinned at Alf like an aging wolf, and smote his thigh. "Ha! At last! A match for our old fox. Tell me, sir oracle. Which sly Greek serpent has sent you to confound us?"

"None, my lord. I speak on my own authority, and perhaps on God's."

"The least and the greatest. You cover all eventualities."

"But of course, my lord. After all, I'm a scholar trained."

Baudouin glared at him. "This camp is infested with priests and spies. Will no one rid of us of this one?"

"No." Baudouin shut his mouth with a snap. The Doge went on unruffled, "No spy would come to us so openly, or led by your brother. A madman might; but a madman is seldom so logical. Sit down, sir pilgrim, and be wise for us. Wisdom is in short supply here."

Alf did not move to obey. "If it's wisdom you look for, my lord, I have little to offer. For you—" he bowed low to them all "—are lords of high degree, and I am but a commoner without name or lineage. Should I presume to counsel princes?"

The Doge's black eyes glittered. "Why not, if princes need good counsel? There's pride in your humility, pilgrim. Sit or stand, I hardly care which, but stay by me. I like the feel of you."

"And I detest it!" Baudouin burst out. "The rest of us can see what comes with it. If this isn't one of His Majesty's ball-less wonders, then I'm—"

"My lord," Alf said gently, "if you would be an emperor, you would learn well that no man holds a throne by setting all his allies at odds."

Baudouin sneered. "I suppose you know intimately how an emperor must act."

"I know what I see," Alf responded. A squire had set out a chair for him; he took it. Thea crouched at his feet. Jehan stood beside and a little behind him, as a guard will, his hands fisted at his belt close to the hilt of his sword.

The Doge smiled and raised a new-filled cup. "To wisdom," he said, "and to foresight." He drank deep.

After a moment Henry followed suit, and Boniface after him. But Baudouin glared and left his wine untouched, though Alf saluted him, smiling wholly without malice.

8

It was very late. The lamp burned low; Alf quenched the wavering flame and sat in the dark that for him was no more than a gray twilight. Beyond the rose-rimmed window the air was warm and close, windless, the stars half hidden in haze. A burning day, a steaming night, a white-hot day thereafter. That had been the pattern for days now.

He looked down at the book open in his lap, and up into the cat-flare of Thea's eyes. She eased the door shut behind her, smiling a little. "You couldn't sleep, either."

"Who can in this heat?"

"You, for instance, when you choose." She came closer. Life in House Akestas had taught her modesty of a sort; she wore a brief shift which left her arms and her long legs bare. Briefly he thought of Saint Ruan's far away in green Anglia, and of the monk who had lived long years there without ever thinking of a woman.

"You never had me to think of." She perched on the arm of

his chair and peered at the book. "What are you reading, little Brother? Theology? Philosophy? Stern moral strictures?"

Without his willing it, his hands moved to close the book. She caught them; he struggled briefly and fiercely. All at once he surrendered. She brandished her prize. "See now! What secret are you hiding?" She opened at random. Witch-light welled through her fingers; she read a few words, stopped and looked up. "Why, this is beautiful."

He sat perfectly still, face turned away from her.

She shook her head, incredulous. "Who would have thought that a monk could have taste? And such taste at that.

'Once, when the world was young,
Tantalus' daughter became a stone
upon a hill in Phrygia;
and the daughter of Pandion
touched the sky, winged as a swallow.
O that I were a mirror,
that you would look at me;
a tunic, that you would wear me,
water to bathe your body,
myrrh for your anointing.
Gladly would I be a cincture
for your breasts, a pearl
to glimmer at your throat,
a sandal for your slender foot,
if only you would tread on me.' "

She touched his cheek. It burned under her hand. "Would you really, Alf?"

He tossed back his hair so suddenly that she started. "No!" he snapped, more startling still in one so gentle. "It's only a book. Irene lent it to me."

"Did she?"

Her eyes were dancing. He stood and sought the window. It was no cooler there, nor had he escaped her. Although she remained where he had left her, her voice pursued him, as relentless as it was beautiful. "Irene is in love with you, little Brother."

He breathed deep. The scent of roses filled his brain. "What is there in this world, that even on the edge of ruin no one has any thought but that?"

"It's the Law," she answered him. " 'Go forth; be fruitful, and multiply.' "

"Even our kind?"

"Especially our kind. If there were any god but the One, and we could choose our own, it would surely be Aphrodite."

"You are an utter pagan."

She laughed; he knew without looking that she tossed her free hair. " 'Immortal Aphrodite of the elaborate throne, wile-weaving daughter of Zeus, I beseech thee' . . . tame for me this lovely boy, who looks on me by day with priestly disapproval and cools these torrid nights with Anakreon and Sappho and others no less sweet."

"The patron of this city," he said deliberately, "is the Blessed Virgin."

"She protects you a great deal better than she's protecting her city."

He turned to Thea then. He had won, for the moment; her eyes yielded although her smile had only begun to fade. "You see it too," he said.

She shivered. All mockery had left her. "I don't have your sight. But I feel it. Something is going to break, and soon."

"Very soon. Alexios is in Thrace with many of the Latins. But Baudouin is here as he wished to be, and the old Emperor is as feeble in mind as in body."

"Old!" She tried to laugh. "He's younger than either of us."

"Do years matter? 'Boy,' you call me, though I've lived longer than most men ever hope to."

"And 'dotard' is what Isaac is. Hopeless, my friends tell me. Completely out of his mind."

"Your friends?"

She twined a lock of hair around her finger and watched him sidelong. "My friends," she repeated. "I have a few, you know.

You're not the only one who goes out and about and explores the City."

"I never thought I was."

She smiled. Alf frowned. There was something suspicious in the way she looked at him, as if she treasured a secret she knew he would not approve of. The last time he had seen her so, she had been frequenting the harem of a Saracen emir.

"In Constantinople?" She laughed. "Hardly. My friends are good Christians. *Latin* Christians. Saxons."

"Saxons? Here?"

"In the palace, in the Varangian Guard."

For a long moment he stared at her, blank with shock. This was worse than the Emir's harem. Or the Lord Protector's kennel. Or the Prince's mews. Or—"How do they see you?" he demanded. "As a cat? As a hound? As a falcon?"

"Of course not. Beasts can't ask questions or make friends with guardsmen."

His breath hissed between his teeth. She was smiling, relaxed in his chair, leafing idly through Irene's book. No sheltered Eastern maiden, she, who had run off in youth with a Lombard prince and ridden to battle with the princes of Rhiyana and gone to the stake as a witch and a heretic. Yet—

"Guardsmen," he said. His voice sounded thin in his own ears, and cold. "Soldiers. If you have no care for your own honor, might you not at least consider that of your hosts? What would Bardas say, or Sophia, if they knew that their guest ran wild among the Varangians?"

Her eyes glittered, emeralds ringed with fire-gold. "Their *female* guest. Don't forget to add that. Their male guest, of course, is far too holy ever to exceed the bounds of sacred propriety."

"I am a fool and a coward, but I know what is fitting. Do you even put on armor and take up an axe? Or . . . is it . . ."

Anger flashed through her mockery. "Why not just say it, little Brother?"

It caught in his throat. But it was in his mind, clear to read.

She said it for him. "You think I've found a cure for my five years' sickness. A great tall Varangian with braids to his waist and arms I can hardly circle with my two hands, and a huge besom of a beard. Someone who'll tumble a yellow-eyed witch with no qualms at all, and laugh with her at the pallid little priest she's been breaking her heart over. A bull to make me forget my white cat from Anglia."

She was standing in front of him. Half of her was laughing; half of her trembled with anger. "You won't be rid of me so easily, Brother Alfred. Nor is my virtue as easy as that, whatever you may think. I can be a man's friend without leaping into his bed."

He flushed, but his voice by some miracle was steady. "You are beautiful. Any man would desire you. Even I, armored in my vows, have never been immune to you. Is it wise, Thea, to walk among men of war who can take by force whatever they wish for?"

She laughed aloud. "I should like to see them try!"

"And then they come to House Akestas and dispose of the witch's familiars."

She sobered abruptly. "No, Alf. That, they will never do. I'm wild and I'm wicked and maybe I'm a harlot, but I am not a traitor."

"Then you'll stop seeing the Varangians?"

"I never said that." She rose and tossed the book to him; he caught it without thinking. "You've done your duty, Father Confessor. I'll do as my conscience bids me. If that is to visit my friends and to look and listen and to catch what rumors I can, what right or power have you to prevent me?"

"I, none. Your conscience—"

"My conscience is my own, and I am my own woman. Whatever you may say."

"I never said otherwise."

"Didn't you?"

She had reached the door. It closed upon her before he could speak; her mind barriered against him with calm finality.

9

"Hell," said Jehan, "must be somewhat cooler than this."

Even in the depths of House Akestas, in high-ceiled dimness, the heat was like a living thing, bearing down with all its weight upon the gasping City, felling the old and the weak and rousing the minds of the strong to bitter rancor. Anna and Irene had already been sent away for quarreling; Nikki, forbidden to play with Jehan's sword, sulked in solitude.

Alf himself was pale and silent and alarmingly abstracted. He had held Jehan's surcoat for him after the other had shown off his panoply; he held it still, crumpled in his lap, entirely forgotten.

"Hell *is* cooler," Sophia said, watching as Jehan knelt on the tiles wrapping his mail-shirt carefully in oiled leather. It made a massive bundle with the chausses and the padded gambeson and the great flat-topped helm. "Especially," she went on, "since no one in Hades is condemned to wear armor. How do you stand it?"

He shrugged. "You get used to it. Though it's never pleasant, damnably heavy as it is, like to rust at a word." He sat on his heels, his task done. "Every time I set my squire to work cleaning any of it, he mutters about entering a cloister. Never mind, I tell him; a few more years and he can win his own spurs, and find some other poor victim to keep his hauberk clean."

"Is that why knighthood perpetuates itself?"

Jehan laughed. "Why else?"

Alf rose, trailing the surcoat, and wandered to the window. The others watched him in sudden stillness. He looked like a wild thing caged.

Sophia's glance crossed Jehan's. His lightness of mood had vanished; he frowned. "How long has he been like this?" he asked softly, though not too softly for Alf to hear if he chose.

She sighed a little. "He's been very quiet for a day or two. Since the rising in the Latin Quarter."

Jehan's frown deepened. "If you'll pardon my saying it, my lady, that was an ill thing."

"You need no pardon," she said. "It was worse than an ill thing. It was a mad thing. For our people to march on the merchants in their own places, burn their shops and houses to the ground, and kill any Latin they found . . . it was despicable."

"Could they help it, when it comes to that? It's hot; it's miserable; there's an invading army camped outside the walls. And no chance of relief from any of it."

"That doesn't excuse murder. Half the people killed were Pisans—Latins, to be sure, but they fought for us; if it hadn't been for them and for the Varangians, the City would have fallen long before it did."

"True," Jehan conceded. "But they were Latins, and they were a target when your people needed one. No; the ill I see is that all your loyal Latins have come over to us. You've lost one of the mainstays of your army."

"A fine strong empire this is," she said bitterly. "You must feel nothing but contempt for us."

"I?" Jehan shook his head. "I'm not that much of a fool. But I am afraid for you. There've been rumblings in the camp.

People are talking about revenge and about making the City pay for what it did to the Pisans."

"And well we ought to," she said. But she had gone cold beneath her veneer of courage.

Alf turned back to the room. Before Jehan could frame a response, he said, "The wind is blowing from the north."

"Ah, good!" she said with more enthusiasm than she felt. "That will cool us splendidly, and blow away any chance of plague."

He shook his head. "No. It's the worst thing anyone could wish for."

Sophia glanced at Jehan. He watched Alf with peculiar fixity; in his eyes was something very close to fear. "What is it?" he demanded. "What do you see?"

Alf shivered convulsively. Jehan's surcoat slipped from his hands to the floor. He stared at it as if he had never seen it before, and bent, lifting it, folding it with exaggerated care. When it was arranged to his satisfaction he laid it gently down upon a table, tracing with his finger the lion rampant that was for Sevigny, and the Chi-Rho which Bishop Aylmer had placed in its claws for the young knight who was also a priest. His eyes were enormous, all pupil; by some trick of the light it seemed to Sophia that they flared red.

He spoke to her and not to Jehan, with quiet intensity. "My lady, if you love your family, keep the children and the servants in the house. Let none of them go out for anything. And send for Bardas. Tell him a lie if you need to. But get him here and keep him here."

"What—" she began.

He cut her off. "See that you have water. All the water you can draw, in every vessel you can find. And food enough for a week at least. Get it now. Get it quickly."

It was madness, surely. Yet it made Sophia tremble. Jehan had risen, death-white under his tan; his sword was naked in his hand.

"No," Alf said to him, "no weapons. Go back to the camp, Jehan. Stay there. Promise me."

"Why? What's going to happen?"

"What you foresaw. But worse. Far worse." Alf looked from one to the other. "Why are you wasting time? Go on!"

He himself was at the door, moving with speed which startled Sophia. Even before Jehan could spring after him, he was gone.

She caught the priest's arm as he passed her. "Wait! Where are you going?"

Jehan stared down at her, eyes wild. "After him. My lady," he added after a moment.

"Is he mad?"

Obviously Jehan was burning to be gone; equally obviously he could think of no courteous way to escape her. "Mad?" he echoed her. "Alf?" He laughed with an edge of hysteria. "I suppose he is. Have you ever seen his back?"

She nodded, wincing involuntarily as she remembered it.

"He was supposed to be burned for a witch. They flogged him instead, as a penance. Then the people canonized him. He has his legend now in the north of Anglia, and even his feast day."

"What does that have to do with—"

"Nothing. But if he's mad, then so are half the saints on the calendar. And all the prophets."

Sophia could find no words at all. Even as she hunted for a response, the door flew open. It was not Alf returning to sanity, but her maid, breathless, disheveled, and scarlet-faced with heat and exertion. "My lady!" she gasped. "My lady! The City's on fire!"

There was something inevitable in it, like the climax of a tragedy. It surprised Sophia that she could think so clearly. She set the woman in a chair, fanned her and refreshed her with a sip or two of wine, and extracted the news from her bit by bit.

It was as Jehan had said. The Latins, incensed by the injury done to their countrymen in the City, had roused to revenge. A troop of them had come armed from the camp, their target the quarter given over to the Arab scholars and merchants. They had sworn to kill Saracens; Saracens, then, they would kill.

The battle had its center in the mosque, the heart of the abomination, a colony of Infidels suffered to live and worship as they pleased within a Christian city. Someone, whether Latin or Moslem or Greek—for Greeks had come to aid their neighbors against the invaders—had brought fire into the battle. By then the breeze which had come to break the terrible heat had grown to a brisk north wind; it fanned the flames despite all efforts to quench them.

"You know how narrow the streets are, my lady," said Katya, almost calm now. "And all the houses are of wood and half of them are falling down. They're burning like logs on a hearth."

Suddenly Sophia was very tired. The servants would be in an uproar; the children would be terrified. And Bardas—if he was in his chamber in the Prefecture, she could lure him home; if not . . .

The hiss of metal on metal brought her eyes to Jehan. He had sheathed his sword; his brows were knit. His face, pleasant and rather foolish in repose, was suddenly hard and stern. "My lady," he said, "you'd best do as Alf told you, and soon. I'm going after him."

"He told you to go back to camp."

"He should have known better, and he should never have left like that before he'd packed me off."

"You know where he's gone?"

"To the fire." Jehan took up the hooded mantle with which he had concealed his foreignness, and threw it on. "I'll come back for my things. Leading Alf, or carrying him."

10

The City was deceptively quiet, basking in the respite from the relentless heat. But beneath the surface, terror had begun to stir. Jehan won passage through the midday crowds with his size and his determination, searching with desperate hope for a familiar white-fair head.

He had hoped for it, but he did not credit his eyes when he saw it under the arch of a portico. For an instant he feared some calamity, illness or violence or perhaps true madness. But Alf met Jehan with clear eyes and a forbidding frown. "Why are you following me?"

"Why are you waiting for me?" Jehan countered.

Alf's frown darkened. "You're an utter fool." He gripped Jehan's arm with that startling strength of his and drew him forward. "Stay with me and keep your head covered."

They heard and scented it before they saw it, screams and cries and an acrid tang of smoke that caught at the throat. As they rounded a corner, fierce heat struck them like a blow.

Flames leaped to the sky, dimmed and thinned by the sun's brightness.

All the strong current of the crowd rushed away from the fire, carrying everything in its wake. Alf breasted it like a swimmer, battling it, borne backward one for every two steps he advanced. Once he stopped; Jehan braced himself, expecting them both to be hurled down and trampled. Yet, although the panic-scrambling was as wild as ever, Alf made his way forward again all but unimpeded.

The roaring in their ears, Jehan realized, was not simply the clamor of many voices raised in terror, but the fire itself as it devoured everything in its path. He saw it leap from roof to roof across the narrow street, take hold upon dry timbers and flare upward like a torch. Black demon-figures leaped and danced within it, casting themselves forth, shrieking as they fell.

Here and there amid the inferno were islands: lines of people struggling to hold back the flames, beating at them with cloaks and blankets and rugs, running from the cisterns with basins and buckets and jars; winning small victories, but losing ground steadily as wind and fire conspired to overrun them.

Alf passed them. The air shimmered in the fire-heat; as if by a miracle the crowd had thinned to nothing. Figures staggered about: a man bent under a heavy chest; a small child clutching at one still smaller and crying; a charred scarecrow with a terrible seared face, that wheeled about even as Jehan stared, and plunged into the flames.

Alf halted so suddenly that Jehan collided with him. "God in heaven," he said softly but distinctly in Latin. Jehan, peering at his face through eyes smarting with smoke, saw there neither fear nor pity but a white, terrible anger. He swept the children into his arms, murmuring words of comfort, and passed them to Jehan. "Take them to safety," he said.

The children were limp, passive, worn out with terror. Jehan settled them one on each arm, with the absent ease of one who had had numerous small siblings. "And you?"

"I'll come back to you," Alf answered.

Jehan hesitated. But the children whimpered, and Alf's eyes were terrible. He retreated slowly at first, then more swiftly.

Left alone, Alf stood for a moment, his face to the fire. It tore at him, buffeted him, strangled him with smoke. He reached inward to the heart of his strangeness, gathered the power that coiled there, hurled it with all his strength against the inferno. The flames quailed before it.

He laughed, the sound of steel on steel, with no mirth in it.

Yet the fire, having no mind, knew no master. It surged forward into the gap it had left, and reached with long fingers, enfolding the slim erect figure. Enfolding, but not touching. That much power he had still.

He laughed again briefly, but his laughter died and with it his anger. Pain tore at his sharpened senses, mingled with terror. There were people in the heart of that hell, alive and in agony or trapped and mad with panic. He set his mind upon a single thread of consciousness, and followed where it led.

Jehan, setting the children down within the safety of the fire lines, saw Alf cloaked in flames. He cried out and bolted forward; a stream of fire like a shooting star drove him back. He would have advanced again, but hands caught him and held him in spite of his struggles.

"Will you show some sense?"

The voice was sharp and familiar. He stared blankly at Thea, who glared back. She was dressed as a boy, her hair caught up under a cap.

"You kept him from being burned," he said. "Now he's gone and done it, and where were you?"

"Don't be an idiot." She let him go. "He's perfectly safe. The last thing he needs is to have you blundering after him and getting killed before he can stop you. Here, see if you can talk these people into getting upwind and staying upwind, and keeping the fire back."

Already she was drawing away from him. "Where are you going?" he called after her.

"To be an idiot." She vanished as Alf had, into a wall of fire.

* * *

The sun crawled across the sky. Beneath it, steadily, inexorably, the flames advanced. Not only wood but fired brick and even stone fell before them. With the sun's sinking, the City wore a girdle of fire from the Sea of Marmora to the Golden Horn.

Jehan lowered his burden to the ground and coughed. Pain lanced through his scorched throat. The woman he had carried from her smoldering house moaned and twisted, overcome more by hysteria than by the smoke. She could heal herself, he thought with callousness born of a long day's horrors. He coughed again, more weakly, and nerved himself for another foray.

A shape grew out of fire and darkness. Its face seemed vaguely familiar, but he saw only the cup it held out, brimming with blessed water. He snatched eagerly at it, caught himself with a wrenching effort, dropped stiffly to his knees. The woman gulped the water greedily and cursed him when he took the cup away half full to give the rest to the boy who lay beside her.

Gentle hands retrieved the cup, returned it filled. "That is for you," Alf said firmly.

He drank slowly in long sips. With each he felt his strength rise a little higher. When no more remained in the cup, he surrendered it. Alf hung it from his belt and set his hands on Jehan's shoulders. They were warm and strong, pouring strength into him, soothing his hurts.

"Where—" Jehan croaked. "Where—"

"We've opened Saint Basil's as a field hospital. Thea is there, and Bardas—Sophia had no luck in fetching him to safety."

"But you—the fire—"

"We've been bringing all the worst wounded to Saint Basil's. Come with us and help us." Carefully, without waiting for an answer, Alf raised the boy who had drunk the half of Jehan's first cup. The woman he ignored, though she tugged at him, whining.

Saint Basil's lay on the very edge of the inferno yet separated from it by a circle of garden. Streamers of fire, wind-driven, seemed to pass over it or else to fall short of it. The air felt cooler there, and cleaner; even amid the cries of agony and the bodies crowded into every space, there remained a sense of order and of peace.

After Alf had seen the wounded boy settled, he brought Jehan to a tall hard-faced man in blue who surveyed them with a grim eye. Jehan knew how unpromising he must seem to a master surgeon of Constantinople: filthy, stumbling with weariness, his mantle long lost, the rest of his garb charred, tattered, and all too obviously that of a Latin priest.

Alf laid an arm about his friend's shoulders and said, "I've found the man I spoke of, Master. He's trained as well as I am, if not better, and he speaks excellent Greek."

"Do you now?" said Master Dionysios. "Prove it."

"He flatters me, sir," Jehan answered, "but then, he did the training. I suppose he's entitled to brag a little."

The Master glanced from the soot-streaked young face to the one which was somewhat cleaner and seemed a good deal younger. Whatever his thoughts, he only growled, "I suppose you know what a bath is for. When that's done, you can find work enough to do."

Jehan bowed.

"And," Master Dionysios added grimly, "mind you, sir Frank. If anyone dies here, he won't be sent to Heaven or Hell by a heretic. We can use your hands, and your training if you have any. Leave the prayers to those who can say them properly."

Jehan's eyes smoldered, but he held his tongue and bowed again with frigid correctness.

Deep night brought no relief, no slackening in the flood of wounded and dying. With all the hospital's rooms and corridors filled, Master Dionysios sent the rest into the garden to be tended by the light of lamps and of the fire itself, a fierce red glow all about them.

Bathed and shaven and dressed in a fresh tunic that strained at every seam but was at least clean, Jehan labored in the garden. The scent of flowers was sweet and strong even over the stench of smoke and burning flesh; it refreshed him as the water had when he came out of the fire. Sometimes he saw Alf, marked by his luminous pallor, tending those whose hurts were greatest. Once he thought he recognized Bardas' heavyset figure, if truly it was His Majesty's Overseer of the Hospitals who held a man's head while a surgeon cut away the remnants of a hand.

Thea attached herself to Jehan soon after he began, still in her boy's clothes but without her cap. "I thought you'd be helping Alf," he said.

She handed him the knife he had been reaching for. "He doesn't need any help."

"And you think I do?"

"I have no talent at all for healing," she said, "but I'm good at holding heads and at talking sense into people."

"And at keeping fire away from hospitals?"

"Maybe."

"Well enough then," he said. "If anyone asks you, you're my apprentice." He had a glimpse of her swift smile before she bent to comfort the child who lay at their feet, his eyes fixed in terror upon Jehan's knife.

Alf saw the sunrise from the roof of Saint Basil's, whither Master Dionysios had driven him with orders that he not return until he had rested and eaten. Food, he could not face; his body, stronger than a man's, was not yet desperate for sleep. Others of the healers tossed and murmured under a canopy drenched with water to keep off the fire, with Jehan among them sleeping like the dead.

He sat on the roof's edge and clasped his knees. The dawn light seemed a feeble thing beside the fire which raged still in the City. It had retreated somewhat from the hospital, feeding now to the southward; flames had crept forth to lick the dome of Hagia Sophia. All between blazed or smoldered or crumbled in ruins; tenements, gardens, palaces, churches, and the arches and columns of the fora.

"People are saying that it's the wrath of God," Thea said, settling beside him.

"The wrath of man can be well-nigh as terrible."

She leaned against him and laid her head upon his shoulder. "If you're tired," she said, "I can shield us alone for a while."

He sighed. "I'm not as tired as that. House Akestas is safe; Saint Basil's will be now, I think."

"Unless the wind changes."

"Pray then. God ought to hear one of us."

She was silent. His arm had settled itself about her shoulders; he seemed unaware of it, staring out again over the ravaged City. His eyes were bleak. "All our power," he murmured, "great enough in old days to make us gods. But neither of us can do more here than keep the fire away from a pair of houses."

"Have you tried?"

"A little." He shivered. "Not enough to do any good at all."

"It's too big now for only two of us, and one all but untrained."

"I know that. It's only . . . I saw this, Thea. I *saw* it. And when it started, when I could have done something, I couldn't move. I could only stand and gape like a fool."

"When I was in Rhiyana," she said, "the King's sister fell ill. She was mortal, you see, and not young. Gwydion has great powers of healing, almost as great as yours, and his Queen has no less. They stayed with the Lady Alianora through every moment of her sickness and did everything they could do. But she died. We all mourned her, Gwydion most of all. She had been his favorite, his little sister who loved her changeling brother more than anyone else in the world. But . . . she died. Some things none of us can change."

"Death and fate and the destruction of cities. I can bear that because I must. What's unbearable is that I have to know it all before it happens."

"*Have* to, Alf?"

"I've always been able to see at will in that place inside of me where my power lies. It looks like a tapestry with its edges stretching away into infinity. But when fate is strong or disaster imminent and inevitable, I can hardly think or feel or see. I only know what must be, and what no effort of mine can change."

"It's been heavy on you ever since Jerusalem."

He nodded. "When Morwin died, he wanted me to find peace in the Holy City. For a little while I did find it. But I forgot what I should have known, that neither happiness nor peace can long endure. Not in this world."

"Of course not. We need to be miserable to know what it really is to be happy." She rose, drawing him with her. "We can't work as much of a miracle as this city needs. But we can do more than most. Especially when we've put a little food in our stomachs."

"I'm not—"

"Hungry," she finished for him. "You never are. But you're feeling very, very sorry for yourself. How much sorrier you'd feel if you'd lost your house and all you owned, and most of your family, and a good part of your skin besides."

He started as if she had slapped him; flushed, and paled. "I could learn to hate you," he said.

"You could. I'm too fond of telling the truth, aren't I, little Brother?"

"And I can't become a falcon to fly away from it."

That struck home, but she laughed. "See? You've caught it from me. Come down with me and be kind to your poor body for once, the better to fight the rest of this battle."

He hesitated. She turned her back on him and began to pick her way among the sleepers.

As he followed her, the sun climbed at last over the rim of the world, its great orb the color of blood or of fire.

11

The fire was dead. The last embers smoldered sullenly, while here and there among them figures moved, searching for the dead, beginning the long labor of clearing away the ruins and building anew where they had been. Even lamentation was muted, cursing subdued, numbed by the immensity of the destruction.

Alf lay in his own bed in House Akestas, its softness strange after so many nights of catching what rest he could wherever he might. To be clean, to breathe air which bore no taint of smoke, to have no pain about him but only the peace of a sleeping household—he could not yet believe that it was so. In a little while Master Dionysios would wake him, or a bolt of agony would pierce through all the levels of his sleep and thrust him back into the battle.

His mind slid away from remembrance. He had passed beyond weariness to a state like drunkenness, all his inner defenses weakened or cast down. His body seemed made of air, the hand he raised before his face a thing of mist and moonlight. It turned, flexed—wonderful creation, so to yield to his will. His eyes ran from it along his arm to his shoulder, down the long line of his body to his distant feet. He did not often stop to consider himself. Feet had to be shod or sandaled for walking; hands served one's needs; hair had to be washed and cut and kept out of one's face. Everything between, one kept clean and fed and covered as much as one might, and tried to forget.

It was not an ill body. Somewhat too thin perhaps, but strong, with few enough needs. Its curse it shared with his face: its moon-white skin which could endure no sunlight without the shielding of power, and its beauty. He had seen its like along the Middle Way, in old gods and in the marble *kouroi* which smiled inscrutably upon the City, shameless in their nakedness.

He breathed deep. The air smelled of roses and of rain. Idly, without thought, he let his hand follow the lines of hip and thigh. There was a lazy pleasure in it, in tracing the planes and angles, the taut play of muscles beneath the skin, so different from a woman's smooth curves. From one woman's, from one body he had never had the courage to learn, nor the will to cast away.

He was on his feet. Supple and serene this body was, when the clamoring mind would let it be. It could glide, it could turn. It could dance, great sensuous sin, to the music that was in it. Heart and blood, lungs and brain, set the measure, ceaseless, complex, inescapable. He spun; his hair whipped his shoulders, scarred flesh oblivious, whole flesh struck with a lash of pleasure. His eyes blurred darkness into light, and light into nameless splendor, and nameless splendor into the sheen of bronze and gold.

He dropped exhausted. The glory died. He was mere mud, sweat and earth shaped in a form that men's eyes reckoned fair. Fair and foul, stained with sin and the will to sin, centered on flesh, who had vaunted his knowledge of God. He had never known more than his own vanity.

His fingers raked his hair. Thick as a woman's, fine as a

child's, tear it, tear it out. The face, the beautiful beardless face, rend it, mar it—

"Alfred!"

All his body snapped taut, arched back from the vise that bound his wrists. It tightened into pain, into agony. Without warning it let him fall. His dream, formless light, had taken flesh; it glared down at him, bronze and gold and unbearably beautiful.

He swallowed. His throat ached. She was splendid in her anger, and surely she knew it; she was always angry. "You always give me reason to be." Thea dragged him up and shook him. "Idiot! How long since you slept? How long since you ate?"

"You made me," he said, "or Jehan. I forget." He willed her into focus. "You went away."

"I've come back." She was still holding him. He touched her cheek. For all the fire of her temper, it was cool, and she did not shake him off. It was he who drew back, who gathered himself together, who found a blanket to cover his nakedness.

"I ate," he said with care, with a touch of bitterness. "Sophia saw to it. I drank honeyed milk with the rest of the children. No wine, milady nurse."

"No sleep either, and no sense at all."

He lay where she willed him, where his own will would have him. Her temper was shifting, changing. Her eyes were more gold than bronze. She was as bare as he, and he had not even seen. She bent over him.

He thrust her back, spinning her about, felling her with force that shook them both. He had forgotten how hideously strong he was.

He fell to his knees beside her, choking upon self-disgust. He had bruised her, hip, breast, cheekbone.

She sat up. He could not read her eyes within the tangle of her hair. He smoothed it away from her face. His fingertips brushed her cheek; the hip he had dashed against the floor; and, hesitantly, her tender breast. His hand might have lingered there; he forced it to fall. "I'm sorry," he said, meaning more than the simple words, the simple wounding. "I'm . . . most . . . sorry."

She shook her head. "Don't be." Her gentleness was worse than any scolding, her kiss more terrible than a blow, chaste upon his stiff cheek. "Sleep now," she said, "and forget. We all have our midnight madnesses."

"I—" His voice died. She began to walk away. The words fought free. "I love you, Thea."

She was gone. He sank down where she had left him, drawing into a knot, trembling deep within. So easily it had come out, so suddenly and so irredeemably. And she had not even stayed to hear.

In a moment he would laugh. In a moment more, he would weep.

12

Sophia closed her account book firmly and laid her pen aside. "No more today," she said to the house steward. He bowed with Arab formality and withdrew.

Once he was well gone, she indulged in a long delicious yawn and stretched until her bones cracked. Voices from outside came clearly to her ears as they had throughout the morning; she rose and sought the window. In the garden below, her guest and her children sat in a circle, three dark heads and Alf's fair one. They all had pens, even Nikki, and writing tablets; when Alf spoke they wrote. Greek now. It had been Latin earlier. The cadences were familiar. Homer?

Alf paused. The girls continued to write; he bent toward Nikki. From her vantage directly above them, she could see the tablet in her son's lap. The scribbles on it looked remarkably like letters.

Her fingers clenched upon the window frame. No, she thought. They had all told her, doctors, priests, astrologers: He would never speak or read or write. "Raise him as you may," the most learned of the doctors had told her in ill-concealed pity. "Train him as you would a puppy or a colt, else he will run wild. More than that, short of a miracle, none of us can do."

For a moment Alf's hand guided Nikki's. He drew back. Nikki paused, head cocked. Suddenly he nodded and bent over his tablet. If he had been any other child, and if any word had been spoken, she would have said that he had been instructed; had questioned and been answered; and had returned to his task with new understanding.

She drew a breath to calm herself. She hoped for too much; it made her see only what she wished to see. What could one young Latin do, however brilliant he might be, where all the wise men of Byzantium had failed?

In the garden Anna said, "There. All done. Now will you teach me a new song? You promised!"

Though Alf's voice was stern, Sophia could have sworn that there was a smile in it. "Patience is part of your lesson, demoiselle. Come, let me see if anything written in such haste can be perfect."

"It is," Anna insisted. "Alf, what's *dem—demi—*"

"That means 'young lady' in Frankish," Irene informed her virtuously, "and he's being much more polite than you deserve."

"Every man owes a lady courtesy," said Alf in a tone which so withered Irene's pretensions that Sophia stifled laughter. "Yes, Anna, it seems that you've done the impossible. There's not even an iota out of place. However—"

It was Irene who cut him short. "Then you'll sing for us? A new song, please."

"Ah," he said. His voice had deepened a full octave. "A conspiracy. For that I should give you ten more lines apiece to teach you how to treat your master." As they burst into loud protests, he added, "But since we've already had our full hour and more, just this once I will yield to your impudence."

Even Nikki laid aside his tablet, leaning forward eagerly. Alf's voice in song was at once deep and clear: like the rest of him, an uncanny mingling of potent maleness and almost feminine beauty. It caught Sophia and held her fast. She did not move when all too soon it fell silent, but stood by the window, gazing out with eyes which saw only sunlight.

Someone came to stand beside her. "There doesn't seem to be much he can't do," Bardas said.

The rough familiar voice called her back to herself. She smiled and took his arm and walked with him out of the workroom. "It's a bit of a scandal, you know. How can we allow a Latin—a boy—to teach our nubile young daughters? Are we positive that he's only teaching them Latin and tutoring them in Greek, with a little music on the side?"

"That sounds like my sister," Bardas muttered.

"Well, yes. Theodora was here yesterday. We visited the schoolroom." Sophia's eyes glinted. "Alfred, as usual, was infallibly polite. Theodora, as usual, completely failed to captivate him with those famous eyes of hers. And she suggested that maybe we weren't entirely wise to expose him to such temptation, with Irene growing so pretty, and he so young and evidently a man entire."

" 'Evidently,' " he said. "I like that."

They paused just past the door which led to the garden. Alf and the children were out of sight round a corner of the house, but they heard Anna's tuneless treble and Irene's sweet soprano rehearsing the song Alf had sung. "It's obvious enough to me," said Sophia, "but I think I'd trust him with any woman living. Except perhaps for one."

He raised an eyebrow.

She raised both. "Well? Have you ever seen anyone look at a woman the way he looks at Thea?"

"It seems to me," mused Bardas, "that I saw a boy or two mooning after you in your day. And you inveigled your father into marrying you off to an old man from Constantinople, purely and simply for his money."

She glared at him. "Money, forsooth! I had enough of my own. Good sense, that was what I admired in you. No fumbling, no foolishness. You knew what you wanted and that was that."

"Two of a kind, weren't we? Though as I recall, the first

time I saw you you were flat on your behind in a dungheap, roundly cursing the half-broken colt who'd thrown you there. I admired your vocabulary. And," he added after some consideration, "your trim ankle."

"You saw more than that, that day." Sophia smiled, remembering. Bardas sat on a stone bench against the house wall where the sun was warm, drawing a breath, of contentment perhaps, that caught and broke into a spasm of coughing.

Sophia sprang toward him, but he waved her away. His breathing had steadied; he leaned back. "Something in my throat," he muttered.

He said that every time. Often lately, since the fire. She looked hard at him. He seemed as strong as ever. A little thinner, maybe. A little grayer. He would be sixty on Saint Stephen's Day.

"It's true," he said in almost his normal voice, "those two children seem unduly interested in each other. Has anyone caught them at it yet?"

She knew he was leading her away from himself, but she did not resist him. "I can't imagine Alfred doing anything of the sort. He's too . . . well . . . *young*."

"Is he?" Bardas smoothed his beard. "How old would you say he was?"

"Seventeen, maybe. Eighteen. But that's not what I mean."

"I know. In some things he's a complete innocent. Blushes like a girl if he hears a coarse word. It's the other things that concern me. He can tell a rare tale when he has a mind. Ever stopped to wonder how he could have been a monk and a priest, taught that great clever ox from the camp, gone on pilgrimage to Jerusalem—the last of which, by his own account, took years, with a year at least in the holy places afterward—and all before he's even grown a beard?"

"Latins take vows almost blasphemously young, sometimes."

Bardas frowned. "There are times when I think he's about fifteen. Other times I'm sure he's as old as the Delphic Oracle. Those eyes of his—he's no boy, Sophia. Whatever else he is, he's no boy."

She shivered in the sunlight. "I know," she said very low. She remembered the doctor in Chalcedon and shivered again. "I don't think he means us harm. The children love him, and I think he returns it. The servants quarrel over the privilege of waiting on him."

"He's bewitched us all, hasn't he? You should hear the stories they tell in and around Saint Basil's. He's supposed to have walked unscathed through the fire, carried any number of people out of it, and worked authentic miracles of healing, aided by a golden-eyed angel in boy's clothes and another disguised as a Frankish priest."

"Jehan is no more uncanny than you are," Sophia said quickly.

"You think so?"

"Of course I think so. He's a good deal brighter than he looks, and he knows more about Alfred than he's telling, but he's no more than he seems to be."

"That still leaves the other two."

Bardas shifted slightly; Sophia sat beside him. "You aren't going to send them away, are you?" she asked him.

He regarded her in honest surprise. "Why would I do that?"

"The stories—"

"Are just stories until they're proven otherwise. I don't deny that I'm highly suspicious, and I'm not at all sure what we're harboring here. But I agree with you. Neither of them means us any harm. Whatever they are."

"Maybe, after all, they're only a pair of pilgrims."

Bardas snorted and stifled another cough. Before he could answer her, a procession rounded the corner: Anna running ahead with Nikki, Irene walking more sedately behind, and Alf in the rear most dignified of all.

Sophia could not quite suppress a guilty start. What if Alf had heard them?

He showed no sign of it. The younger children paused only briefly before vanishing in the direction of the stable; Irene excused herself to attend to her studies—"A love poem, *I* bet," Anna said, and was firmly ignored—and Bardas had business in the City.

Which left Alf, and Sophia sitting in the sun. There was an awkward pause. "I should see to the kitchen stores," Sophia said to fill it.

Alf sat where Bardas had been, with no show of self-consciousness. Since he neither responded to her inanity nor looked at her except to smile his quick luminous smile, she stole the chance to look at him. His face was smooth, unlined, with no mark or blemish that she could see; the last scar of the burning was gone wholly, without a trace. It could have been a cold face, white and flawless as it was. But the tilt of his brows warmed it, gave it a hint of the faun; and when he smiled it could melt stone.

"Should you be in the sun?" she asked.

His eyes flicked to her. They seemed to change whenever she saw him, sometimes gray, sometimes silver, sometimes colorless as water. Now they were palest gold, with the same sunstruck sheen as his hair. "I'll go in in a little while."

"Soon, then." He was silent; she added, "I liked your song. Was it Latin?"

He nodded. "A hymn for Rachel bereft of her children. 'Why are you weeping, maiden mother, lovely Rachel?' " he sang very softly in that marvel of a voice: " '*Quid tu virgo mater ploras, Rachel formosa?*' "

He sang no more than that, although she waited, expectant. After a moment she spoke. "Do you miss your monastery?"

She could hear his breath as he caught it, see his fists clench in his lap. For an instant his face was truly cold. Yet he spoke quietly, without either pain or anger. "Yes. Yes, sometimes I do miss it. The peace; the long round of days from prayer to prayer and from task to task, with now and then a feast or a guest or a villager who needed healing or comfort. I miss that. The Brothers whose faces I'd known all my life; my Abbot who was my friend . . . there are times when I ache to take wing and fly back and never leave again."

"Why don't you?"

He startled her with a flicker of laughter. "For one thing," he said, "I don't have wings. For another, I don't belong there anymore. My Abbot is dead; the world has claimed me."

"Has it?"

"Do I look so much like a monk?"

"You look like a gentleman of the City."

"Who longs for his cloister." That had been her precise thought; she stared at him, silenced. He smiled bitterly. "I suppose one can't repudiate one's whole upbringing in a day or even a season. But I'm going to have to do it."

"Why?"

He paused. His eyes had darkened almost to gray. "Many reasons," he answered, speaking as quietly as ever. "I killed a man, you know that."

"Against your will and in defense of your Abbot."

"No," he said. "It started that way. But when the stroke fell, I knew exactly what I was doing, and I wanted to do it. I took a human life; for that I was truly repentant and atoned in every way I knew how, even to Jerusalem. I shall never free myself from that guilt. Yet that I killed when I did, whom I did—he was mad, and he wanted to destroy three kingdoms, and he murdered my friend who had never raised a hand against any living thing. I rid the world of him. I've not been able to regret it."

She took his hand. It was the left, his writing hand, its fingers stained with ink. Black, not blood-scarlet. "You killed one man. How many have you healed?"

"That's what everyone says. I know about sin and repentance and absolution; who better? But I can't go back to Saint Ruan's. It's more than the act of murder long since atoned for. It's that I could do it and feel as I do about it. I've changed too much. They raised me to be a ringdove, Thea says; I grew into an eagle."

"Thea has a clear eye."

"Thea has a gift for irony. She also says that no one can turn a leopard into a lapcat. By that, I suppose, she means that I'm innately vicious."

"She means that you were stifling in your abbey. Maybe

someday when you've had all the world has to offer, you'll be ready to go back and find peace."

The bitterness had left his smile. It was gentle and a little sad. "Maybe," he said without conviction. He rose. "Master Dionysios will be looking for me. Good day, my lady."

When she found her voice again, he was gone, and she had asked none of the questions she had meant to ask. She realized that she had crossed herself; cursed her own folly, and turned her back on the garden.

13

Though the sun shone almost with summer's brilliance, the wind which scoured the City was icy cold. Alf drew his hat down lower and huddled into his cloak.

"The worst thing about this city," his companion said, "is its climate. A furnace all summer; then before you can get your breath it's winter, with a wind howling right out of Scythia."

Alf smiled. The other's tone was as cheerful as his words were glum, his round cheeks bright red with the cold; he grinned up at Alf and clutched at the hat which threatened to take flight and leave his bald crown bare. "There's your turning. I suppose I'll see you tomorrow then?"

"Wait." On impulse Alf said, "Let me walk you home."

The smaller man's grin widened. "Are you being protective, then? Eh, brother? They aren't hunting doctors today, only Latins."

"I want to walk," Alf said, "and I'm not expected home quite yet."

"First time you've ever left Saint Basil's when you're supposed to, isn't it? Trust Master Dionysios to know when you're working too hard."

"I'm not—"

"Oh, no. Thin as a lath and white as a ghost, and you're not overworking. Of course not. And half the people who come in insist that no one but Master Theo tend them. If we weren't so fond of your pretty face, my friend, we'd all hate you with a passion."

"I can't understand why you don't."

"Didn't I just tell you? It's your face. Besides the fact that you're the best doctor we've got. And don't glower at me like that. Fat old Thomas is babbling on again as usual, but it's the truth and you know it. There are some who'd gladly see the last of you, but most of us are happy enough; you do all the work, and we get to watch and collect some credit." Thomas grinned and patted Alf's shoulder, which was as high as he could reach, for he was a very small man. "Look, I've talked us right up to my doorstep. Come in and warm up before you go back."

Somewhat later, Alf strode away from Thomas' house with a cup of wine warming his belly and a smile on his lips. Strange that in this half-burned and crumbling city he should have found more and better friends than he had in his own country.

What's strange about it? I've always known you're a Greek at heart.

He looked about. In the throngs about him he could not see Thea's face. Though perhaps the striped cat in the doorway, or the pigeon which took wing in front of him—

Close by him scarlet blazed, a pair of Varangians leaving an alehouse. They were big men and young; he had seen faces like theirs on many a villein in Anglia, long Saxon faces thatched with straw-fair hair. As he paused, one stared full at him and grinned. The eyes under the blond brows were startling, golden bronze.

He knew he was gaping like a fool. The Varangians parted almost within his reach; the one whose eyes and mind were Thea's stopped short in front of him and swept him into a muscular embrace. "By all the saints! Alfred! What are you doing abroad at this hour?"

Behind the strange male face, the deep voice, Thea laughed at his discomfiture. Her mockery steadied him. "I'm walking home from Saint Basil's," he answered her. He looked her over and laughed a little. "No wonder you were angry when I read you my lecture on mingling with guardsmen. What a pompous fool I was!"

"Weren't you?" Thea drew him into a passageway away from prying eyes. Almost at once she was herself again, stripping off her bright gear and bundling it together, dressing in the gown she had worn when he saw her that morning, drawn it seemed from air. The trappings of the Guard vanished as the gown had appeared; she turned about with dancing eyes. "How do I look?"

"Beautiful, of course," he said. "You'll have to show me how you do that."

She paused in adjusting cloak and veil. "What? Shape-change?"

"No. Make things vanish."

"It's easy enough." She took his arm and entered the throng again. "Tonight after everyone's abed, I'll show you."

He smiled.

"You're cheerful today," she said.

He shrugged slightly. "There's a man at Saint Basil's who seems to have decided that I'm worth troubling with."

"Don't tell me you honestly doubted it." He did not respond; she added, "He can make you smile. That's a power to equal any of mine."

"Am I always so morose then?"

"Not morose. Preoccupied, mostly. It's a game in House Akestas to get a smile out of you; the day someone tricks you into an honest-to-God grin, we'll have a festival."

He stared at her in dismay, until he caught the mirth behind her eyes. "On me," he said, "a grin would be a disgrace."

"You're vain."

"Surely." A vendor passed them, balancing a tray laden with hot and fragrant cakes. Alf tossed him a coin and gained a napkinful that warmed his hands and set his mouth to watering. "Here," he said to Thea, "aren't you hungry?"

They ate as they walked, Alf more than usual but still very little. The rest of his share he wrapped and secreted in his robe.

"Nikki will have a feast tonight," Thea said.

"And Anna, and Irene if her dignity will allow it."

"You should have had a dozen brothers and sisters and an army of cousins."

"I had hundreds. Fellow novices when I was a child, and pupils for years thereafter."

They paused upon the steps of Holy Apostles. Over the roar and reek of the City, they heard chanting and caught the sweet strong scent of incense. "Novices and pupils aren't the same," she said.

"Close enough."

"Did you ever know any girls? Or teach any?"

"A few," he said. "Enough to learn that girls need be no less intelligent than boys. Though most change when womanhood comes, forget logic and philosophy and think only on husbands and children."

"Or at least on young men and on what gets children." Thea stood a little apart from him with a cold space between. "I have been rebuked."

"I said *most*. Not *all*."

"There is Sophia," she agreed.

"And there is you."

"I don't know any philosophy. And as for logic, Aristotle would be appalled. All I know is the pleasure of the body."

A sigh escaped him. "You know a great deal more than that. But if you think you have any need at all for what I can teach, I'll be glad to be your master. If you will teach me—"

She leaned forward, breathless.

"If you will teach me the ways of power."

There was a silence in the midst of the City. Suddenly Thea laughed. "It's a bargain. Power for philosophy, and we'll see who makes the better student." She linked arms with him again and plunged into the crowd.

* * *

"Filthy Latins!"

With an effort of will Jehan kept his hand away from his sword. It was as much as any Frank's life was worth to walk unconcealed in the City, but both he and his companion were well cloaked and hooded. The cry of hatred had not been meant for them.

He stopped to get his bearings. Left here round the bulk of the church. The wind was cruel. He shivered and wrapped his cloak a little tighter; turned to speak to the man beside him, and caught too late at his hood.

"Barbarians! Murderers!"

Something whistled past his ear. He whipped about, sword half drawn. An iron grip stayed his hand. "No!" hissed the other.

Jehan fought free. The crowd had thickened about him, the murmur of their passing turned to a snarl. In the instant before he let go the hilt, they had seen naked steel.

He drew up the deep hood and made himself advance. Left past Holy Apostles. Left—

Alf stopped short as if he had struck a wall. Thea whirled, every muscle taut. Behind them the crowd eddied, drawing in those who paused upon its edges, rumbling ominously.

A shout won free. "Frankish bastards!"

Without a word, both sprang toward the uproar.

Two men filled its center. One lay in a pool of black and blood-red. The other stood astride him, holding off blows and missiles with the flat of his sword.

"Hold!" bellowed a deep voice. "What goes on here?"

A giant in scarlet shouldered through the mob, ignoring blows and curses, wrenching a stone from a man's hand, roaring for silence. His uniform and his rage and the axe which he carried lightly in his great hands cowed all but the boldest. Those he faced, bulking before the Frank with the sword; his beard bristled and his tawny eyes blazed.

A stone flew; he caught it with his axehead, shattering it.

"One more," he growled. "Just one more. Who fancies a year or six with the Emperor's jailers?"

For a long moment the balance wavered. Teeth bared; hands drew back to throw. The Varangian shifted his grip on his axe and braced his feet.

Slowly the mob melted away.

A figure in healer's blue slipped round the Guardsman and dropped beside the fallen man. Blood stained the tonsured crown, pouring from a deep gash there.

Alf looked up into the eyes of the Lord Henry of Flanders. "Sheathe your sword," he said, "my lord."

As Henry obeyed, Alf explored Jehan's wound with light skilled fingers. The young priest stirred under his hands and groaned. His touch stilled both voice and movement; he probed the gash again. It was deep though not mortal, and bloody. He wiped the blood away with a corner of his mantle, drew up his outer robe and tore ruthlessly at the fine linen of his undertunic.

Without his willing it, his power gathered and focused. He could only slow it, turn it aside from full healing as he bound up the wound.

He slid one arm beneath Jehan's shoulders. "Help me," he said, breathing hard for Henry's benefit. Together they raised the great inert body, supporting it on either side, its arms about their necks. But Henry hesitated, glancing about. "The Guardsman. Where did he go?"

"Back to his barracks, I suppose, my lord." Alf bent his head and stepped forward. The young lord followed perforce.

Jehan swam up out of darkness to a raging headache and Alf's calm face hovering over him. "What did you keep me under for?" he demanded of it fretfully.

"Convenience," Alf answered.

Jehan glared and winced. "Did someone hit me over the head with a mace?"

"A stone with sharp edges." Alf laid a cool hand on his brow. The pain faded; his sight cleared. He could see other faces:

Thea's, Sophia's, Henry's. He reached out to the last. "You're all right? You're not hurt?"

Henry smiled. "Scarcely a bruise," he said. "They tell me you'll live."

"Maybe," Jehan muttered. He sat up dizzily, saw that they had stripped him down to his shirt. His head was bandaged, his hair damp from a washing. "How long was I out?"

"About an hour," said Alf, propping him with pillows. This, he realized, was Alf's own bed.

They settled about him, Alf at his side, an arm about his shoulders. The support was somewhat more welcome than he had thought it would be. *You're all but healed,* Alf's soft voice said in his mind, *but the shock to your body was severe. You'll need to sleep, and sleep deep.*

Jehan yawned, thinking of it, and clenched his jaw. He would not sleep like a baby while the others talked. *And none of your sorcery!* he thought at Alf.

His friend smiled, perhaps at him, perhaps at Henry. "Well, my lord, how is it that we see you here of all places?"

One of the servants entered with wine. Henry accepted a cup with a murmured courtesy, all the Greek he knew. As he spoke Thea whispered in Sophia's ear, the Greek of his *langue d'oeil.* "I came back from Thrace a week and more ago with the rest of our forces and the young Emperor. Life in camp can be stifling after one's been on the march. When my priestly friend told me he was going to dare the City—which is more than anyone else will do—I invited myself."

Alf's smile faded. Henry met his level stare for a moment, then looked away. "I am no one's prophet," Alf said very softly.

"I do not ask," Henry responded more softly still.

"You," said Alf, "no." His voice changed; a hint of his smile returned, then flickered away. "You were foolhardy, both of you, to venture here in so poor a set of disguises. Next time you should have the sense to dress as Greeks, and you, Jehan, to wear a hat. If anything maddens the City more than a Latin knight, it's a Latin priest."

"It is bad," Henry agreed soberly. "I hadn't known precisely how bad. Out in Thrace we were victors; here we're monsters. Pierre de Bracieux and his men quit the palace this morning in terror of their lives, though milord is howling for revenge."

"He's too brave for his own good." Jehan caught Alf's eye and flushed. "I know what I am, damn it! and he's a fighting fool. He had plenty of tales to tell. People are strengthening the City's walls, do you know that? Quietly, without fanfare, and without asking anyone's leave."

"Neither Emperor seems to be objecting," Henry said. "Isaac's mind is at least half gone, and Alexios has immured himself in his palace where neither we nor his own people can come near him. If my lady will pardon my saying it, this city is not well ruled."

Sophia's eyes sparked. "I know it," she said through Thea, "and I deplore it. But not all of us are cowards. Some of the nobles are beginning to take matters into their own hands."

"You among them, my lady?"

Her lips met in a thin line. "I'm only a woman, and my husband is a bureaucrat, not a prince. I have no power. Only anger."

Henry bowed to her in sincere respect. "I regret that we've come to this, my lady. If I had my wish, we would be in Jerusalem and your city would stand intact."

"Regret!" she snapped. "You should have thought of regret when you sailed up the Horn. Admit it, sir Frank; your holy war has turned into a merchants' quarrel, and this is the richest city in the world. Now you've seen how rich it is, you'll not be bought off except with all we have."

He did not deny it. But he said, "We've done as we contracted to do. His Majesty has not. He owes his throne to us; and we need food and money, and winter is coming. What little he's given us is far from enough. Already many of us are urging that we put aside our patience and take what we need."

"And in the City," Thea said on her own account, "they say that enough is enough. They never chose the Emperor you've set over them, and the one of their own choosing is beneath contempt. They've endured for nigh a thousand years by discarding rulers who can't rule and setting up those who can. One morning, my lord, you'll wake and find that there's a new head under the crown."

"Will it be any better than the ones before it?"

"Who can tell?" She glanced at Alf, who listened without expression, offering nothing. "The walls aren't repairing themselves. There's a man commanding it, one of the Doukas; people call him Mourtzouphlos, Beetle-brows, an alarming man to meet in a dark corridor. He married a daughter of the Emperor you so valiantly cut down in Thrace, and he hasn't forgotten it; and he's far enough into the new Emperors' confidence that they've made him Protovestiarios. That, my lord, is more than a noble valet and esquire or even a steward; he controls the Private Treasury, and through it the imperial favor. You'd do well to watch him."

"So we do," Henry said. "Why do you think we took Alexios off to Thrace?"

"You're giving away state secrets," Sophia murmured.

"No, Lady. I'm saying what everyone knows. Before I left we were more allies than enemies. Now the balance has shifted. I'd like to see it change again."

Alf stirred beside Jehan. "It was the fire. Whichever side kindled it, no one has forgotten that the Latins struck first that day. No one will forget. The hate is too strong and runs too deep."

"On both sides," said Thea. Her face twisted in sudden fierce anger. "By God and all His angels! Can't a one of you think of anything but hating?"

Alf reached out to touch her clenched fist. Face to face, they looked startlingly alike. Gently he said, "The root of it isn't hate. It's fear. Every stranger is an enemy, and every friend could turn traitor. Yet each side shares the same thoughts, all unknowing."

Light dawned in her eyes. "If they could know—if their minds could be opened—"

He shook his head. "No, Thea. No. They're not made for it. It would drive them mad."

"They're sane now?"

"Perfectly sane. Only blind and afraid. Yet there are some who see." His eye caught Sophia, who had just begun to understand through Jehan's translation, and Henry, whose face displayed a mingling of confusion and fascination. "We can pray that they may rule."

"When has good sense ever had the upper hand?" She pulled away from him. "We women aren't pleasant to listen to, are we? A pity there isn't a lady or two of sense and breeding in the camp. We'd put an end to all this idiocy, and quickly too."

"What can a woman do that a man can't?" Alf demanded of her.

"Make a peace we can all live with. And we'd have done it long since, too. Held off the fleet, talked them round, and saved more lives and property than anyone can count. Unfortunately," she added bitterly, "there was neither woman nor wise man at the head of either side that day."

"There was Dandolo," said Henry, "who knows what he wants; and Marquis Boniface, who wants what he can get; and my brother, who won't settle for the leavings. And for the Greeks, a mindless mob and a coward. The usurper died of wounds taken in battle, and every one was in his back."

She faced him. "Why don't you rule?"

"I?" He seemed truly shocked. "My lady, I'm my brother's loyal vassal. Whatever he commands me to do, I do, for honor of my oath."

"Regardless of the dishonor of the command?"

Jehan sighed heavily. "Yes, there's the rub. Thea, if you can persuade the people to elect you Emperor, I'll be your most avid supporter. But at the moment I have a splitting headache, and it must be past time for us to go back."

"Yes," she said tartly, "go back and try to open some eyes. If the sight of your bandages doesn't rouse the whole army."

"No fear of that. More likely they'll cheer the marksman who brought down the Pope's varlet."

"Go to the Doge," Alf said, cutting short her sharpness and Jehan's bitter levity. "Tell him what we've said here. Tell him too that he can win this war, but it will bring him no joy. And if he loses, his death will most cruelly hard."

Jehan paused with his cotte half on. Before he could speak, Henry said, "Those are perilous words to say to the Master of Saint Mark."

"He asked for them. Did he not?"

Henry was silent. Slowly, with Alf's help, Jehan finished dressing. His headache, feigned when he spoke of it, had begun to approach agony. "We'll tell him though it kills us."

Alf's fingers brushed his brow. They were warm and cool at once, drawing away the pain, lending him strength. "Dear friend," Alf said, "I'd never send you to your death. Nor do I ask you to come back here. It's too much danger for too little cause."

"I hardly saw you at all." Even to himself Jehan sounded faint and fretful, like a tired child.

"But you did see me." Alf eased something over Jehan's bandage, a hat, broad-brimmed and much worn.

Jehan's groping hand found the braided band and froze. "I can't take this away from you!"

"You can keep it till I come for it. Now, your cloak. You'd best be quick; it will be dark soon, and you won't be able to find a boat to take you across the Horn."

Jehan grasped at the little that mattered. "You'll come for it?"

"Or you'll bring it. When it's safe, and only when." Alf embraced him briefly, tightly. "Take care of yourself, Jehan."

14

Nikki pulled at Alf's hair. *White,* he wrote on his tablet. And at Alf's coat: *Blue*. And his own: *Red*.

Alf swallowed laughter, for Nikki's eyes were mischievous. *No,* he said in his mind; scored through the last and waited, pen poised.

Green! Nikki cried, snatching the pen and writing it in a jubilant scrawl.

Alf's mirth won free. *Yes, green,* he said, *and well you knew it. Now what is it?*

Coat, Nikki answered with his pen. *I wear—him?*

It, Alf corrected him. He nodded, brows knit, forcing himself to remember. Words were a wonder and a delight, but they were hard to keep hold of, shifting and changing as quickly and inexplicably as people's faces. He thought tiredness at Alf, and the other nodded. *Enough now. Go and rest.*

Not rest. The picture in his mind was of the stable and of the three kittens there. He clasped Alf's neck in a quick embrace and left him, skipping as Anna had taught him to do.

Alf tidied the nursery which did duty as a schoolroom, thinking of the one in Saint Ruan's with its gray walls and its hard benches and its rows of novices in their brown robes. Brother Osric, who had been master there when he left, was Abbot now; young Richard had taken the mastership. Though he would not be so young after all—thirty-five? forty? He had been a very hellion when he entered the abbey, fifth son of a poor baron, determined in his contempt for the monks with their pious mumblings. But under the contempt there had been a brain, and a reluctant fascination for the words which the monks had mumbled.

They had sent him a gift through Bishop Aylmer in Rome: his own *Gloria Dei*, copied and illuminated by the best hands in Saint Ruan's, with a commentary over which both Osric and Richard had labored for long years. It lay now in his clothes chest, its beauty hidden in the plain cover which Brother Edgar had made for it to turn aside thieves, nor had he opened it since it came to him.

His will reached, *so*, and it lay in his hands. He sat at the worktable and opened it. His fingers trembled a little. It was even more wonderful than he had remembered.

There folded within was the letter which had come with it, written in Osric's minute precise hand. News of the abbey, small things, this Brother ill and that Brother recovered, a splendid apple harvest and enough mead to make everyone tipsy on Saint Ruan's Day; Duke Robert had given a magnificent bequest, and Lord Morfan was maintaining that the southwest corner of the oak forest had belonged to his family since King William's day. And among all of this, the lines which with the release from his vows had sent Alf from Jerusalem: "Already the younger ones make a legend of what you did, and tell the tale of the Archangel Michael who came to be Our Lady's champion and slew the Abbot's slayer in her Chapel; and there is the sword hung over the altar as proof of it. You yourself we've let them forget, all of us old dodderers, because you asked it, nay demanded it, in the letter the King of Rhiyana sent to us; and because, the world being what it is, maybe it was wisest. We put it in the Necrology: *'Dead on the winter solstice in the tenth year of the reign of His Majesty, Richard, called Coeur-de-Lion: Alfred, foundling, novice, monk and priest of Saint Ruan's upon Ynys Witrin; master of the school, author of the* Gloria Dei, Doctor misteriosus. *May the peace of the Lord rest upon him.'* "

He smoothed the parchment, staring at it, not seeing it. The pain was piercing, as he had known it would be. But not as it had been before. This he could bear. It was pain, not agony. And half of it he had had to force with a flood of memory.

In spite of himself, he was healing. He looked at the book which he had written, and he saw not the cloister but the schoolroom of House Akestas. The words of the monk from Anglia seemed strangely distant. Someone else had written them long years ago, someone he no longer knew. Even the person who had wept when the letter came, only a year past, was not the one who read it now. This new Alfred had no tears to spare for a man five years dead, or for an abbey whose walls could only be a cage.

Carefully he closed the book. He could not read it. Not yet. That pain was real, and deep enough to make him gasp.

He turned. Sophia stood in the doorway, her face reflecting his own, white and shocked. For an instant she had seen in him the full count of his years.

"My lady," he said.

"I wish you wouldn't call me that," she said more sharply than she had meant. In a gentler voice she added, "Are you feeling well? You look ill."

"I'm well." He straightened, brushing his hair out of his eyes, and smiled as best he could.

"Corinna said you were in here at dawn."

That was when Nikki liked to be taught and he to teach, while everyone else slept. It was their secret, theirs and Thea's, for sometimes she came to sit with them, bringing them booty from the kitchen, most of which Nikki ate. Honey cakes this morning, and a bowl of raisins. "I'm well," he repeated.

"But won't you have any—" she began.

He was already gone, his book under his arm.

Alf woke to a timid shaking and a voice calling his name. Sophia's maid bent over him, her hair down, a nightrobe clutched to her ample bosom. Her grief and fear, mingled with embarrassment, shocked him into full consciousness.

"Master," she said, "Master, I'm sorry, but my lady wouldn't let me send Diogenes." She was very careful not to look at him save in quick glances. "It's Master Bardas. He's—"

Alf was up, pulling a tunic over his head, striding forward even before it was settled about him.

He heard Bardas' coughing in the passage, stilled as he opened the door. "Damn it, woman!" Bardas said hoarsely. "You didn't have to wake the whole household."

Sophia moved aside as Alf came to the bed. By lamplight her face was death-white. But Bardas' was gray, clay-colored, filmed with sweat. The hands which tried to thrust Alf away had no strength. "What did you get up for? You don't sleep enough as it is." His voice cracked into a cough; he groped for a cloth, snatched it from his wife's hand.

As the spasm passed, Alf reached for the napkin. Bardas gripped it tightly, but the strong slender fingers pried it away and smoothed it. The stains upon it were scarlet.

Alf met Sophia's eyes. They were brave and steady, but beneath lay terror. She had seen the death in her husband's face.

Alf folded the cloth and laid it beside Bardas' hand. "This isn't the first time," he said.

"It's a touch of lung fever, that's all. I'm getting better. No need to drag you out of your bed."

Alf knelt by Bardas' side. Fear was thick in the room, Katya's, Sophia's; and Bardas', a deep well of it overlaid with anger. *Dying, I know it, damn this body; dying, and what will they all do? War's coming, Sophia's as good as a man but who'll believe it, little as she is, no bigger than a child. Sophia, the girls, poor half-made Nikephoros who was all the son I could manage; some bull of a Frank will trample them all and leave them for dead.*

Alf examined him with the light sure touch which so comforted the people who came to Saint Basil's. In spite of himself Bardas sighed under it. Pain stabbed his lungs; his eyes darkened as he fought back the spasm. But the hands were there, deft and gentle, and the face like a lamp in the gloom. There was nothing boyish in it, nothing even youthful. *No,* it seemed to say to him without moving its lips. *No one will harm you or yours. Nor will you die. Not yet. Sleep, my friend. Sleep deep.*

Bardas fought to hold to the light. But he had no strength against that gentle, implacable will. His eyes closed; his breathing eased and deepened.

"He'll sleep now," Alf said, "and be better when he wakes." He straightened, drawing a long breath. His face was drawn, his eyes staring blindly into the dark. But the gray pallor had left Bardas' skin; he slept easily, without that terrible rattling of breath which had frightened Sophia even before the coughing began.

Alf was turning away, wavering a little. She caught his cold hand, though once she had it she could think of nothing to say. He swayed visibly. She pushed him into a chair and held him there while Katya ran to fetch wine. A sip or two seemed to strengthen him; his eyes lost their blind look, and a ghost of color tinged his cheeks.

Relief made Sophia's voice sharp. "Don't you go too," she snapped at him.

"I can't," he said faintly, or perhaps she imagined it. A moment later he spoke in a different, stronger voice. "Bardas is very ill. I won't hide that from you. But if he rests and refrains from fretting, he can recover somewhat. Enough to see this war to its end."

She had known it, but the blow brought her to her knees. Alf reached for her; she shook him off. If her knees had given way, her mind had not. "You're not well yourself. Go to bed now and give me one less thing to worry about."

"It was only a passing faintness."

"Go to bed, I said!"

It was the same tone which she used with a recalcitrant child. She saw a spark of anger in his eyes—after all, she had sent for him and made use of him and thanked him not at all—and with it a glint that might have been amusement, but he obeyed her meekly enough.

He had left his wine almost untouched. She raised the cup, stared at it for a long moment, and drained it to the dregs.

But the strong vintage of Cos had no power tonight to dull her wits or to lull her body to sleep. After a wakeful while she left Bardas in Katya's care and went where her feet led her.

The garden had succumbed to frost some time since; the waxing moon lent a cold beauty to its ruins. Sophia walked through the brittle grass among flower beds covered thickly with leaves until spring. Although the air was cold, the wine warmed her.

A flicker of light, a murmur of voices, drew her to the far corner. The moon glinted on Alf's pale head as he sat cross-legged on the ground, a white dove nestling in his hands. Even as Sophia paused, shrinking back instinctively into the shadows, he said in a soft clear voice, "You know I can't do that."

The dove stirred, ruffling its feathers.

"I've tried," he said. "I can't. I do everything just as you've told me; and when the change begins, when nothing inside me is solid or stable, terror drives me back into myself."

The white bird spread its wings. His hands were empty; a hound stood before him, glowing white as if its coat had trapped the moon. Its ears were the color of blood.

Something moved in Alf's shadow. A small figure danced about the beast, and the beast leaped with it, licking its laughing face.

Alf's grave expression softened. "Yes; that's my favorite shape, too." His hands gathered light, fingers flying; he wrapped Nikephoros in shimmering strands like jewels, or like chains.

Sophia sprang forward in fear, in consuming anger. She snatched up her son, hardly aware that the cords of light had thinned and fallen away, or that the witch-hound had fallen back leaving her face to face with the creature she had begun to love as a kinsman.

"Sorcerer!" she hissed at him.

He flinched as if she had struck him, but said no word. He looked very young, and wounded to the heart.

He had ensnared them all and corrupted her son. Nikki struggled wildly in her arms, not knowing her at all, aware only that she had taken him away from his delight.

"You're hurting him," Alf said softly.

She tightened her grip. "Better I than you. How long have you had your spell on him? How long before you make him one of you?"

"Since we met," he answered, "and never. No human can become what I am."

Surely his candor was a trap. Nikki had quieted, chest heaving, each breath catching in a sob. She held him more lightly and turned him to face her. A sharp pain wrung from her a cry; he broke free.

His teeth had drawn blood. She pressed a corner of her shawl to the wound and stood still, watching without comprehension. Alf had not drawn the child in or otherwise sealed his victory. Nikki clung to him with frantic strength; gently but firmly he pried the clutching hands away and set Nikki on his feet. For a moment his hands rested on Nikki's shoulders. They stiffened, then sagged. Nikki turned slowly, drew his mother's arm down, kissed the place where he had bitten her. His face was wet with tears.

She kissed them away. His arms locked about her waist. But only for a moment. He stood back, head up, and turned his face from her to Alf and back again. His pleading was clear to read.

She hardened her heart. "Who is your master, witch-man? The Lord of Lies?"

"No," he said, the flat word, no more.

"Why? Why did you turn out to be like this? We took you

in. We trusted you. We loved you. Why didn't you—oh God, why didn't you keep me from seeing this?"

He touched her hand. She recoiled. But he pursued, rising, towering over her. His fingers closed about her wrist; he turned her arm, uncovering the wound. It had bled very little, but it ached fiercely. He brushed her skin with a fingertip, rousing a deep shudder, yet the touch was warm. The pain ebbed away; the marks faded like smoke in the sun.

He let her go. She drew back step by step until she was well out of reach. "*Why?*" she cried to him.

"I wanted you to know from the first. You wouldn't listen. The doctor knew in Chalcedon. You wouldn't heed him. And I was weak enough to let you be. Tonight . . . Bardas is dying, Sophia. Within a year he will die, nor can any power of mine do more than slow his dying. And before he slept he wanted me to tend you as a grown son would when he should be gone. Could I let either of you depend upon a lie?"

Her voice caught in her throat. She forced it out. "Does—does he—"

"He knows."

"But when—"

"Before I made him sleep. He said he always knew I wasn't like anyone else. He didn't want you to know. You are a jewel among women, he said, but after all you are a woman."

"But he didn't *say* any of that!"

"He thought it."

There was a silence. Sophia gathered her scattered wits into what order she might. Alf stood unmoving. The moon had caught his eyes and kindled them.

She rubbed her arm where the pain had been, slowly, eyes fixed upon him. "What would happen," she asked in a steady voice, "if I called a priest?"

"He would be extremely annoyed to be roused so late."

She strangled laughter that was half hysteria. "And for nothing, too. I can't hate you, Alfred. I may be endangering everyone who's dear to me, but I simply can't."

"I'll go away," he said. "I should have done it at the first."

Sophia wanted to hit him. She seized his hand instead, too quickly for either of them to shrink away, and held it fast. "Don't be ridiculous. You have a place here. There's no point in running away from it."

"I'm corrupting your children."

"You're keeping my husband alive."

He bowed his head. His face was in shadow, the lids lowered over the strangeness of his eyes. He was a legend, a tale of wonder and of terror. Yet she realized that she felt no fear of him at all. His hand was warm in hers, made of flesh like her own; she had seen him ill and she had seen him well, healing where men had destroyed.

"No," he said, "don't judge me now. It's only the wine and your anxiety for Bardas, and guilt that you spoke to me as you did, though you had the right."

"I had no right!" she countered sharply. "I forgot everything I'd ever seen of you. I spoke to wound you who'd already worn yourself to a rag for Bardas and for me; and I thought things of you that no man would ever forgive. And you never moved to defend yourself. Whatever you are, Alfred of Saint Ruan's, you're far closer to Heaven than to Hell."

"You've seen what I can do."

"Would you harm me or any of us?"

"No." He answered at once, without doubt, though the rest was soft, almost hesitant. "I couldn't. It would hurt me too much."

She embraced him tightly. "You're safe now," she said. "No more fears and no more secrets. There's only one thing."

He tensed.

Sophia drew his head down, the better to see his face. "Do you always know what everyone's thinking?"

His eyes widened in dismay and in understanding. "Oh, no! Only when there's need, or when the other wishes it; or when there's no help for it."

She let him go, oddly comforted. "Of course," she said. "There would be laws and courtesies. And you are a philosopher."

"Of sorts."

"You're not as young as you look, are you?"

"No," he answered, "I am not."

"Sometimes it shows." She touched him again, a brief caress. "Thank you, Alfred."

"For what?"

"For everything. Even for telling me. I still trust you with my children."

He bowed low, unable for once to speak.

15

"Aristotle," said Thea, "was a mere maker of lists. Plato was a philosopher."

"Plato lacked a system." Alf closed his book, rose and stretched.

Thea watched him from her corner of the window niche. "A philosopher has to have a system?"

"If he wants to capture the fancy of the schoolmasters."

"And you?"

"I prefer Plato." He sat down again, close but not touching, and took up his book. "I'm illogical, old-fashioned, and very probably a heretic."

"Very probably," she agreed. "I'm tired of the *Categories*. Where's the book you found in Master Dionysios' library?"

"The Plato? In my room. Shall I fetch it?"

"Let me." She set it in his lap, snatched out of air. Their hands touched; his withdrew quickly. He opened the book more quickly still.

His eyes ran over the words, but his mind reflected Thea's face. He stole a glance at her. She sat with knees drawn up, head cocked to one side, waiting. A difficult pupil, she; lethally quick-witted and well aware of it, acknowledging him her master but allowing him not an instant's rest upon his laurels.

She would catch him now if he did not bring his mind to order. But it would not shape itself as he willed it. He watched his hand stretch out to trace the curve of her cheek.

She smiled with the familiar touch of mockery. "Was that in your book?"

"Dreams," he said, "are shadows of the life we live, and life a shadow of the Reality."

"Have your dreams been strange of late?"

"My body is seventeen years old. My mind in sleep follows it and it alone. What are six decades of philosophy in the face of that?"

"What use is philosophy at all? Except to keep dry old men busy and to put young ones to sleep, where they dream of love and wake to foolish shame."

"My teaching bores you then? Do you want to end it?" He managed to sound both eager and regretful.

She laughed and weighed their two books in her hands, Plato and Aristotle. "Bored? I? How could I be? You're the best of teachers, and you know it. But I'm a poor philosopher. All those wordy old men with their heads in the clouds . . . even Socrates, who knew a thing or two of the world, what was he doing but escaping his termagant of a wife and finding excuses for his poverty?"

"There's more to the world than what we see."

"Who should know that better than I? And I like to give my mind a bit of exercise. But I can't look at all those sober speculations in the proper light. If you and I are only shadows, or faulty conglomerations of the four elements, or a dance of atoms in the void, why is life so sweet?"

"To you perhaps it is."

"And to you it isn't? Humans have trapped you, little Brother. They live a little while, bound in flesh that must decay; some do the world a bit of good, but most, like angry children, destroy as much of it as they can before they're snatched away. Or they make up stories about the foulness of flesh to convince themselves that they don't want to stay in it. They forget how to live, and say that God, or the gods, or the Demiurge, or whatever power you will, set them here to test them and prove them worthy of an afterlife. Or else, and worst of all, they deny that there is any meaning in anything and give themselves up to despair."

"Would you rather that no one thought on his fate at all?"

"Too much of anything is dangerous. Look at you. The monks made you in their own image and taught you to shrink from the world. Maybe they were made for Heaven, but you weren't."

"Then I must have been made for Hell."

She glared at him. "Don't talk like a fool. You were made for earth, which stands precisely between. And which means that you can reach for both. Heaven if you live as you were meant to live, in full realization of what you are. And Hell if you deny any part of yourself."

"If I turn my power loose, I can destroy the world."

"That's arrogance, and a denial of your conscience. We are gifted with one, you know. Or cursed if you prefer."

"*We*, you say. What are we? Changelings, say people in Anglia. But all the legends tell of human children stolen and monsters set in their places, troll-brats or mindless images which shrivel away with the dawn. Not elf-children of the true blood."

"Who's to say what real elf-children are like? Maybe we are monsters, too hideous or too incomplete to be endured, or else miserable hybrids whom none of our lofty kin would acknowledge. Though I've talked with beings of the otherworld, ghosts, and once a demon; and I've heard tell of one of us who met a Power under a hollow hill. None of them could or would tell us what we are. Maybe we really are changelings. Maybe we're God's joke on humankind. Maybe we don't exist at all. Who knows? There are only a few of us that I know of, and those few have all gone to Rhiyana or known its King."

"Gwydion, for all his wisdom, knows no more than you or I."

"Yet you asked me, woman that I am, and anything but royal. I'm flattered."

"I was shouting in the dark."

"And avoiding the main issue as usual. Your body isn't as easy to distract as your mind is. When are you going to listen to it?"

"When it stops bidding me to sin."

"Is love a sin?"

"Love, no. This is lust."

"Can you be so sure of that?"

That was her essence: to shake the foundations of his world. He unclenched his fists, took the books from her, rose. "I can't separate the two when I think of you, but I will do it. Then we shall see."

"Then you shall no longer have me to trouble you."

She spoke so quietly and so calmly that she frightened him. He moved by instinct, closer to her; standing over her, looking down into her face. The books weighed him down; he willed them away and set his hands upon her shoulders. So thin she was, all brittle bones like a bird. She had had no more sleep or food or peace of mind than he had.

Without conscious thought, he bent and kissed her. She responded with more warmth than he had looked for or dared to hope.

"Yes, damn you," she said angrily, "I love you, God help me. Love you, lust for you, and snatch with shameful eagerness at any crumb you deign to drop in front of me."

He stroked the smooth softness of her hair. She closed her eyes and shivered. "Damn you," she whispered. "Oh, damn you."

He knelt face to face with her and took her cold hands. "Marry me, Thea," he said.

Her eyes opened wide. He met them, baring his mind to her, all defenseless. *I mean it,* he said. *I want it. Marry me.*

Her eyes, then her hand, freed from his, explored his face. Her fingers tangled in his hair. "I love you," she said.

He waited, heart hammering, unable to breathe.

"I love you," she repeated, speaking carefully, "but I don't want to marry you."

His heart stopped. All the blood drained from his face.

She played with his hair, smoothing it, stroking it. "You want me almost as badly as I want you. But you're afraid of the sin. Marriage, you think, will take away both the sin and the fear. You don't see yet that words mean nothing; that love, not a priest's mumbling, is the sacrament."

"I do see it," he said in a voice he hardly recognized as his own.

"Only with your eyes. In your mind, Alfred of Saint Ruan's, you're still in your cloister, though the Pope has given you a writ that says the opposite. And I won't marry a monk."

For a long while he knelt there under her hand. Little by little his heart went cold. She saw it; he watched the dismay grow in her eyes. But she said, "I would be your lover if you were the Lord Pope. Your wife I cannot and will not be."

He rose slowly. He understood now why she had flown from him in Petreia. But her anger had been fiery hot. His was ice-cold. "I beg your pardon, my lady," he said. "I have offended you. I shall not repeat my error." He bowed with careful correctness and began to turn away.

"Alf!" she cried.

He turned back. She faced him, and he saw a stranger, a woman beautiful in her anger, who after all meant nothing to him.

Her own passion froze; her head came up, her chin set. "No," she said, "do not offend me again."

Once more he bowed. This time she did not try to prevent his leaving.

16

This was going to be a bad day, Sophia thought. The children had been quarreling since they woke; the cook was in bed with a fever and breakfast had been all but inedible; and Bardas had risen from a sleepless night, dressed, and announced that he was going out and be damned to them all. Even the sky wept, a gray cold rain that would turn to sleet by nightfall.

She paused in the passage between the kitchen and her workroom and rubbed her aching eyes. "God," she prayed under her breath, "give me patience, or at least a decent night's sleep."

Swift light footsteps brought her erect. Alf descended the stair from his room, fastening his cloak as he moved. He slowed when he saw her; his eyes warmed.

The world seemed a little lighter for his presence. Sophia put on a smile for him and said, "Good morning. I didn't see you at breakfast."

"I ate in the nursery with Nikki." He drew up his hood and settled a hat over it. All his face receded into shadow save for the uncanny ember-flare of his eyes. Yet even that comforted her, in its own fashion.

He touched her cheek, the merest brush of a fingertip. "Bardas won't harm himself," he said gently.

"In this weather?"

Alf smiled, a white flash in the depths of his hood. "He'll be well. I've seen to that. And he's better off as he is, working and making himself useful, than fretting in his bed."

Her answering smile was faint but genuine. It faded as she sensed a change in him like a sudden, freezing wind. Thea stood at the end of the passage, stiff and still. Alf inclined his head to her politely, as to a stranger; bowed to Sophia, murmuring a word or two of farewell; and took his leave.

"A gray morning," Thea said. Now that Alf was gone, she seemed her usual self.

That cold moment had brought back Sophia's headache in full force. She could find no smile for Thea and barely a pleasant word. "Gray? Black, rather. Have you ever had days when the whole world seems out of sorts?"

"Too many." Thea's arm settled about Sophia's shoulders. She had not Alf's gift of heart's ease; she was fire and quicksilver, bracing rather than comforting.

Sophia sighed and let herself lean briefly against the other. "You two," she said. "What would I do without you?"

Although Thea's voice was light, Sophia felt the tension in her body. "Don't go thinking of us as angels of mercy! We're like cats; we look after our own comfort. If it adds to anybody else's, why then, how pleasant for him."

"You're too modest."

They walked toward Sophia's workroom. It was warm there, a warmth which crept up through their feet from the hypocaust below. Thea went to the window and stood gazing out at the rain which lashed the barren garden. Her face in profile was unwontedly still.

"Is something wrong?" Sophia asked her.

She did not turn. "No," she answered, "of course not. What makes you think that?"

"You and Alf. You've been avoiding one another for days now. Has something happened? Is there anything I can do?"

"No," Thea said again. "It's all right. It's nothing."

Sophia approached her and laid a hand on her arm. "If I'm prying, I beg your pardon. But it's *not* nothing when the whole family can feel a difference. All's not well between you. Is it?"

"You are prying," Thea said in a thin cold voice. She clasped herself tightly, tensely, dislodging Sophia's hand. But she did not move to go.

The other waited, silent.

Suddenly she spun about. "Stop thinking sympathy at me!"

"I can't help it."

"You aren't trying."

"I'm sorry."

"You aren't." Thea drew a shuddering breath, controlling her face and voice, mastering her temper. "I . . . sometimes we forget; humans have eyes too. Has it been so obvious?"

"Rather. It's Alf, isn't it?"

"How can you tell?"

"I have eyes," Sophia said without irony. "For all his sweetness, he has a temper. A terrible one, with staying power. You're much quicker to anger, and to forgive."

"Sometimes," Thea muttered. "Sometimes not. God, what fools men are!" She prowled the small room, restless as a cat. After a circuit or two she stopped. "He asked me to marry him."

"And you refused?"

"Of course I did! He doesn't want a wife any more than I want a husband."

"Then why did he ask?"

"Temporary insanity. Why else? But now he's got his pride to think of, and a wound in it that he won't let heal. Does he think I don't have any of my own? Marriage is bad enough for any woman without her having to contend with a husband who's still more than half a monk."

"You could cure him of that, if you would."

"Not by marrying him," Thea said. "He was a monk for

longer than you'd ever believe, with no more thought for his body's needs than a marble saint. The first time he realized he was made of flesh, and warm flesh at that, he hardly knew what was happening. When he found out, he was terrified. Terrified and disgusted, as if God hadn't made that part of him too."

"Can you honestly blame him?"

"For being afraid, no. Not even for being ashamed; that's only his upbringing. But I won't marry him. He has to come to me without shame, with no more fear than anyone might expect of a man who's never taken a woman; as a lover, or not at all."

"You're proud too," Sophia said. "As proud as he is. One of you is going to have to yield."

"He won't. And I refuse to crawl at his feet."

Sophia shook her head. "Stubbornness never solved anything. God forgive me for encouraging a sin; but if I were you, I'd go to him tonight and stay there until I'd broken this deadlock."

"No," said Thea, immovable. "I'm done with begging. He'll come to me or he won't come at all."

Sophia sighed. Quarrels, she thought. What had they ever brought but grief? And this one shadowed the whole household.

She bit back angry words, tried to speak gently. "Whatever else God gave you beyond what He's given the rest of us, He didn't take away your capacity for foolishness."

"Probably not," Thea agreed willingly. "I have business in the City. Is there anything I can do for you there?"

You know well, Sophia thought, but she held her tongue.

Thea left pleasantly enough, even with a smile, leaving Sophia to her accounts and to her troubled thoughts.

Alf was late in coming to Saint Basil's. Even as he shed his sopping cloak, a throng of students, doctors, and walking wounded converged upon him. He had promised to teach a class in anatomy; Stephanos was much better but still in pain; he was not permitted to tend the women, but this one surely, he must advise, such symptoms, no one here had ever seen . . .

"Master Theo!" a voice called over the din. It was one of the students, her high voice pitched even higher with urgency. "Master Theo! You must come at once. Master Dionysios—"

The name freed Alf from the pressing crowd and sent him striding swiftly toward the Master's study.

Just within the door, he stopped. Dionysios sat in his accustomed chair, a book in front of him fallen open to a brilliantly painted page. But he was not alone. On either side of the door stood a guard in splendid livery, and across from the Master sat the most elegant creature Alf had ever seen.

"This is the man called Theo?" The voice was soft, cultured, and contralto, yet not a woman's. Nor, though the face was beardless and beautiful, was it a woman's face. It registered some little surprise, and perhaps amusement. "So; for once the tales were true."

"What did you expect?" Alf asked coolly, offering no more greeting or courtesy than he had received.

The eunuch smiled. "Less than what I see. Oh, much less. They said that you were tall; fair; angelic in face and humble of bearing, but at the same time royally proud. Well then, I looked for a light-haired man of middle height or a little more, with some claim to handsomeness, and an air of ill-concealed arrogance. Who would have thought that for once the rumors would be true?"

Alf glanced at Dionysios. "Sir," he said, "have you called me here for a purpose? Am I to amuse your noble guest?"

"He's noble certainly," said the Master without either awe or pleasure. "His name is Michael Doukas. He's come from the Emperor."

"Truly?" Alf's calmness did not waver. "Which one?"

"Need it matter?" asked Michael Doukas softly, toying with one of his many rings. "Yet if it concerns you, I shall be formal. His Sacred Majesty, Isaac Angelos, commands you to attend him in his palace at Blachernae."

Alf's eyes widened slightly. "I am of course greatly honored. But why?"

The Emperor's messenger looked him over slowly, dark eyes glinting. "You are a very famous man, Master Theo. Even our exalted Emperor, set aloft upon his throne, has heard your name and wondered at it. Wondered indeed which of the many tales is true. Did you will the fire of accursed memory, great master? Or did you will it away?"

Dionysios stood abruptly. "Emperor or no Emperor," he rapped, "I'll not have courtiers' games played in my presence. If you have to take my best man away from me on a day when I can ill spare him, do it, and let me get back to my work."

"Certainly His Majesty has no intention of keeping you away from your duties." Michael Doukas rose with languid grace. He was nearly as tall as Alf, and slender as a woman. "Come, Master Theo. You are expected."

Beneath Dionysios' annoyance Alf sensed fear. It was most irregular, this summons. The Emperor, Dionysios well knew, was not sane. And Michael Doukas was as deadly as he was elegant. Who knew what trap had been laid, or why?

Alf met the Master's gaze and smiled. Dionysios scowled in return. *Go on,* his eyes said, *get yourself killed. Should I care?*

"Come," said Michael Doukas.

17

The Emperor Isaac Angelos sat upon his throne with his crown upon his head and in his hand the orb of the world. Beside him on a second throne lay the source and center of his power, that which alone might rule the Lord of the Romans, the Heir of Constantine, the voice of God on earth: the book of the Gospels laid open to the image of Christ the King. All about the double throne stood the high ones of the court. Above them arched trees of gold bearing fruits of diamond and ruby and emerald, and on the branches jeweled birds; before them crouched a lion of brass.

The lion, Alf noticed, was tarnished, and tilted at a precarious angle; the birds neither moved nor sang. The living courtiers seemed splendid enough, yet most looked bored beyond words. He caught at least one ill-concealed yawn before he turned his eyes away from them to the man upon the throne.

By rite and by custom the Sacred Emperor was more than a man. His every moment was hedged about in ritual as ornate and as holy as the Mass itself. His every thought was shaped in and for his office. Or so the makers of the empire had ordained over the long years. Like the beasts and the birds, the office was failing, the man marred.

Isaac Angelos might have been handsome once. His features, though strongly drawn beneath the graying red-gold beard, were furrowed deep with pain and petulance. Over his ruined eyes he wore a band of silk, imperial purple, that gave him the look of the blinded king in a play.

Every step of Alf's approach from palace gate to the dais' foot had been a step in a solemn hieratic dance. It should have brought him into the sacred presence in a state of mindless awe; but he was only weary, fastidiously distasteful of the robes which he had been made to wear. Magnificent though they were, of priceless Byzantine silk embroidered with gems and gold, they had not seen a cleaning in all the reigns since they were made.

He bowed as his guide directed him, the last and deepest of many such obeisances, full upon his face as if before a god. Above him the Emperor stirred. His voice rang out unexpectedly deep and rich. "Is he up yet? Eyes—where are my Eyes?"

Alf rose. A small figure had come to stand beside the Emperor. Despite its size, it was no child but a slim honey-brown youth with a proud wisp or two of beard. With his great dark eyes fixed upon Alf, he began to sing. He had a clear tenor voice and a relentless eye for detail, and the gift of painting a portrait in words. What he sang, the Emperor saw, even to the slight wry smile as Alf heard the inventory of his robe's smudges and stains.

The sweet voice stilled. The Emperor sat in all his majesty. Beneath the bandage his cheek twitched slightly, spasmodically. His fingers loosened upon the golden orb; it rolled from his lap, fell to the floor with a leaden thud, bounced like a child's ball upon the steps of the dais. It halted at Alf's feet.

No one dared to touch it, although several of the guards and eunuchs had started forward aghast. Nor did Alf move to pick it up. Among the courtiers, some had stirred, alive to the portent. Magicians, those: sorcerers; diviners and astrologers.

They watched him avidly, some with knowledge and perhaps with fear.

"Sire," Alf said in the silence, clearly and directly as if this had been a Western king and not the sacred Emperor, "surely you did not summon me merely to look at me."

The Emperor started a little, his fingers opening and closing, finding only air. "To look? To look, you say? With what?"

"Why, Sire, with your Eyes."

"My eyes are gone. Right in my palace he did it, my brother, my little brother who always swore he loved me. Do you have eyes, child?"

"Yes," Alf answered. Off to the side a courtier drooped against his fellow, limp with ennui.

"Cherish your eyes, little one. So beautiful they are, so clever to take in the light." Isaac Angelos trailed off. For an instant he seemed to subside into a torpor; abruptly he drew himself up in his seat. His fists clenched upon the arms. "You," he said in a new voice, a strong one. "They call you Theo. What is the rest of it? Theophilos? Theodoros? Theophylaktos?"

"Only Theo, Sire."

Above the bandage the Emperor's brow clouded. "No man has but half a name."

One of the sorcerers made his way to the Emperor's side. He was a prince of his kind, a turbaned Moor with a smooth ageless face the color of ebony and a fixed, serpent's stare. "Your Sacred Majesty," he said softly in perfect Greek, "no man may have so little of a name. But is he a man?"

Michael Doukas stirred beside Alf, as languid as ever. "A boy then. A youth, in courtesy, and quite likely to become a man. Of that, learned master, I can assure you."

No one quite ventured to smile. Skeptical of the Moor's magics they might be, but they knew enough to fear his influence.

He did not deign to reveal anger. "I questioned not his gender but his species. Look, sacred Eyes. Is that the face of a mortal man?"

"He is very fair," sang the dwarf, "like to the old gods."

The sorcerer bent, speaking in the Emperor's ear. "Your

Majesty, his name, his face, hint at great mysteries. The tales you have heard, the marvels of which your servants have told you—"

"Marvels," Isaac Angelos echoed him. "Magic. Mysteries. An angel in the fire. It burned, my City, like old Rome. But nobody sang its fall to the lyre. He was working miracles. A house fell down and he walked out of it, no scratch or burn, and in his arms a man of twice his bulk. He laid on his hands and men healed. He healed them. He heals them. Come here, child, and lay your hands on me."

Alf spoke gently, with compassion. "Sire, if I have a gift or a skill, it is of God's giving. But He has granted me no power to restore what is gone. I cannot give you back your eyes."

The Moor was a basilisk, the courtiers carrion birds, circling, waiting for their prey to fall. None yawned now or wished for release.

The Emperor turned his head from side to side as if to scan the audience. "No healing? No recompense? A throne—how easy after all to win it back. But I would rather have my eyes." He leaned forward. "They said there would be a miracle. They said one would come. It was in the stars, and in the crystal, and in the fires."

"Aye," intoned the Moor. "The time will come, beloved of God, when you will see again. You will have your eyes, your youth and strength, your empire in all its glory. You shall rule the world."

Alf stooped and lifted the orb. Its fall had dented it, shaken loose a jewel or two, bent askew the cross that crowned it.

The courtiers had taken up the sorcerer's proclamation, an interchange of verse and response, caught up short as Alf raised the sphere of gold. Suddenly he was weary of all this, the ritual, the tarnished splendor, the Emperor whose mind wandered on the paths of madness. They had made him so, these fawning servants, ruled by men who boasted of power and magic. Charlatans, all of them. Liars, sycophants, parasites.

The Moor, who had more knowledge than most if no wisdom, drew back a step. In his eyes Alf saw himself, a frail figure in a great weight of soiled silk, grown suddenly terrible.

"Sire," Alf said quietly in silence thick enough to touch, "your empire has fallen from your hand."

"Then," said Isaac Angelos, reasonably, "give it back to me."

"I cannot."

"I am the Emperor. I command you."

"I cannot," Alf repeated. "It has gone the way of your eyes. There is no healing for you, Lord of the Angeloi. Your eyes are gone. Your empire is gone. Your city will fall because you have not ruled it but have sat upon your throne dreaming of miracles; paying heed to these false prophets who gather like jackals about you."

"Lies!" thundered the Moor. "Who has sent you, O liar without power? The Doge? Marquis Boniface? Or," he added with a venomous glance at Alf's guide, "our own Doukas?"

Alf regarded the sorcerer calmly. "His Majesty summoned me, as you know well who brought my name to him. What was it that you wished for? That I add my voice to yours, echo your feigned foreseeings, strengthen your lies with mine? Or that I speak the truth as all my kind are bound to do, and perish for it, thus removing the threat of my presence? For true power must not endure if smooth words and conjurors' trick are to prevail."

The Moor's lip curled. "A poisonous serpent, you are, bloated with lies and twisted prophecies."

With a sudden movement the Emperor smote the arm of his throne. "Prophesy, boy. Prophesy!"

"No one commands my power," Alf said softly, "not even His Sacred Majesty."

"Command it yourself then," snapped Isaac Angelos.

Alf did not quite smile. "Very well, Sire. What would you know?"

That took even the Emperor aback. "What? There are no incantations? No fires or crystals or arcane instruments?"

"I am not a sorcerer, Sire. My power comes from within. Ask and I will answer."

The Emperor paused for a long while, stroking his beard. At last he spoke. "Where is my gold sandal?"

In the breaking of tension, one or two of the courtiers laughed. Alf betrayed neither scorn nor fear. "You asked me to prophesy, Sire, not to find what you have lost. Your sandal," he added coolly, "lies with its mate in the dragon chest which came from Chin, under your robe of crimson silk embroidered with pearls."

The Emperor's fingers knotted in his beard. "Prophesy," he said. "Prophesy!"

Alf looked up into the haggard blinded face, with the orb a dead weight in his hands. The crowd of courtiers waited, minds and faces set for mockery. He drew a long breath and loosed the bonds of his seeing.

18

This must be how one felt after love: this glorious release, this utter lassitude. Alf's power, sated, returned docilely to its cage; he turned from it to the outer world, sighing a little, suddenly aware of his body's weariness.

Rough hands seized him. Voices roared in his ears, shaping slowly into words. "Liar! Impostor! Latin spy!"

The hall was in an uproar. Even the Emperor was on his feet, howling like a beast. "Kill him! *Kill him!*"

The hands began to drag him away. They belonged to Varangians, he realized. Even yet he was too numb and spent to be afraid. The last thing he saw before a scarlet darkness enfolded him was the Emperor's mad rage, and beyond it the Moor's wide white smile.

As the tumult receded, Alf struggled free of the Guardsman's cloak which had wrapped him about. They half dragged, half carried him down a long glittering corridor, marble-cold and deserted.

Alf fought to walk; after a step or two they let him, keeping still a firm grip upon his arms. "Where are you taking me?" he asked them.

Neither replied. Nor did their faces tell him anything. The eyes of both were blue and hard.

The palace was a labyrinth, their passage through it tortuous and interminable. Once they passed from building to building under the sodden sky. Alf's feet ached; he might have laughed at himself, the tireless pilgrim, grown too soft from his months in the City to walk any proper distance.

Abruptly the Guards halted. A door opened; they thrust him through it and slammed it behind him.

He had fallen to one knee. He straightened slowly, shaking back his hair. This was no prison cell. A reception room, he thought, furnished with a chair or two, a wine table, a divan beside a glowing brazier. The walls shimmered with mosaics, beasts and birds in a garden, a golden fish leaping high out of a fountain spray.

His eyes returned from the wall to the divan. On it reclined a languid smiling figure. "Greetings," said Michael Doukas.

There was a chair nearby; Alf took it.

"No doubt of it," observed his host, "you have style. Courage, too, or should I call it folly? To prophesy so calmly, in such exquisite detail, and to his own face, the downfall of an emperor."

"He asked for it," Alf said.

"He asked for a web of soothing lies. It's well for you, sir prophet, that he never asked your true name or nation, and that his sorcerer knows you only as the healer of Saint Basil's."

Alf's entrails knotted. Michael Doukas smiled, arching a delicate brow. "So, Alfred of Saint Ruan's, is your courage not absolute? Or do you fear for your friends in House Akestas?"

Alf clamped his jaw, but the other read the question in his eyes.

"I have my spies. The Doge admires you, I understand, though you've never performed for him as you have for us. We're enormously flattered, if somewhat disconcerted. Has anyone ever called you Cassandra?"

"Yes."

"Indeed?" Michael Doukas was interested. "Someday you'll have to tell me the tale. I plan to survive this, you see. The others will tell themselves that you lied, that all your dooms were simply empty words. I shall build upon them."

"Can you be sure that I tell the truth?"

"How not? I've read a book and I've heard a tale or two. I know what you are, Master Alfred. Alf—Theo—who named you so wisely and so well?"

"A monk in Anglia and the Master of Saint Basil's." Alf raised his chin. "You aren't alone in your wisdom, sir. The Moor too knows what I am."

"What. Not precisely who. Or," added Michael Doukas, "where."

"So," Alf said. "What will you do with me?"

The dark eyes glinted upon him. "I have you in my power, don't I? It's not often I have to deal with one quite so good to look on. More than good, if truth be told. What is it like to look in the mirror and see what you see?"

He expected an answer. Alf gave it, shortly. "Maddening."

Michael Doukas laughed. "Indeed! You're behind it and can't enjoy it. There's a tragedy for old Euripides."

"Aristophanes," Alf muttered.

Again that sweet, sexless laughter. "Such wit! You have an alarming array of talents, master seer. And very little patience to spare for me. I play with you, you think, like a cat amusing itself before the kill. No doubt you expect me to keep you here until I tire of you, then hand you over to His Majesty's torturers."

"You don't serve the Angeloi," Alf said. "You only seem to. Are you going to make me prophesy for your black-browed cousin?"

"No," answered Michael Doukas, "of course not. My handsome kinsman has no use for a seer. I serve myself, Master Alfred, and perhaps the City. If what you foretell comes to pass, there will be great need of a man with wit and intelligence and a thorough knowledge of the empire's workings. Rulers may change with dismaying regularity, but a competent administrator is worth more than a hundred kings."

"And I, who know all of this, am in your hands. In all senses. The Emperor has decreed my death. You know all there is to know of me; most particularly that while I have no dread of my own death, I feel quite otherwise about the deaths of my friends. Again I ask you. What will you do with me?"

"I like you, Master Alfred. Yes," Michael Doukas said, "I like you very much indeed. Brave as only a Latin can be, clever—almost—as a Greek, and completely unafraid to tell the truth. Would you enter my service?"

"What would I be? Your prophet? Your bedmate? Your fool?"

"Fools are a Frankish affectation. A prophet you've already been. The other . . . you are heartbreakingly beautiful. But you are also quite obviously, and quite tiresomely, the sort of young man who cares only for women."

Alf's face was stony. Michael Doukas smiled. "No, I want you for other things. To look at, perhaps. To tell me the truth."

"Then you should find yourself a slave. Or an intelligent lapdog."

"And not a Latin wanderer who tries to pass as a Greek? Rather successfully, I might add. Your accent could merely be provincial."

"I've refused to serve the Franks, who after all are my own people. Should I turn traitor?"

"Some might say you already have. You're here, are you not?"

"Not of my own accord."

"No one forced you to come to the City."

"I came as a pilgrim. I remain as a healer. To which occupation I would like very much to return."

"Well then, you shall be my physician."

Alf regarded him with a clear pale stare. "You are in excellent health and likely to live to a great age if your intrigues do not bring you to a sudden end. You have no need of my services, Michael Doukas."

"How proud you are! Lucifer before his fall." Michael Doukas rose and smoothed his robes. "You are adamant?"

"Yes."

"So." The eunuch raised his voice. "Guards!"

They came at once, filling the room with their presence, no longer the Emperor's Varangians but those who had accompanied the chamberlain to Saint Basil's. He indicated Alf with a languid hand. "If the Emperor should ask, this man is dead. He died in most exquisite agony, as befits a spy and a traitor. Upon his death, in the way of sorcerers, his body shriveled and fell to dust."

"And if the Moor asks?" Alf inquired.

"If the Moor asks, we cut you up and fed you to the menagerie." Michael Doukas paused, half smiling. "You had better not appear at Saint Basil's for a time."

"Until His Majesty is well distracted?"

"You know your own prophecy." He beckoned. "Take him away."

Alf stood in their hands, eyes upon the eunuch. "Why?" he asked.

Michael Doukas shrugged. "I like you. And," he said, "you might be of use to me later. Remember what I know, and what I have not done."

"Could I forget?" Alf smiled suddenly, startling that polished courtier into a brief, wide-eyed stare. "You are an utter villain. But for all that, a strangely likable man. Look for me at Armageddon."

19

The City was like a beast crouched to spring.

Across the Horn the Latins held to their camp, although the bitter wind clove through their tents and the sleet hissed in their watch-fires and their bellies knotted with hunger.

Within the walls, the Greeks nursed their hatred.

Alf could taste it, a vileness upon his tongue; could sense it as a throbbing in his brain. House Akestas offered no refuge, his shields no defense; even barricaded with all the power he could muster, his head ached with dull persistence.

"I said," Bardas' voice was slightly raised, "Master Dionysios has been inquiring after you."

With an effort Alf focused upon his surroundings. They were all staring at him: Anna and Irene with a book between them, Nikki playing on the floor with a kitten, Sophia in the midst of a letter; and Bardas on a couch, sitting upright in defiance of all his nurses but leaning more heavily on the cushions than he wished anyone to see. His eyes upon Alf were sharp in a face thinned and grayed with sickness. He raised a brow. "Well, sir? The Master wants to know, will you be coming back from the dead before winter ends?"

"Yes," Alf said. He willed his voice to be steady, even light. "Soon, in fact. A month in the tomb is quite long enough for any man."

"Is it safe?" Irene asked barely audibly. "After all, Master Dionysios knows the truth about you, but no one else does. Except us. And the Emperor—"

"His Majesty is mad beyond recall." Alf closed his eyes. It did nothing for the ache, but it kept him from seeing the others' concern. "I did that, you know. I told him what would be; and it thrust him over the edge. He's convinced now that he's God's deputy on earth; that when the sun comes round into the Lion he will slough off his skin like a snake in spring and emerge with his eyes and his youth restored, and proceed to rule the world."

"Could he do that?" Anna asked seriously.

"Of course not." Her father snorted and stifled a cough. "The young fool isn't thriving either, from what I've heard. He's tried to get back into favor by turning on the Latins, but it's too late for that. People are beginning to look round for a new emperor."

"Beginning?" Sophia shook her head. "It's gone past that. Isn't the Senate meeting in Hagia Sophia?"

"It is," Bardas answered. "Without a word from the palace."

"And not a man in all that assembly will accept the crown." Alf rose slowly. "Your pardon, but I think . . . I need to lie down."

They all would have sprung to his aid, but he waved them away. "Please, no. I'll be well enough. It's only a headache."

In the end he had to submit to Corinna's brusque and competent ministrations. She saw him undressed and laid in bed with a pungent herbal brew mixed with wine inside him and a cold compress on his brow. When she left him alone in the darkened room, he sighed with relief.

A small hand slipped into his; another touched his cheek. He opened his eyes to meet Nikki's wide worried stare. Through the shields which guarded his power, he loosed a dart of reassurance.

It had little effect. *Sick,* Nikki responded. *Father's sick. You're sick. The air feels bad. I'm afraid.*

Alf sat up, casting aside the compress, wincing as the movement set his temples throbbing.

Nikki's face twisted. *You hurt!* He held his own head in his hands. *You shut it in. That makes it worse. It hurts me.*

Carefully Alf knelt and smoothed Nikki's hair. His hands healed where they touched. *Better?* he asked.

After a moment Nikki nodded.

Alf smiled. *I have to go out. I'll come back as soon as I can. Will you wait for me?*

Nikki's brows knit. But he stepped back and watched Alf dress. Before the other was well done, he had fled.

Alf paused. He had seen no tears on Nikki's face, nor sensed aught but anxiety and a mind-picture of consolation in the form of a kitten. He shrugged slightly and reached for his cloak.

The Emperor Alexios prowled his privy chamber, gnawing his nails. His chamberlains watched him in white-faced silence. He was not an imposing man, this youngest of the Angeloi. Tall enough, handsome enough, with his father's strong features, but both his face and his movements lacked something. Resolution perhaps, or strength of will.

Suddenly he spun and smote his hands together. "Where *is* the man?" he cried.

The servants glanced at one another. After a moment one ventured forward, bowing to the ground. "Most sacred lord, His Excellency the Protovestiarios has gone as you requested to—"

"I know where I sent him!" Alexios resumed his pacing. "I sent him across the Horn. The Marquis must help me. The cursed mob will elect an emperor and kill me after, I know it. Marquis Boniface was my friend. He will stop them. He'll do anything if he's paid well enough, and I've offered him the richest bribe I can think of. For his priests, our Church—what's a word or two in the Mass if I survive this?—and for him the palace we're standing in. It's no loss. We can move to the Sacred Palace next to Hagia Sophia. It was good enough for Justinian and Basil and half a dozen Constantines. It's good enough for the Angeloi. Oh, sweet saints in heaven, let my lord win safe to the Marquis and bring him back with his knights!"

In the rear rank of chamberlains, eye met eye. One of the eunuchs, young and darkly elegant, nodded infinitesimally and slipped away.

Alf drank deep of the open air. He had not left House Akestas since he came back from the palace; his body, long inured to confinement as any monk's must be, nonetheless rejoiced in freedom. No matter that the sun was shrouded, the clouds heavy with rain. Even his pain had lessened, as if the walls of the house had gathered it all into too small a space.

While his feet bore him through a dim alleyway, his mind opened slowly, lowering each shield with care. The mood of the City washed over him, hate and fear and slowly hardening determination.

And something else. A very small thing, a pricking on the edge of consciousness. He probed, met nothing. A random thought then, nothing to fear. He dismissed it and bound mind again to body, making his way through the narrow crowded streets.

"Sire! By all that's holy, man, let me through to His Majesty!"

Alexios whipped about. The grating voice sawed through the sudden tumult at the door, harsh always, harsher now with emotion. Close upon it came its owner, a thickset man in rich garb now rumpled and soiled, with black eyes glittering under a single heavy bar of brow. He stopped short just within the door, breathing hard as if with exertion yet ghastly pale. As his eyes found the young Emperor, he plunged forward to fall at Alexios' feet. "Disaster, Your Majesty," he gasped. "Utter disaster!"

The Emperor stood with his mouth open, speechless.

The black-browed lord raised himself with visible effort.

"Sire, it's worse than we ever dreamed. My embassy is discovered; the people are up in arms, howling for your blood. That an heir of Constantine should sell his Church and his empire to barbarians with his palace for a surety—"

At last Alexios found his voice, an octave higher than its wont, almost a shriek. "Blood? My blood? The Marquis—"

"He consented. But there's no time for him to move. Even now the mob converges on the palace. Sire, by your leave, all your guards and soldiers have fled. Only the Varangians remain loyal to you. Let me set them to defend the walls and to delay the attack."

Alexios clutched at his minister, half blind with terror. "It's all lost, I know it, I know it. They'll catch me, rend me. I'll die!"

The Protovestiarios seemed to have regained much of his composure if none of his color. "No, sacred lord. Not yet, if your loyal men have any power left. The mob will come—it must. But you need not be here. I know a place, a safe place where you may rest and restore yourself and work to regain all you have lost."

The young Emperor was close to collapse. But some remnant of strength stiffened his back and sharpened his voice. "There is no safe place for me, my lord Mourtzouphlos. I shall be recognized and cut down."

Something glittered in the other's eyes, anger perhaps, or contempt. "My lord knows how well I have always served him. Will he not trust me now? I have the Marquis' promise of sanctuary, and loyal men waiting to bring us both to him. Come, Sire, I beg you. Come."

Alexios wavered. Mourtzouphlos knelt. "Sire, I beseech you, before it's too late."

The Emperor stared at him. "Too late?" he repeated. All at once he crumpled. "Oh, anything, anything! Only get me out of here!"

Mourtzouphlos gestured sharply. Men came forward with a heavy cloth. "My lord will pardon this indignity. Only for his life's sake do we subject him to it."

He was limp in their hands, all strength gone out of him with his brief resistance. They wrapped him in the rug and lifted him as if he had been no more than that, bearing him away.

Mourtzouphlos followed. On his face was the beginning of a smile.

The palace loomed in the dusk like a rock out of a tide-race. Beyond its walls a triple line of Guardsmen held off a mob alit with torches. The axes of the Guard glittered, raised to defend but not yet to strike.

Alf paused for breath on the edge of the tumult. All the wide space between himself and the palace gate was a tossing sea of humanity, and over it the flicker of fire.

He had all but forgotten the small prickle in his mind until it came again, slightly stronger. This time his swift probe caught something and gripped, drawing it to him.

A figure stumbled out of the throng to fall against him. He stared down at it in astonishment and growing horror. "Nikephoros!"

Nikki drew himself erect, hand to head. *You hurt me,* he accused.

Alf's fear for him turned to wrath, swiftly throttled. Nikki felt it and paled, though he did not flinch.

You hurt me, he repeated.

You followed me. Alf's mind-voice was cold. *You hid your mind from me.*

Nikki paled even further. He was close to tears. *I wanted to see where you went,* he said. *People always go out, but I never do. I'm tired of being locked up. I want to go out like everybody else.*

"Sweet Jesu," Alf said aloud. Nikki watched him with eyes gone huge, bracing himself for dire punishment. When Alf raised a hand, he fell back a step.

Alf caught his shoulder in a light strong grip. *Of all times for you to turn rebel . . .* He held Nikki's eyes with a white-hot stare and spoke to him even beyond mind-words, a wave of pure will. As Nikki responded with acquiescence, he took the child in his arms under his cloak and plunged forward swiftly into the mob.

It was quiet in the palace, an eerie quiet like the deeps of the sea while a storm rages overhead. Alf passed as a shadow among shadows, unseen even by those few servants who, out of ignorance or courage, went about their accustomed duties.

In a hall all of gold with pillars of golden marble, Alf met one who had eyes to see him.

"Too late," said the Varangian with Thea's eyes burning in his Saxon face. "The young Emperor is taken. The old one—"

"Is safe enough. I know." Alf spoke coolly, as to a stranger. "I was looking for you. I would prefer that you not risk yourself in this madness."

"You would prefer?" The unfamiliar deep voice was rich with scorn. "You can have a preference? And stand here to tell me of it with the heir to House Akestas in your arms?"

"He followed me," Alf said shortly. "Come home, Thea. This is no place for any sane being."

Thea's jaw set. "Here, my name is Aelfric."

"Appropriate," he observed, unyielding. "Come. Or are you going to wait until the battle comes this far?"

"It won't," she said flatly. "But you had better go back where you came from. It's death for you to be seen here."

"All the more reason for us to be quick."

She made no move to obey him. In this form she was as tall as he, broader and probably stronger, and in power, for all his native strength, she had the greater skill. He met the eyes which remained hers for him whatever shape she took, and held them.

For a long moment they did not waver or fall. Then they slid away.

"Come," he said.

When he turned, she followed him.

* * *

Mourtzouphlos inspected himself in the glass a servant held up for him. He looked well in imperial purple; the purple shoes of an emperor were an excellent fit. Better, he thought with the hint of a smile, than the green ones of the office he was forsaking. He adjusted his girdle slightly and smoothed his beard. "That will do," he said.

His men ranged themselves about him, the vanguard of those who held the palace. Soon the Varangians would learn that they had a new emperor to defend. But the head did not matter to the Guard, nor the feet, nor the body between; only the crown and the buskins that marked the Emperor.

Torchbearers waited on the balcony, the mob below, in spreading silence. He stepped forth.

A roar went up, as sudden and as mindless as the cry of a beast. But the closest and the keenest-eyed marked the face of the man above them. His name ran through the crowd, a manifold mutter: Alexios Doukas, Mourtzouphlos. "Mourtzouphlos. *Mourtzouphlos!*"

He let them shout their fill. It was like wine, sweet and heady. He allowed himself a smile. The mob here, the young idiot safe in irons, the Senate bickering uselessly in Hagia Sophia; he had them all precisely where he wanted them.

The tumult had died to a mild uproar. Mourtzouphlos beckoned; a torchbearer moved closer, raising his brand high. Its light flashed upon the regalia of an emperor. Save the crown. That, Mourtzouphlos held in his hands, raising it for all to see. Another shout rose, hushed when he lowered the crown and handed it to his elegant young chamberlain.

A thin wind ruffled his hair, struggling to lift his heavy mantle. He set his hands upon the cold stone of the balustrade and raised his voice. Though rasping-harsh, it had power; it carried easily. "People of the City," he said. "Romans. You know me."

He paused to let them bellow their assent, and continued. "You know me," he repeated. "I have served the empire for all the years of my manhood, and the emperors to the best of my ability. In this past grim year, I have done all that I may to protect the City from her enemies. I have fought in her battles; I have strengthened her walls. I have counseled her rulers and shown them the enemy where they looked for friends."

The mob began to seethe again. "The Latins! The filthy Latins!"

Mourtzouphlos raised his hands but not his voice. "Yes, the Latins. The wolves are at the gate, the fire in the field. I have shown Their Majesties what their allies are. I have beseeched them to cast the barbarians out; I have implored them to destroy this plague before it destroys us all. And yet—" His voice thickened with emotion; he fought to clear it. "And yet, while they pretended to listen—while they smiled and promised to take thought for their imperiled people—all the while, they were betraying us."

This was a lion's roar, deafening and deadly. Scarlet flared in torchlight, the ranks of the Guard swaying under a sudden assault. But it wavered and dissipated before the threat of the Varangians' axes.

"This very day," Mourtzouphlos said, "the Emperor Alexios sent a message to the Frankish camp." He had won silence, a multitude of ears straining to catch what he could tell. "He has struggled in recent days to make us forget who set him upon his throne. Yet the City has never forgotten. We, loyal to the City and the empire, have never let ourselves forget. And today, with our remembrance clear for him to see, he revealed his true allegiance. He sent to the Latins to ask their aid. Against the City and the empire he asked it. As surety"—Mourtzouphlos choked upon the words he had to say—"As surety, he offered two things: this palace, home of emperors since the great days of the Komnenoi; and our Church. Not only our city but our very souls would lie in thrall to—"

What more he would have said was drowned in the people's rage. It rose to a crescendo, so powerful and so prolonged that Mourtzouphlos began to be afraid. If this mob escaped his tenuous control—

He set his teeth. He held it. It raged, but it did not surge forward to overwhelm the Guard and the palace.

When at last he could be heard, he spoke again, hoarse with the effort of carrying his voice over that multitude. "I have served the emperors as best I can. But when service to the ruler becomes betrayal of the empire, then must that service end. You, people of the City, have seen this for long and long. I, blinded by my loyalty, have looked only now to the full truth. The Latins gave us their puppet and called him our Emperor. His father, once our rightful lord, has lost his wits with his eyes. And I have come at last to the end of my devotion. What have the Angeloi gained us? A hostile army outside of our walls, and half the City within destroyed by fire, and grief for all our people. It is time we remembered who we are. We are Romans, the sons of Augustus, of Constantine, of Justinian; rightful heirs to the empire of the world. Shall we permit a stinking rabble, a pack of unwashed barbarians, to trample us into the dust? Shall we bow to the Doge, whose eyes we took for his spying and his treason, and acknowledge him our master? Shall we surrender even our ancient faith to worship at the altar of the schismatic and the heretic, to yield our will to the Pope who tyrannizes over ruined Rome? Tell me, people of Constantinopolis! Must we do these things?"

"No!" they thundered back in one voice.

"No!" he echoed them. "No, and no, and no. The empire is firm, yet it needs a head. Those lords who are both loyal and wise have beseeched me to place mine beneath the crown. I know I am not worthy. But I am willing to take up the burden for the empire's sake and with your consent. And I vow to you, whatever you choose, whomever you set up as your Emperor, I shall labor ever and with all that is in me to rid us of the scourge across the Horn. The Latins shall fall; the City shall be free again, so help me God!"

He had them. Aye, he had them. "Mourtzouphlos!" they roared. And in counterpoint that slowly overwhelmed the rest, the acclamation of the Emperor: "Long life! Long life! Long life to His Sacred Majesty!"

Slowly, carefully, and with great satisfaction, Mourtzouphlos set the crown upon his head.

20

"It's done now."

Alf did not glance back at Thea, who walked behind him still along the lighted ridge of the Middle Way. She had spoken in her own voice; a long stride brought her level with him and revealed her as herself, glaring fiercely at him. "The City has a new Emperor," she said with more than a touch of sharpness.

"I know. The storm has broken; I can think again." Alf halted and set Nikki down. The child stood unmoving, great-eyed with the wonder and the terror of all he had seen that night; as a wagon rattled past he started, reaching instinctively for Alf's hand.

It shakes, he said in his mind. *It hits the bottoms of my feet.* Safe in Alf's grip, he surveyed this new and frightening world.

How ever did you manage to follow Alf so far?

He looked up at Thea. She frightened him no more than Alf did, for all her pretense of fierceness. *I was busy,* he answered her. *I was following. I had to keep him from feeling me. But the people got to be too many and too—too pushing.*

It's a miracle you didn't get trampled.

He shook his head. *Not that kind of pushing. That wasn't hard to get out of at all. But they were thinking so much. So many and so much and in so many places at once.*

Thinking? Alf dropped to his knees, heedless of any who passed, and searched Nikki's face with eyes gone slightly wild. *You heard them thinking?*

"That's not the worst of it," Thea broke in upon Nikki's assent. "Humans can do that easily enough if they have to. It's the least of our powers. But how did a human child manage to shield his mind from you for as long as he did?"

"I was preoccupied," Alf said.

Thea made a sound which was neither delicate nor feminine. "You're not a tenth as inept with your power as you want me to think, little Brother. He shielded from you. Which is something even I was far from skilled at when I was five years old."

Nikki watched their faces. He could follow the thoughts behind their words, but he could not understand what they meant. They were excited and angry and puzzled and perhaps a little afraid, staring at him with eyes that were like no one else's and looking up to glare at one another.

He reached for Thea's hand. It was cold and tense. Carefully, covering up his thought with not-thinking, he brought their two hands together. They had clasped before they knew it, the glares turned to frank amazement. "He did it again," Thea said. "But he's not one of us!"

"Are you sure of that?" demanded Alf.

"He's human," she said with certainty. "Do you realize what this means?"

Alf rose abruptly, letting go her hand as if it burned him. "I realize that we are in the middle of the main thoroughfare of Constantinople. And it's begun to rain. Come, Nikephoros."

Thea drew breath to snap at him. But Nikki shivered and sneezed. She took the hand Alf had not seized, and spread her cloak over the small cold body. Alf moved to do the same. They checked, eye flashing to meet eye, and relaxed all at once, advancing in step with Nikki warmly content between them.

* * *

Nikki accepted his punishment with new-won fortitude: abrupt separation from the two who had brought him home, a bath at Corinna's hands, a bite or two to eat, and confinement to bed under her grim eye.

His mother, whose eye had been grimmer still, sank into a chair when he was gone and covered her face for a moment with her hands. When she lowered them, she was calm but pale. "I thought we'd lost him," she said.

Alf paused in nibbling at the supper she had set before him, and touched her hand. "Before God, Sophia, I'm most sorry. If only I'd known sooner that he was following me—"

"How could you have known? It's not your fault. If it's anybody's it's mine, for not realizing that he'd do such a thing. He's not a baby anymore, to hide in my skirts. And he's not an idiot or a monster that I should keep him locked up out of sight."

"He is certainly not either of those."

She looked down at her hands. Without knowing it she had taken a bit of bread and reduced it to crumbs in her lap. Carefully, fighting to keep her fingers steady, she brushed the remnants into a napkin, folded it, and laid it on the table before her.

Alf stopped even pretending to eat. "Sophia," he said, "you have no cause to grieve for him. Or to blame yourself for anything he is or does."

"He's my son."

"And one to be proud of."

Her eyes blazed with sudden, uncontrollable anger. "Stop it, will you? Just stop it! I may be a weak and foolish woman, but I know the truth when it slaps me in the face. My son is a deafmute. A deafmute he was born, and a deafmute he will always be. And no amount of weaseling words can ever change it."

"Maybe not." His quiet voice shocked her into stillness. "But he is also a human being. I know it. I can talk to him; I can speak so that he can understand."

"But not so that *I* can—" She broke off. "No. You said . . . of course. Being what you are, how can you not? And—can he—"

"Yes."

That was hope, that frail battered creature which staggered to its feet and began feebly to crow. She had taught herself to forget hope. A morning of early autumn; three children with their teacher in the garden, and letters on a tablet. "All this time," she said slowly, "and you never told me. You never even hinted."

"It had to find its time."

"Now?"

Alf nodded.

She had to take it in little by little. It was too much, losing her son and then finding him again, and learning that he had walked unprotected through a raging mob, and now this. "You aren't telling me of a miracle. 'The eyes of the blind shall see, and the ears of the deaf shall hear'—that's not what you can offer. This is . . . plain . . . magic."

"Power, we call it. Mind-seeing. For Nikki it's speech."

"But it's not speech!" Her vehemence brought her to her feet. "It's *not* speech. He'll never talk as other people talk."

"Maybe not." Alf poured a cup of wine warmed with spices and set it in her hand. "He's learning to read and to write. He knows what words are, and why people's lips move so often and so strangely. He's not the young animal all your wise men proclaimed him to be. He's a boy who one day will be a man. A good man, if his promise fulfills itself. Can you ask for any more?"

"Can I—" She was perilously close to breaking. "Why can't you make him whole? Really whole?"

Alf's face was white and still. "I am neither a god nor a saint."

"Then what are you?"

"I don't know," he said wearily. "I really don't know."

His words calmed her as no proper answer could have done. With calm came awareness of what she had said, of what wounds she had dealt him. He watched her with pale tired eyes, and waited for her to strike again, making no move to defend himself.

Sophia sat with care and drank deep of the wine. Its warmth gave her strength to speak. "Whenever you bare your soul to me, I trample it under my feet. How do you keep from hating me?"

"Why would I want to?"

"Oh, you are a saint!" She drained the cup and set it down. "I have to think. Will you pardon me if I go away to do it?"

"You needn't. I can—"

"Don't be noble. You've been ill and you're still wobbling on your feet, and you have a supper to finish." Once more she stood. She tried to smile. "When all of this has sunk in, I expect to be deliriously happy. Or absolutely terrified."

"Of me?" he asked very low.

"Of this whole mad world. I used to think I understood it, you see. I was very young then." She leaned over the table and kissed his cheek. "Good night, Alfred."

He was still there when Thea found him, the wine cold in his hand and the food untouched. His face did not change as she took Sophia's chair and began to fill a plate, although he passed the bread to her before she could ask for it.

"Thank you," she said, biting into the loaf. "Ye gods, I'm hungry. I can't remember the last time I ate."

There was no stiffness in her voice or manner, no hint of coldness. He gathered himself to leave her, noting meanwhile that she had bathed and washed her hair, and that she had put on a robe which precisely matched her eyes. Bronze shot with gold, that in certain lights seemed all gold.

Strange how very beautiful she was to look on, and yet how utterly of earth she seemed when she spoke. Such beauty should never speak, or should give utterance only to the sweetest of words.

"How unspeakably dull." Thea filled a bowl with stew. "On the other hand," she added as she reached for a spoon, "it would suit you to perfection. Mystic stillness alternating with verses even more mystic in the fashion of the Delphic Oracle . . . in no time at all you'd have people pouring libations to you."

He rose somewhat more abruptly than he had meant to, lips tight. "It's late," he said. "I'm tired. Good night, Althea."

"You see?" She downed the stew with relish, helping it on its way with bread and cheese and sips of wine. "Sophia says you hold grudges and I don't. You can certainly sit on a grievance as long as anyone I've ever seen. Do you intend to detest me for the rest of your unnaturally long life?"

"I do not detest you," he said through clenched teeth.

"Wasn't I precise enough? Very well then: I irritate you, annoy you, and drive you to distraction. In that order. You're a frightful prig, do you know that? And a bit of a pedant besides."

"I'm very well aware of it."

Her eyes widened, miming astonishment. "Who'd have thought it? Brother Alfred can see his hand in front of his face. Shall we try for the arm? You're arrogant too, assuming I'd come to heel in the palace just because you ordered it."

"You did, didn't you?"

"What else was there to do? I wasn't about to let old Beetle-brows prove me a fool and have me holding off the mob while he stole the crown. On my way to tell the truth to my friends I found you slinking about, mildly suicidal as usual and fancying yourself clever. Naturally I humored you. Why not? My mission was a lost cause in any case, and I saved your precious skin."

His nostrils were pinched and white; his eyes glittered.

She clapped her hands. "Ah, joy! At last I see you in a temper. Go on, hit me if you like. I don't mind."

His fists clenched, but he did not raise them.

She reached for the roast fowl in front of her, dismembering it neatly, biting into the leg. Her teeth were white and sharp; she ate like a cat, at once delicate and fierce. "The trouble with you," she said, "is that you don't know how to handle your temper. Either you crush it all into a tiny box and sit on the lid, or you nurse it and pamper it and tend it like a baby till it grows into a monster and devours you. Why don't you just let yourself go?"

"The last time I did that," he said, low and controlled, "I killed a man."

"No." She finished stripping the bone and turned it in her fingers. "Even that, at the last, was coldly logical. An execution, not a murder. There's passion in you, no doubt of it, but every time it makes a move toward freedom, you either throttle it down or go out of your mind with fear of it, or escape it by telling yourself its object means nothing to you. Doesn't it go against all your priestly training to lie to yourself so much?"

Her light dispassionate voice struck Alf deeper than any torrent of abuse. She had done with her meal; she sat back, sipping wine and watching him over the rim of the cup.

"You don't care for me," she said. "Oh no. You would have come to the palace for any stranger, ignoring all your instincts, that, sir prophet, should have told you there was no danger at all for me. Can it be that after all you're blindly and hopelessly in love with me?"

He drew a sobbing breath. Without warning he struck her.

But she was not there. She stood just out of reach, not quite smiling. "So," she observed with a world of understanding in the single word. "I've flattened you twice for saying the same thing to me. Do you want to try again? Do you love me, little Brother?"

"Yes!" It was a cry of pain.

Thea drew closer to him and laid her hands on his shoulders. He trembled and would not look at her, staring fixedly at the air above her head. "There now. Old grudges die hard, don't they? And the truth can be agony. Will you believe me if I promise you that your pride will recover?"

He shook his head from side to side, tossing it. "It should die the death."

"That's not wise, either. Look at me, you lovely idiot. Do you know what you've been doing to me with all your cold-shouldering? The best friend I've ever had, for all your shortcomings, and you've cut me off as if I were your worst enemy. For nothing."

"You call it nothing?"

"Wasn't it? You asked me to marry you. I said no, and told you why. You stalked off in a rage. And stayed in that rage for well over a month. You're still in it. Are you always like this when you can't have what you want, precisely when you want it?"

That startled him into meeting her gaze. She regarded him steadily, neither yielding nor resisting. His throat constricted; he forced words through it, painfully. "You . . . said I had to be the one who ended this battle."

"You came to the palace for me."

"I didn't intend—" That was not exactly true, and he knew it as well as she. "You were going to alert the Guard. That would have precipitated a civil war with you in the very middle of it. Could I lie here safely out of the way and let you do that?"

"By then, of course, I'd come to the same conclusion. I understand oblique apologies, little Brother, though this one is more oblique than most. I accept it. Now kiss me, to put the seal on it."

He hesitated. Her eyes laughed; her hands linked behind his neck. Laughter bubbled up within him for all that he could do. With sudden resolution, he bent his head and did as she bade.

21

Cartwheels rattled on the road; cattle plodded behind and among the wagons, lowing their complaint, while sheep milled and bleated and herdsmen hemmed them in with cries and curses. Over all rang the clamor of iron on iron and iron on paving stone: the heavy destriers, each bearing an armed and armored knight.

Jehan looked back along the column. As far as he could see before trees and the road's curving concealed it, the army advanced ponderously but in good order, each knight or squire or sergeant in his place, mail-coif up and helm ready at his saddlebow. One or two caught his glance and grinned. Victory had lifted all their spirits, the town taken and plundered behind them, its booty safe here among them or sent ahead to the camp, food and drink enough to sustain the army for a full fortnight.

His red stallion fretted, sidling, threatening the bay beside it with flattened ears and bared teeth. He brought the beast sternly to order and grimaced at the bay's rider. "He hates to drag along at a walk."

"Don't we all?" Henry of Flanders eyed the trees which closed in upon the road. "I'll be glad to come out into open country again."

Jehan nodded. "I like to see where I'm going, and what's waiting for me. Though this road is better than anything I ever saw in a forest at home. Deer tracks, those were. This is a *road*."

"We're spoiled. All this Eastern luxury: roads and baths and spices, and silk by the furlong. Do you know, I have it on good authority that the Greeks don't heat their houses with simple fires. They put the fire in the walls or the floor and stay warm all round."

"That's the old Roman way. Furnaces and hypocausts. I saw it in House Akestas."

There was a small silence. Henry brushed dust from his helm, saying slowly, "I . . . heard something in one of our councils. A rumor only. Before the new Emperor seized the throne, old Isaac had his fortune told. It wasn't to his taste. The soothsayer—he was, they said, no more than a boy, but he wore the robe of a master surgeon. They . . . disposed of him."

"I know."

There was no expression in Jehan's voice. Nor could Henry read anything in his profile with its strong Norman arch of nose and its stubborn jaw.

After a little Jehan said, "It was Alf. Who else could stand up in front of an emperor and say what he said?"

Sudden anguish twisted Henry's face. "How could he let himself die like that? So horribly, and for so little."

"He didn't."

Jehan had spoken so quietly and so calmly that for a moment Henry did not trust his own ears. "He—"

"He's alive," Jehan said. Face and voice had come to life again; Henry saw a touch of mirth there and a touch of compassion. "Not that he isn't capable of running after his own death. But it would take a good deal more than a senile old fool to finish off the likes of him. You can lay wagers that he read the future for His Majesty and didn't soften the truth to the smallest degree, and that afterward he arranged to drop from sight for a while to keep his friends safe."

"He sent you a message." It was less a question than an accusation.

Jehan shrugged. "Not really a message. Just . . . I know he's alive and well. I'd know if he weren't. Don't ask me to explain, my lord. Alf's not precisely amenable to explanations."

Even to himself Henry could not admit the depth of his relief. He turned aside from it to consider the road ahead. Nothing moved on it, not even a shadow; above the laced branches of the wood the sun was shrouded in cloud. The trees were thinning; beyond them he could see the open sky and the long stretch of winter-bared hills rolling down to the camp.

Somewhere behind, a pair of sergeants argued. Their voices carried on the cold still air, both amiable and contentious.

"Well now," drawled one, a light voice with the liquid accent of Provence, "surely one emperor is as good—or as bad—as another. By the time anyone learns how to pronounce the name of this latest eminence, we'll be princes in Jerusalem."

The other spoke in a rumbling basso, a solid Flemish peasant's voice with a hard head behind it. "I can say it already. Mourtzouphlos—Mourtzouphlos. Mourtzouphlos the warmonger. He's no coward of an Angelos. You don't see him sitting on his behind listening to soothsayers, or dithering about from Latin to Greek and back again. Hasn't he opened war already? Shoring up the walls, bricking up the gates, building those towers on top of the towers he already has, to keep us out; and riding abroad whenever it suits him to harry our foraging parties. He'll give us a good dose of cold steel before he's done."

"Empty defiance," said the southerner, undismayed. "He'll never go beyond a threat or two. These Greeks are lazy; effete; effeminate. One show of genuine force and they'll topple."

The Fleming grunted. "Tell that to the Varangians. If you can persuade them to lay down their axes long enough to listen to you."

"Ah, but those are mercenaries. The Greeks are made of

lesser stuff. Haven't we just overrun a whole town full of them?" The southerner laughed. "Oh no, old friend. We've nothing to be afraid of. Come spring, we'll twist the Greeks' arms to get our money and sail down to Outremer."

Henry sighed a little. He had not thought that anyone clung still to that dream.

The Fleming most certainly did not. "If we leave this place, it will be by fighting our way out of it. Or conquering it, if it comes to that. Never trust a Greek, boy, and never underestimate him."

The southerner's laughter rang clear and mocking above the myriad noises of their passage.

Abruptly it stopped.

Before Henry's mind woke to alarm, his body had hauled his horse about, his eye flashed to find the armored figure toppling slowly from its saddle. One eye was wide, astonished. The other had sprouted an ell of black arrow.

Someone thrust Henry's helm into his hand. Jehan's was already on, the priest reaching across to aid his friend. One of the cattle bellowed, struck by a dart; men cried out, screams and curses and prayers to every saint in heaven.

The bay destrier wheeled upon its haunches. The wood swarmed with Greeks, an army all about the Frankish column, and at its head under the imperial banner, the Emperor himself, crowned, cloaked with purple. His soldiers slipped beneath the lances of the knights to strike at the horses with swords and daggers, or shot from the branches of the trees where none could reach them, or plunged a-horseback into the howling chaos of men and cattle and wagons.

Henry filled his lungs. "Drop lances!" he bellowed. "Out swords! Form up round the wagons!"

Even as he spoke he let his lance fall, drew his great sword, spurred the charger forward. A Greek plunged toward him, a wild-eyed fool who wore no helmet, only a circlet of gold about his brows. Henry's blade swept down; the man's face dissolved in a spray of scarlet. The young lord laughed; for he realized suddenly that he was himself without a helm. He had dropped it somewhere, he knew not where, nor cared. "To the wagons!" he roared. "To the wagons!"

Jehan's world was a clamorous darkness lit by a thin line of light, the eye-slit of his helm. He heard Henry's voice, his lance already forsaken, his sword red with blood, and in his mind a bitter clarity. *What fools we were,* it observed, watching his sword cleave its way through the massed attackers, *riding like ladies on a holiday and never looking for an ambush. If we survive this, we'll take no credit for it.* And: *It's an honorable death, I suppose.* And: *By our Lady! What bold brave knights we are!* He whirled his dripping blade about his head and whooped, and drove his stallion into the midst of the enemy.

Shapes whirled past him, a blur of blood and steel. A banner whipped in the wind, bright, strange, heavy with purple and gold. A mailed knight matched blade to his blade; another crept up behind, a crawling in his spine. He touched spur to his stallion's side. The great horse gathered and leaped, lashing out with deadly heels even as Jehan's blade clove the helmet of the man in front of him.

An image floated above the press, a shimmer of gold and jewels: a gentle Lady whose great eyes stared serenely into nothingness, whose lips smiled, impervious to the clamor of battle. Beneath her rode a figure of splendor, a knight in gold-washed armor upon a milk-white mare, his helm surmounted with a cross; for surcoat he wore a garment of cloth of gold, across its breast a cross of gems and gold.

Jehan grinned within his helm. A poor priest, he was, in his plain steel with his surcoat all bloodied, and the Patriarch of Constantinople flashing and glittering under the icon of the Virgin.

Not all the Latins had gathered about Henry. A bold handful raged among the Greeks. Jehan called out to them. "To me, my lads! To me!"

They came as the cubs to the lion, a shield for his back and his sides. He raised his sword and sprang forward full upon the Patriarch.

The guard of Greek knights scattered. The Patriarch hauled

at the reins, but his mare jibbed, shying. Jehan's blade swept down. In the last instant it flickered. The flat of it crashed upon the nasal of the Patriarch's helmet. The reins fell from nerveless fingers; the mare bolted, her rider clinging blindly to her neck.

The icon swayed dangerously upon its great ark of gold and jewels. One of its four strong bearers had fallen, trampled under a charger's hoofs. Another stumbled.

Jehan shouted something only half coherent and leaped from his saddle into the very midst of the Greeks. They scattered before his sword. The icon was falling. He thrust his shoulder under the ark and staggered, eye to staring eye with a Greek well-nigh as tall as himself. The Greek yawned and dropped. A burly man in tattered surcoat and dented helm filled his place; and another, heaving up the mighty weight, raising it again toward heaven. The Virgin smiled her secret smile; the gems glittered about her, set in pure gold.

Henry saw the icon fall and rise again upon Latin shoulders. The Franks lifted a shout; the Greeks faltered in dismay.

Now, Henry thought. And aloud: "Now!"

All his gathered men drew together with Henry at the head of the spear. The enemy held before the charge; weakened; broke. Mourtzouphlos himself, within a circle of chosen princes, saw all his guard felled or driven in flight; and Henry's sword smote past his shield to send him tumbling over his horse's neck, sprawling ignominiously upon the ground.

Sick, half stunned, he staggered to his feet. The charge had swept past him. His mount was gone; his army was an army no longer but a fleeing mob. Over the Latin helms swayed the icon that was the luck of his City, and the bright banner of his empire.

No one paid him any heed, not even the crows that had gathered to feast on the dead. His dead, save for the one reckless Provençal whose laughter had roused the ambush.

He cast off his shield and his crowned helmet. Pain stabbed his right arm, the mark of Henry's sword. He set his face toward the distant City and began to run.

22

Bardas slept as easily as he ever did now, freed for the moment from the torment of coughing which racked his whole body, granted the release from pain which was all the healing Alf could give. His face, though thinned to the bone, wore a semblance of peace.

Sophia combed out her black braids. Freed, they tumbled to her knees: her one beauty and her one vanity. This morning she had found a thread of gray. Well; it was time. She was thirty-four.

Across the bed, Alf straightened. In lamplight and intent on his task, he looked strangely old, an age which smoothed and fined rather than withered and shrank, like the patina of ancient ivory.

She was obsessed with time tonight. As he began to gather the packets and vials from which he had made Bardas' medicine, she asked, "How old are you, Alf?"

A bottle dropped from his fingers, mercifully falling only an inch or two, striking the table with a sound which made them both start. Very carefully Alf picked it up again and laid it in his box of medicines. His voice was equally careful, his face completely without color. "How old would you like me to be?"

"As old as you are."

He tightened the knot on a bundle of herbs, head bent. His hair hid his face, whiter in that light than Bardas' yet thick and youthful. "That," he said, "could be embarrassing. Or frightening."

"To you or to me?"

"Both." He looked up. It was a boy's face with the barest hint of white-fair downy beard. But a man's voice, well settled, and eyes too unbearably ancient to meet.

He laughed as a strong man will, in pain. "I'm not that old! If I were like anyone else, I could conceivably be still alive."

"Then—"

"I was seventeen when I took vows in Saint Ruan's. Bardas was a very young child. In too many ways, I'm still seventeen."

"I'm neither embarrassed nor frightened."

Wide-eyed, surprised, he looked younger than ever.

She smiled. "I'll tell you a secret. I'm still seventeen too. I just don't look it, and I try not to act it. At least not in public."

"It doesn't matter? That I—"

"Why should it? I only wanted to be sure. I hate mysteries." She finished her combing and began to bind up the gleaming mass again. "It's reassuring, in its way. All that wisdom and experience, and a body strong enough to last out any storm."

"But also, all too often, at the mercy of its own unnatural youth."

"Unnatural, Alf? Did you buy it? Or induce it?"

"Saints, no!"

"Well then," Sophia said, "for you it's natural. It certainly looks well on you."

Alf closed the lid of the box and fastened it. He was smiling wryly. "There are two kinds of people in the world. People who want desperately to burn me at the stake, and people who take me easily in their stride."

"Not easily. Just . . . inevitably. What must it have been like for you? Raised as you were, trained as you were, and being what you were. Even with the monks' acceptance, or tolerance at least, you still had to face the Church. My poor little prejudices are nothing to that."

"I'm trapped in this body. I have to endure it. You have no need."

"Don't I? You're so wise about the rest of the world, and such a fool with yourself."

He bowed his head. "I don't think I understand people very well."

"You do. Perfectly. Except when your own person comes into it. The monks triumphed with you, I think."

That brought his head up, and won reluctant but genuine laughter. "I begin to see what I missed in all that lifetime without women. A clear eye, an acid tongue, and a wonderfully illogical logic."

"Only a man would find it illogical. It makes perfect sense to me."

"Of course it does." He came round the bed, took her hand and kissed it. "You're good for me, Sophia."

"Like one of your medicines: bitter but bracing."

He laughed again. She watched him go, smiling even after he was gone. "Naturally," she said to Bardas who slept on unheeding, breathing almost easily, "I'm in love with him. Who isn't?"

Alf's laughter died beyond the door. He was grave and almost sad when he stood in his own room, setting the box of medicines with his blue mantle, running a fingertip over the fine wool. It was early still, hours yet to midnight; he felt no desire to sleep. A bath he had had. A book? He had a new one, given him by Master Dionysios when he returned to Saint Basil's. "Take it," the Master had growled, glaring at him as if he had committed some infraction. But behind the glare lurked the joy no one else had even tried to hide.

He set the book beside his chair and undressed slowly. He glimpsed himself in the silver mirror that lay upon the table. Diogenes had left it that morning when he cut Alf's hair. Alf turned it face down and reached for the loose warm robe he always wore for reading at night. Settling into the chair, he opened the book.

This was not Dionysios' volume of Arabic medicine.

The moon and the Pleiades have set.
I lie in bed,
alone.

Irene's love poems. He moved to close the book, found himself turning the page instead.

Immortal Aphrodite of the elaborate throne,
wile-weaving daughter of Zeus,
I beseech thee,
vanquish not my soul, O Lady,
with love's sweet torments.

Bardas was dying. The Emperor had lost not merely a skirmish but the fabled luck of the City. Jehan lay cold and sleepless in the camp, rolling on his tongue the bitter dregs of his victory. And Alf could think of nothing but the fire in his flesh. He set the book down with exaggerated care and rose. The house slept about him, even Sophia drowsing on the cot she had had the servants set up near Bardas' bed, with Corinna stretched out at her feet in mountainous repose.

Softly on bare feet he ventured into the corridor. Something stirred, startling him: Nikki's kitten, mewing and weaving about his ankles. He gathered it up, settled it purring in the curve of his arm. Its thoughts were small feral cat-thoughts, warm now and comfortable.

The women's quarters, though called that still, had been given over to the children; beyond it at the top of House Akestas Thea had claimed a room of her own. Its door was unlocked. Alf opened it slowly, fighting every instinct that cried out to him to flee.

Dim light met his eyes. A lantern hung on a chain from the

ceiling, shaped like a hawk in flight. It illumined a small room simply and plainly furnished, almost like a servant's. The only extravagance was the bed's coverlet, a blaze of flame-red silk embroidered with the phoenix rising from its pyre. Thea sat cross-legged upon it in a woollen robe, her hair free, mending a shield strap. That was so very like her that Alf smiled without thinking and was in the room before his terror could master him.

She returned his smile, not at all disturbed to see him there where he had never come before. "Welcome to my empire," she said. "Sit down and keep me company while I finish this."

There was nowhere to sit but on the bed. Alf sat stiffly at the very end of it. She had returned to her mending, frowning with concentration. Her hair had fallen forward; he wanted to stroke it back. But he did not move.

The kitten yawned hugely, stepped out of its nest, negotiated the descent to the bed. After some thought, it curled in a hollow beyond the crest of the phoenix and went complacently to sleep.

Thea took the last stitch and tugged at it. Satisfied, she laid the shield down beside the bed, tossing back her hair. The lamp caught the gold lights in it, deepened the shadows to black-bronze. "Inspection tomorrow," she explained. "His Majesty, having run home from battle with his tail between his legs, wants to assure himself that he still has enough power to make an army miserable."

"Isn't he claiming the victory? A few Greeks fell, to be sure, and he lost his horse. But he routed the Franks and brought the icon and the standard back to the treasury where they belong."

"So he says." She stretched like a cat; her loose robe clung to breast and thigh. "A few people believe him. The rest know he has to save his skin. Before he took the crown he promised his supporters that he'd rid the City of the Latins in a week. A month, he's saying now. Soon it will be a season. And he may not last that long."

He found that he had moved closer to her, close enough to touch. His hands were icy cold. His heart beat hard. *Coward,* it mocked him. *Coward, coward, coward.*

She stroked the kitten, rousing it to a drowsy purr. "Under Mourtzouphlos," she said, "for all that he's had his failures, the palace feels different. He may have lost a battle today, but he's won others; and he's willing to *act*. The Angeloi never even began to try."

Alf listened to her in growing despair. He had succeeded; he had convinced her that he could not give her more than he ever had. Love, but love of the mind only, that of the body twisted and made powerless by his lifetime in the cloister. Companionship, friendship, even kinship he could give, for after all he was the only being of her own kind in this part of the world. But nothing more.

She had fallen silent. He could have wept to see her so beautiful, and he too little of a man even to touch her except as a brother. He would have been better as a eunuch, like Michael Doukas, who had never known how to desire a woman and who could never know it.

No, said a voice deep in his mind. *Even this is worth the price.*

If he could live his life again, he would have her in it just as she was now. Watching him, saying no word; ready to be hurt, more than willing to be loved.

Even though I am no maid?

He stared blankly. He had never even thought of that. "For me," he said, "only one thing matters. That you are you. Thea. None other." He heard himself speak and realized that it was the truth. And that she too was afraid. Not of her body—that, she had mastered long ago—but of that which had been between them since they met in Anglia, and was like nothing she had ever known. Beside that, his own terror was a small thing, a child's whimpering in the dark.

It doesn't frighten me. He held her hands and met her wide eyes, and remembered as he so seldom did that she was younger than he.

"Do you know what it means?" she cried. "We're bound. One soul, the humans say. They don't know the half of it. Wherever you go, I must go; whatever you do, I must be with you. If you hurt, I hurt; your joy is my joy. We can never be free again."

"Free?" He kissed her palms and held them to his cheeks. "What is freedom?"

Her fingers tensed; he felt the prick of nails. But she did not try to pull away. "Bodies are simple. An hour's play, a moment's pleasure, and there's the end of it. But this is forever. Forever, Alf!"

"It's not an easy thing to face. And yet . . . many a time I've wished you far away, or regretted the day I met you; we've quarreled and I've come close to hating you. But if you left and never came back, I know that I could not live."

"It's a trap. A vicious, impenetrable, eternal trap."

"So," he said, "is all this wonder of a world. See what blessings we're given to make it easier. Beauty and agelessness and power, and the bond which has held us together from the moment of our meeting. Although I'm not much of a blessing for a woman, nor indeed much of a man at all."

"Who lets you think that?" Indignation put all her fears to flight. She pulled away from him, only to take his face in her hands and kiss him on the lips, shivering him to his foundations. "You're a man," she said with conviction.

"I'm afraid." And of that he was, folly though he knew it to be.

"Of course you are. So was I, my first time, and it's worse for a woman than for a man. I soon got over it."

"I—I don't think—I'm not ready—"

"No?" She looked down; he blushed. "Your body most certainly is."

"I can't," he said in sudden desperation. "It's useless. I was a monk for too long. I'm still a monk. I'll never be anything else. Let me go!"

She was not holding him. Nor did he take flight. Even as he begged for release, his fingers lost themselves in her hair; her arms circled his neck.

"The body knows," she whispered in his ear. "Trust it."

The body, yes, and the power. Gently, delicately, he wove

himself into the web of her mind. All its threads were air and fire, eternally shifting and changing, yet at the center of them ever the same. Whatever shape she chose to bear, she remained herself.

Her awareness enfolded him. For an instant it turned upon itself; he saw through her mind a structure of perfect order, a temple of light, its center a sphere of white fire. Himself as she knew him, taking shape about the fire, a slender youth in the habit of a monk that bound him like chains. Yet as he watched, his bonds melted away; he lay beside her clothed only in his skin, drawing her into his arms.

She was warm even to burning, and supple, and slender-strong, slim almost as a boy yet curved where a boy would never be. What his eyes had known against his will yet unable entirely to escape, his hands now explored in wonder and delight. "Oh, you are beautiful!"

"And you." She kissed his brow and the high curve of his cheekbone, and after an instant his lips. She tasted of honey.

Before he had truly partaken of her sweetness she withdrew, turning, drawing him with her. He was above her now, her arms about him. Her hands ran down his back along the knots and ridges where the whip had gouged deep. "I love you," she whispered. "I have never loved anyone else as I love you. Nor ever shall."

She had forsaken all the armor with which she faced the world, all her sharpness and her mockery and the hard fierce glitter of her wit. Her eyes were meltingly tender; she tangled her fingers in his hair and brought him down to meet her kiss.

Deep within him a seed burst and sprouted and grew and put forth a blossom, a flower of fire.

She moved beneath him, opening to him. His blood thundered in his ears; his body throbbed. He was all one great song of love and terror and desire, and of sheerest, purest joy.

Behold, thou art fair, my love, behold, thou art fair!
Thou art beautiful, O my love, as Tirzah, comely as
Jerusalem, terrible as an army with banners.

I will get me to the mountain of myrrh, and to the hill of frankincense. . . .

To all his words and songs and fears she had but one, and that one lost in light. "Yes," she breathed, or thought, or willed. "*Yes!*"

23

Thea sighed with contentment and settled more comfortably in the circle of Alf's arm. His free hand, moving of its own accord, found her breast and rested there, as Nikki's kitten curled purring on the curve of her hip.

She traced an aimless wandering pattern on his chest and shoulder to make him quiver with pleasure, and let her hand come to rest over the slow strong pulse of his heart. "I love you," she said.

"Still?"

She laughed softly. "Still! I knew there was fire under it all. And such fire!" She kissed the point of his jaw, paused, nibbled his neck with sharp cat-teeth. "There are lovers and lovers. With some, once is enough. With others passion lasts for a little while, then fades. But a few—a precious few—are like the best wine in the world. The more one has, the more one craves, and one never grows weary of it. You, my little Brother, are one of the last."

"I know you are." His lips brushed her hair. "Now I know why the Church calls it a sin."

"Only the crabbed old men in their cloisters. Which you, my love, most certainly are not."

"Not anymore." For the first time he sounded almost glad. "So this is what all the poets mean. *Dulcis amor!*"

He sang the Latin so sweetly and so passionately that her heart stopped. Then she laughed. "Sweet indeed! Now I'm sure of it; you were born for this."

"To each living creature its own element."

She drew back a little to see his smile. Their eyes met and kindled; their bodies twined, to the kitten's utter and heartfelt disgust. Even in the midst of the fire they could laugh as it stalked to the bed's farthest corner and sulked there, lamenting its lost sleep.

Sophia woke abruptly. The lamp was guttering, the room silent save for Corinna's soft snores.

It began again. Bardas' coughing, deep rending spasms that shook the heavy bed. She half fell from the cot, stumbling over Corinna, groping blindly for the medicine Alf had left. But she could make no use of it while the storm lasted. It was long, agelong.

At last it ceased. Bardas lay gasping. His face was a skull, his eyes deep-sunken in black sockets. Open though they were, they saw nothing, but stared blankly into the dark. He swallowed the potion by instinct, without even his usual grimace at the taste.

Corinna loomed beside her with a bowl of water and a cloth. Silently the woman began to sponge the fever sweat from Bardas' body. There was so little of him now, skin and bare bone and the horror that devoured his lungs.

Resolutely Sophia bit back tears. Bardas needed a level head and a steady hand, not a flood of weeping.

The new storm struck without warning, longer and even worse than the last. When it subsided, it was only a lull. Bright blood stained the sheet, a thin stream which did not cease.

She had lived with fear through all that black winter. But this was stark panic. "Alf," she whispered. "Alfred."

Corinna straightened. Her deep voice was calm and calming. "I'll fetch him, my lady."

"Please," Sophia said. "Please bring him."

Left alone, she took up the cloth Corinna had laid down and gently wiped away the blood from Bardas' lips and chin. But more flowed forth, a great gout of it as a spasm shook him. There was no awareness in his eyes. There was only his pain and the battle for his life.

Corinna was gone for an interminable while. Sophia did not, would not, count the crawling moments. Nor would she yield to her terror. Deep in her mind, a child shrieked and pummeled the walls.

The door opened. She spun toward it in an ecstasy of relief.

Corinna's chin was set, her scowl terrible. No tall pale figure stood behind her. "He's not in, my lady," she said in a flat voice.

Sophia drew a shuddering breath. "Of course he's in. He must be in. Did you look in the schoolroom? In Nikki's room? In the bath? Or maybe the garden. He might be in the garden. Go, look there. Go on!"

"I looked there. Also in the library, the kitchen, the stable, and the garderobe."

Sophia's hand went to her mouth. She would not scream. She would not. If only she could think. "I'll look myself. You stay here. Don't let Bardas—don't let him—" She broke off before her voice spiraled into hysteria. "I'll come back. Watch well."

Everyone lay in his bed where he belonged, save Alf. His lamp burned still; a book lay on the table, his clothes folded neatly on the stool but his bed untouched. Sophia stood upon the Persian carpet and forced her mind to work. Where had Corinna not looked? The servants' quarters—no. Her workroom. The larger dining room for guests, and the lesser one for the family alone. No, and no. He might have gone out for some reason of his own, duty or the compulsion of prophecy.

No. He could not have done that. Not tonight. Then where—?

Abruptly she knew. She sprang forward half running.

She flung open Thea's door, panting, hand pressed to her side. Three pairs of eyes met her own, wide and startled. One was the kitten's, differing from the others' only in size. Sophia released what little breath she had in a cry of relief. "Alf! Thank God!"

He was already on his feet, snatching at his robe. She reached for him as a drowning man reaches for a lifeline. "Bardas—blood, so much blood, it won't stop, it won't—"

He clasped her hand for the briefest of instants. Then he was gone and Thea holding her up, clad only in her tumbled hair. Sophia clung to her with desperate strength. "I couldn't find him anywhere. I thought I would go mad."

"But you did find him." Thea drew on her robe, dislodging Sophia's hands with some difficulty. Once clad, she half led, half carried the other down the passage. "Alf will do all he can. You can be sure of it."

At the head of the stair, Sophia stopped suddenly. "You—you were—and I—"

Thea smiled. "It doesn't matter."

"But—"

"Come," Thea said in a tone which suffered no resistance.

With Alf laboring over Bardas and Corinna lending aid where he asked, Sophia regained her self-control. Thea brought wine for her, warmed with spices; she drank it without tasting it, mechanically, intent upon Alf's face. It was grave, absorbed, yet otherwise unreadable. She struggled to decipher it.

The coughing eased. Alf knelt now very still, one hand on Bardas' chest, the other smoothing the sparse white hair with absent tenderness. His face froze into a mask, white as death but with burning eyes.

Thea moved softly to stand behind him, hands resting on his shoulders. Sophia waited hardly breathing for she knew not what. The only sound was the rattle of Bardas' breath and the creak of Corinna's aging bones as she lowered herself to her knees. She crossed herself and began to pray.

A priest, Sophia thought. *I have to send for a priest.* But she did not move or speak.

Alf's face tensed. Sweat beaded his brow; almost invisibly he began to tremble. Light shimmered about him, a faint sheen like stars on silver.

A sound brought her eyes about. The door opened barely enough to admit a child. Nikki crept into her lap, blinking sleepily but holding her hand in a warm firm clasp. She held him to her and rocked him, knowing full well that it was not for his comfort that she did it but for her own.

The long night wheeled into dawn. The lamp flickered and failed; cold gray light crept into the room.

Alf sank back upon his heels. The rumble of Corinna's prayer caught and died. Bardas lay still, gasping but no longer coughing.

Sophia had no voice to speak. Alf raised his face to her, the same white mask but with eyes bereft of all fire. "I cannot heal him," he said softly and clearly, with all the weariness in the world.

She rose, setting Nikki on his feet. Slowly she made her way to the bed. Bardas turned his head a fraction. His eyes were clear but a little remote, as if his soul had already begun to withdraw from his body. He smiled at her; his lips moved with only the breath of a whisper. "It doesn't hurt anymore. It's just . . . a little hard to breathe."

Alf slid an arm beneath his shoulders and raised him a little, propping him with a cushion.

"Better," he sighed. "Come here, Sophia." She came and took his hand. It returned her clasp with a faint pressure, soon let go. All his strength bent upon the battle for breath. Yet he was losing it, inch by inch. It was not only the corpse-light of the winter dawn that touched his face with death. Slowly it spread, robbing his limbs of their warmth, advancing inexorably toward his heart.

His breathing faltered, rallied, caught. She covered his lips with hers. His eyes smiled his old, private smile. As she straightened, the smile touched his mouth. Slowly she drew back.

His body convulsed. Even before the spasm had ended in a torrent of blood, she knew that he was dead.

24

Sophia had no use for the extravagance of Eastern grief. She would dress all in black as befit a widow; she would forsake her perfumes and her jewels and refrain from painting her face. But the servants had their orders. No wailing; no excesses of lamentation. The house was still and silent, even the children muted, stunned. Later, when she thought of the day which followed Bardas' death, her first memory would be of Anna's face when she heard that her father was dead: the huge shocked eyes and the cheeks draining slowly of color, leaving her as pale as the corpse upon its bier. Irene wept immediately and wildly. Anna did not. She looked long at Bardas; touched his cold hand, half in love, half in revulsion; and went away without a word.

Alf found her in the stable, currying her pony till the dust flew up in clouds. It was warm there from the bodies of the beasts in their stalls: the pony, and the mules that drew Sophia's carriage, and the old dun mare which Bardas had ridden on his travels outside of the City. She whickered as Alf passed; he paused to stroke her soft nose and to feed her a bit of bread.

Anna ignored him resolutely. She laid down the currycomb; he took it up and began to groom the mare. There was a moment's pause before she reached for the brush.

He kept his back to her, working diligently. As he bent to inspect the mare's hoof, Anna sneezed. He did not glance at her. She had stopped her brushing altogether; he felt her eyes upon him.

He released the hoof and straightened. "Are you going to ride?" he asked.

"It's raining," she said flatly.

"Not anymore."

"I don't feel like it." Yet she clambered onto the pony's back, tethered as he was, and sat there stroking his neck.

Alf left the mare and brought out a crust or two for the pony.

"All he cares about is food," Anna said almost angrily.

"He likes his ease too. And you, when you spoil him."

"When I feed him." Carefully she unraveled a knot in the thick mane. Her brows were knit; her mouth was tight. She looked very much like her mother.

"Alf," she said abruptly, "what happens when somebody dies?"

He sat on the grain bin while the pony nosed his hands, searching for another tidbit. "Many things," he answered. "The body doesn't work anymore. The heart stops; the flesh grows cold. The soul—the self—goes away."

"Where?"

Under her hard stare, he raised his shoulders in a shrug. "I don't know. I've never been allowed to follow the whole way. After a while, the light is too bright. I have to turn back."

"Is that a story?" she demanded.

"No. I don't tell stories."

"Except true ones." Her eyes narrowed. "Why do people die?"

"The world is made so. Man lives his life as he wills, and if he is good, as God wills too. When the time comes, God takes him. Life, you see, is both a gift and a test. A gift because it's sweet and there's only one of it for every man. A test because it can be very bitter, and a man's worth is judged by how well he faces the bitterness. At the end of it he gains Heaven, which is all sweet and no bitter and wholly free from death."

"Father died." She said it as if she were telling him a new thing. "He went to Heaven."

"Yes. He went to the light."

"Everyone dies. Everyone goes to Heaven if he's good. Mother will die. Irene will die, and Nikki, and Corinna. I'll die. When I get old, I'll die." She studied her hands. Small narrow child-hands, sorely in need of a washing. "I'm not old yet. Father was old. Mother's not quite old. I don't want her to die too. She won't die. Will she, Alf? Will she?"

Despite the stable's warmth, Alf was suddenly cold. He spoke with an effort, keeping his voice quiet. "That is in God's hands."

Anna slid from the pony's back and stood in front of him. She was very pale. "Father died and went away. That's not him back there on the bed. Mother will go away too. I'll be alone."

"No." He took her cold hands in his warm ones. "Your mother will take care of you. If ever she can't, I'll be there. I promised your father that. And I keep my promises."

She shook her head slowly. "Everybody dies. You'll die too."

His fingers tightened. He relaxed them carefully and drew a deep breath. "Anna, I'm not like other people."

"I know that," she snapped impatiently. "You and Thea. You can talk to Nikki. You can make sick people well. But not Father. *Why* not Father?"

"God wouldn't let me."

"Then God is bad."

She glared at him in defiance, heart thudding, half expecting to be struck dead for the blasphemy.

He regarded her with a quiet level stare. "God cannot be bad," he said, "but He can let bad things happen for His own reasons. Death is only evil for those who love the dead. For the dead themselves, it's a joy beyond our conceiving. Imagine,

Anna. No more sorrow and no more pain. No more sickness and no more fear. Only joy."

"You were crying too. I saw you."

"Of course I was. I loved him, and I'll miss him sorely. It was myself I cried for. Not your father."

She freed her hands and buried them in the pockets of her gown. He was silent. She wanted to hit him, to make him angry, to rid him of that maddening calm.

"I'm not calm," he said. "I'm only pretending. What good would it do if I screamed and cried and upset the horses?"

"I'd feel better."

"Would you?"

"Yes!" she lied stubbornly. But she added, "You're always pretending?"

"Most of the time. Monks learn how to do that."

"Monks are horrid. You're horrid. I hate you!"

"Why?" he asked.

She stared openmouthed. He stared back with wide pale-gray eyes. She plunged toward him, hands fisted to strike him; but her fingers laced behind his waist and her face buried itself in his lap, and all the dammed-up tears burst forth. He gathered her up and rocked her, not speaking.

It was a long while before she stopped. She lay against him. He was warm and strong and more solid than he looked. "I've got your coat wet," she said in a muffled voice.

"It will dry." He set a handkerchief in her hand; she wiped her face with it, sniffing loudly.

Her hair was in a tangle. He smoothed it with a light hand. She blinked up at him, her eyes wet still, but her mouth set in its old firm line. "If you go away," she said, "or die, after what you promised Father, I really will hate you."

"I swear to you, I'll neither die nor leave you. Not while you need me."

"You had better not." She slid from his lap and stood a moment. The likeness to her mother was stronger than ever. "I think I'll ride after all. Will you come?"

He nodded. "For a little while." He reached for the mare's bridle and turned toward her stall as Anna began to saddle the pony.

Bardas lay in his tomb beyond the City's walls. The long rite of grief was ended, the funeral feast consumed; the guests and the mourners had gone back to their houses. There remained only the Akestas, family and servants, in a house gone strangely empty.

Alf was the last to go up to bed. He had spent a long evening with Sophia, most of it in silence. There had been no need of words.

He bathed slowly, weary to the bone. They crowded him, all these humans, clinging to him, barely letting him out of their sight. He had not even been able to sleep in peace; Nikki had shared his bed every night since Bardas died.

But it was not Nikki he found there tonight. Thea sat in his usual place, combing her long free hair. She looked up as Alf hesitated in the doorway, but did not smile.

His heart thudded against his ribs. He quelled an urge to turn and bolt. "Where is Nikephoros?"

"I sent him to keep his mother company. She needs him. You," said Thea, "have me."

He tried to swallow. His mouth was dry.

"I know," she said. "I've left you alone too long. You've had time to think."

Carefully he closed the door behind him.

She laughed a shade too shrilly. "Poor little Brother. Has guilt struck at last? Thou shalt not look on a woman with lust in thine eye; thou shalt not know her carnally; and most of all, thou shalt not enjoy it."

"Particularly," he said, "when thine host is dying in thine absence."

"He would have died no matter where you were. He should have died months ago. But you kept him alive. In the end, God lost patience and came to claim His own."

Alf left the door to stand near the bed, but not close enough to touch. Her eyes upon him were bright and bitter. "When I was most off guard," he agreed, "God struck. It was His right."

"And now, in atonement, you've vowed to cast me off."

He advanced a step. She tilted her head back, the better to see his face. He spoke with care. "The nights have been long and dark. I haven't slept much. Mostly, I've been thinking. I've pondered sin and guilt and repentance. I've considered all that I am and all that I've taught and all that I've been taught."

Her lip curled; her eyes mocked him.

He continued quietly, weighing each word. "Yes, it is a lot of thinking, even for a scholar. I can't help it; it's the way I'm made. Just as you were made with mind and body in balance, thought and action proceeding almost as one. But even I can come in time to a decision."

"This time," she said, "when I leave, I won't come back. Ever."

He looked long at her. She could not hold his gaze; she glared fiercely at her hands, turning the ivory comb in her lap. She was all defiance over a hurt and a fear which she would not let herself acknowledge. So well she fancied she knew him.

"Thea." She would not raise her eyes. His voice firmed. "Althea, look at me."

She obeyed, a flash of gold-rimmed green.

He met it with cool silver and ember-red. "You know me very well, Thea. Yet you don't know me at all. What makes you think, now I've had all of you, that I'll ever let you go?"

She drew her breath in sharply, a gasp, almost a sob.

"Beloved." His voice was gentle. "Oh, I had all the thoughts you blame me for, and others besides. After all, I was sworn to chastity for a man's whole lifetime. But I was also trained in logic. And logic told me that nothing so sweet, indeed so blessed, could truly be a sin. I found light in it, but no darkness. Not where there was love."

She searched his face and the mind behind it, open wide for her to see. Suddenly, almost painfully, she laughed. "See, even I can be a fool! I knew how you would be. I *knew*."

"I was. I flogged myself with guilt. But I must have imbibed a drop or two of your good sense. In the end, early this past morning when you stood night watch with the Guard, it won. I was going to make Nikki sleep tonight and come to you." He kissed her lightly, with a touch of shyness, for he was a novice still. "It's been a long while."

"Too long." She laughed again, more freely, as he dropped his robe and lay beside her. "How could I have forgotten? You were not only a monk; you were a theologian."

"And the theologian, though late in emerging, always gains the victory. An agile mind in a willing body, and the fairest lady in all the world. So much has God blessed me." He loosed the lacing of her gown. "I love you, Thea."

Her answer had no words, and needed none.

25

At Candlemas, as you know, Your Holiness, our forces took two great and holy trophies: the standard of the Roman Empire and the blessed icon of the Virgin which bears with it the luck of Constantinople. Shortly thereafter we received word that the usurping Doukas had disposed of his rivals, the young Emperor strangled in his prison cell, his father slain soon after by age, sickness, and grief. No bond of honor or treaty now compels us to keep peace. As Lent draws to its end in fasting and abstinence no less devout for that our circumstances force it upon us, we advance inexorably toward the conclusion of this conflict. Count Baudouin has sworn to celebrate Easter in Hagia Sophia. That, he will do, by God's will and the will of our army.

Jehan set down his pen and flexed his fingers. A few sentences more, and that would be the end of His Excellency the Cardinal Legate's latest epistle to the Pope; and His Excellency's secretary would be free for an hour to do as he pleased. The sun was gloriously warm, as if the past bitter winter had never been; he gazed longingly at it from the stifling prison of the Cardinal's tent, and swallowed a sigh.

Soon, he promised himself. Grimly he took up the pen again. Its tip was beginning to splay already after only a line. He needed a new quill. And none in his writing case; he had been meaning to replenish his supply and had kept forgetting.

A shadow blocked the sunlight in the tent's opening. That would be Brother Willibrord returning most opportunely from one of his endless Benedictine Offices. He had little love to spare for a sword-bearing Jeromite priest with pretensions to scholarship, but he carried an exceedingly well-stocked writing case.

"Good day, Brother," Jehan said, squinting at the robed shadow against the sun. "Could you spare a new quill for God's charity, or at least for the Pope's letter?"

Brother Willibrord said nothing. That was one of his few virtues: silence. Even as Jehan turned back to his letter, the monk set the pen in his hand, a fresh one, well and newly sharpened.

"Deo gratias," Jehan said sincerely but rather absently, eyes upon the parchment. Now, where was he? . . . *The will of our army.* Yes. *After much deliberation, the captains have determined to assault the City with all the forces they can muster. The attack will commence before—*

He stopped. Brother Willibrord stood over him still, a silent and hopeless distraction. He looked up, barely concealing his irritation. "Yes, Brother?"

Alf smiled down at him, a smile that turned to laughter as Jehan's jaw dropped. "Indeed, Brother! Has all your labor made you blind?"

"Alf," Jehan said. He leaped up, scattering pen and parchment. "Alf! What are you doing here?"

"Fetching my hat," Alf answered. "Didn't I say I would?"

"That was months ago. *Months!* With every rumor imaginable coming out of the City, and some of them declaring you dead."

"You knew I wasn't."

"I did," Jehan admitted grudgingly. He pulled Alf into a tight embrace. "By all the saints! Next time you commit imaginary suicide, mind that you do it where I can get at you."

"If I can," said Alf, "I will."

"That's no promise." Jehan held him at arm's length and inspected him critically. "You look magnificent. A little tired, maybe. But magnificent."

Alf returned his scrutiny with a keen eye, running a hand down his side. Under the brown habit there were ribs to count. "You, on the other hand, could use a month or two of good feeding."

"It's Lent. I'm fasting." Jehan dismissed himself with a shrug. "All's well in the City?"

"As well as it may be," Alf answered soberly. And after a pause: "Bardas died just after Candlemas."

Jehan's jaw tightened. "I . . . couldn't have known. He was a good man. His family—are they—"

"The Akestas refuse to be daunted by so feeble a power as death. I'm the weak one. Do you know what Bardas did, keeping it secret even from me? Adopted me as his son and made me the guardian of his estate, to hold it in trust for his lady and his children. Not," Alf added, "that Sophia needs my help. She has a better head for business than I'll ever have."

Jehan stared, and laughed amazed. "You're a rich man. You. If only the Brothers could see you now!"

"Thank God they can't. I'm written down in the City as Theophilos Akestas, Greek, doctor, and adopted heir of a minor noble house." Alf shook his head, torn between pain and mirth. "There's irony in heaven and high amusement here below. It serves me right, says Thea, for being such an insufferable saint."

"Bishop Aylmer will laugh till his sides ache."

"He always has been certain that I'm one of God's better jests."

"He thinks the world of you." Jehan looked down at the

unfinished letter and grimaced. "If you'll give me a moment to finish this, we can talk for an hour after."

"Finish it then by all means," Alf said.

Jehan bent to his task. *The attack will commence before the Ides of April.* He paused to dip his pen in the inkpot. *With reference to the quarrel between Father Hincbald and the Abbot of Marmoutier. . .*

Slowly Alf walked round the tent. Before the Ides of April. And March already at its end.

He stopped in front of an ornate crucifix and crossed himself without thinking. The tent walls seemed to close about him. Too many men had dwelt in this place for too long with too little care for cleanliness. And war, war everywhere, a great surge of power and purpose bent upon destruction.

"Alf. Alf, are you all right?"

Jehan was shaking him, peering anxiously into his eyes. "I left the City to get away from this," he said irritably: "fates, prophecies, and the firm conviction that the walls are about to fall on me."

His friend said no word but led him out into the free air. He drank it in great gulps, turning his face to the sun that now seemed less an enemy than a long-sought refuge.

Little by little his mind steadied. He smiled at Jehan a little wanly. "Someday, my friend, I'll manage to get through a day without scaring you out of your wits."

"I'm not scared. I'm used to you."

"I hope I gave you time to finish your letter."

"It's done." Jehan held up a worn and shabby hat adorned with a palm of Jericho. "Here's what you came for."

Alf took it and set it on his head. Arm in arm they walked through the camp, down to the shore of the Horn.

Men swarmed there, repairing and refurbishing the fleet: Saint Mark's mariners, with scarcely a glance to spare for a Frankish priest and his companion. They found a place of quiet amid the tumult, a curve of sand round a pool but little larger than the basin Alf bathed in.

Jehan slipped off his sandal and tested the water. "God's feet! It's cold!"

"It's still winter in the sea." Alf lay on his cloak, hands laced behind his head, hat shading his eyes. "In the City the earth is waking to spring. The almond tree is blooming in our garden; the children are making me teach them spring songs."

"Love songs?"

Alf glanced at Jehan, half smiling. "Irene asks for them. Anna groans and endures them. They're pretty enough, she admits."

"Especially if you sing them."

Alf's only response was a smile. Jehan sat and watched him, asking no more of him than his presence. The Horn stretched beyond him, aglitter in the sunlight, dividing the Latin shore from the walled might of the City.

"You know," Jehan said slowly, "you're an Akestas now. A Greek. An enemy."

"No, Jehan," Alf said, "not an enemy."

"That's not what anyone here would say." Jehan leaned toward him, intent. "Alf. Don't go back there. You don't have to fight, just to be here with your own kind."

"And what of the Akestas?"

"They can leave the City. Don't they have kin in Nicaea?"

Alf shook his head. "They won't go. Nor will I."

"You're all mad. There's war coming, can't you see? *War!* If we win you'll be condemned as a traitor. If we lose the Greeks will turn on you, a Latin in Greek clothing. Either way, the Akestas will suffer for harboring you. Do you want that?"

"They won't leave their city. I won't abandon them. They're my family now, Jehan. I'm bound to protect them."

Jehan stared at him. He was Alf still, but he had changed. Jehan remembered how he had felt in Saint Ruan's when he learned that Alf was gone and that Thea had gone with him. Angry at first, and jealous, and stricken to the heart.

One did not keep a friend by clutching at him. King Richard had said that, without even Jehan's assurance that one day he would see Alf again.

And yet. "There's no safety for you in Constantinople. Won't you see sense just this once, and escape while you still can?"

"I can't," Alf said.

"You don't want to."

"Maybe not." Alf rose and began to walk aimlessly. The other scrambled to follow him. He did not pause or glance aside. "Jehan," he said after a time, "Brother Alfred is dead. He can't rise again. It's not fair even to ask him to."

"I'm not. I only want you to be safe."

Alf gripped his arm and shook him lightly. "I love you too, brother. But I don't need a keeper."

"You need a good whipping," Jehan muttered.

Alf passed him, mounting a low hill. From that vantage he could see all the ordered sprawl of the camp, seething within and without, arming itself for battle. Ten thousand men, swelled with the Latin allies whom the Greeks had driven out of Constantinople: they were a strong army in the reckoning of the West. Yet they faced the greatest city in the world.

He turned toward it. Burned and battered though he knew it to be, riddled with dissension and cowardice, it stood firm about the curve of the Horn, held up with the pride of a thousand years of empire.

"She is old," he said. "She wavers and begins to fall. But no power of the West will long prevail against her."

"You've fallen in love."

"I've fallen into prophecy." Alf shook himself. "This was the wrong place to come to escape from it."

"How did you come here?"

"Witchery, of course," Alf replied.

Jehan nodded, unperturbed. "I thought so. That's what's different about you. You're freer with it. Freer all over. Almost like . . . well . . . Thea."

"She's labored long and hard over me." Alf kept his eyes on the City. "The end was a battle royal. She tried to make a man; the monk fought to remain as he was. She won."

There was a small pause, a bare concession to Jehan's priestly vows. The young knight broke through with a whoop. *"Eia!* I've won my wager."

As Alf stared, Jehan laughed aloud. "I knew you'd come to it sooner or later. Henry swore you never would; you're too saintly. That shows how well Henry knows you. *He* never heard you when you were still a pious monk, coming out with 'Lovely Flora' in place of an *Ave Maria*. And he's never had a proper look at Thea. How ever did you manage to resist her for as long as you did?"

"Ironclad idiocy," Alf answered. "You're a wretched excuse for a priest. Not only condoning sorcery but aiding and abetting it, and now rejoicing in a confession of open and thoroughly shameless fornication."

"Why not? I've just won Henry's best sword. And you look as close to happy as I've ever seen you. Unwanted wealth, forebodings of doom, and all."

"Everything has its price."

"Are you asking me for absolution?" Jehan asked, suddenly grave.

"No," Alf said. "If you gave it I'd refuse it. The Church frowns on everything I am and do."

"Not everything, and not all of us. Maybe I'm lapsing into heresy, but I don't think there's any sin in you."

"Thea would laugh. A theologian, she declares, can reason his way out of anything."

"That's the beauty of our art. How else can the Pope both deplore this war and make the best of it?"

"The same way a renegade Latin monk can throw in his lot with a family of schismatic Greeks." Alf drew Jehan into a brief embrace. "Our paths won't cross again until the war is over. Promise me something, Jehan."

"If I can," Jehan said warily, fighting down an urge to clutch at him and never let him go.

"You can," said Alf. "Whatever happens, victory or defeat, promise me this, that you'll do all you may to protect the women and children. I know in my bones that it's going to go ill for them. Very, very ill."

"I promise." Jehan caught Alf's hand. Once he had it, he could not say what he had meant to say. Only, "God be with you."

"And you," Alf responded.

And he was gone. Vanished like a flame in a sudden wind, and in Jehan's hand only empty air.

26

Alf knew well how Jehan had felt when he refused to take sanctuary outside of the City. For the thousandth time and with patience outwardly undiminished, he said, "Master Dionysios has done all that he may to make Saint Basil's secure. He's repaired the walls and strengthened the gates and hired guards to watch over them all. He's dismissed most of the students, and those doctors and servants who've asked for it; he's sent away the malingerers and the walking wounded. All of us who remain can take refuge in the hospital, with such of our kin as wish to go."

Sophia nodded. "I know that. I understand it. I give you leave to go and to take the children with you."

"But you won't come."

She shook her head. Grief had not changed or weakened her; the certainty of war had roused in her no senseless panic. Yet something had gone out of her. Joy; the deep delight in life which had lain beneath all she did or thought or felt. "This is my house," she said. "I won't be driven out of it by anyone. Not even you."

Alf sighed. "Very well. I stay here. I can't protect two places at once."

"No!" Her tone was almost angry. "I want the children safe and under guard in Saint Basil's, and I want you with them."

"They've lost a father. Will you deprive them of their mother?"

"I intend to come out of this with my life and my fortune intact. My family I entrust to you. If harm comes to any of them, I'll see that you pay a due and proper price."

"No one will touch them while I live. But, Sophia—"

"I'm content." She rose from her chair. "I'll speak with Anna and Irene. Nikki I'll leave to you."

As she passed Alf, he held out a hand. "Sophia," he said, not quite pleading.

She chose not to understand him. "Yes, you'll be wanting a servant. Corinna, I think. She's as strong as most men, if it should come to a fight, and she's loyal to a fault."

Alf opened his mouth and closed it again. Sophia smiled a small smile with no mirth in it, and left him standing alone.

Jehan shifted, searching in vain for a comfortable resting place. Men snored on either side of him, one with an elbow wedged in the small of his back; he winced and eased away from it. Water hissed and slapped against the ship's hull; below, in the hold, the horses stirred, uneasy in their nightlong confinement.

Cautiously Jehan rose. The deck seemed sheathed in metal, shimmering in starlight: rank on rank of armored men, each clad in mail with his head pillowed on his helm. Jehan picked his way through them, rousing grunts and drowsy curses, to lean upon the rail. Shields hung there for ornament and for protection. A fine brave sight they would be, come morning, each with its vivid blazon.

He ran his hand along the rim of his own. Its blood-red lion glared at the City in defiance of the sigil it bore, the banner of the Prince of Peace.

All hope of peace had died long since. The fleet lay off the farther shore of the Horn, heavily laden with men and horses, grotesque with the shadows of the towers built wall-high upon their decks, awaiting the dawn and the assault upon the City.

Soon now. It was black dark, but the air tasted of morning. Far in the east over the forsaken camp, Jehan thought he could discern a faint glimmer.

Among the ships, men had begun to stir, a low muttering that grew slowly louder, mingled with the chink and clash of metal, the thudding of feet on the decks, and the neighing of the horses in the holds.

The glimmer in the east swelled to a glow that conquered all the horizon. One by one the stars faded.

"Can't you sleep either?"

Jehan glanced at Henry. His face was a pale blur in the dawn light. "I never sleep before a fight."

"Praying?" asked Henry.

Jehan laughed shortly. "I save that for afterward. Especially when I'm not at all sure which side God is on."

"Then why do you fight?"

"Why not?" Jehan flexed his shoulders within his mail, and stretched. "His Eminence would be happier if I didn't. But I don't want to sulk in my tent like some shavepate Achilles when my friends are out risking their necks. Besides, I swore an oath. I gave my word when I took the cross, that I'd follow wherever the Crusade and the Doge of Saint Mark led. Should I be forsworn?"

"You have higher vows."

"The Pope himself set me free to follow my conscience. I would in any case, he said; the least he could do was make it legal."

It was light enough now for Jehan to see Henry's smile. "You were wasted on the Church, I think."

"No," Jehan said. "When this is over, if God spares me, I'm going back to being a monk again. Cloisters, hourly Offices, all the study I could wish for . . . I'll be dreaming of it out there when the fighting gets hot."

"You make it sound almost pleasant."

Jehan laughed truly this time, and freely. "Of course it is, the morning before a battle when I'm too shaky to sleep."

Henry grinned and filled his lungs with the morning air. "Fight beside me today, brother."

"Would I be anywhere else?" Jehan turned side by side with him and went to gird himself for the battle.

Well before dawn, the soldiers of the empire had ranged themselves along the walls that faced the Golden Horn. The farther shore was a shadow only, a presence in the night, but a presence grown deadly.

Morning crawled over Asia. Slowly the shadow ships took shape, and after a long while, color. Every ship bore on its sides the shields of its men; from every masthead flew a banner or a pennon. The new sun struck fire upon their blazons.

"They're moving," muttered a voice among the Varangians.

Slowly, weighing anchor, raising sail, striving with oars against the current of the Horn.

A young Guardsman glanced over his shoulder. His eyes were bronze-gold; two minds gazed out of them, Alf's enfolded in Thea's. Within the walls across the half-cleared ruins of the fire rose the Hill of Christ the All-seer. A monastery crowned its summit; upon the hill before the gates spread the vermilion tents of the Emperor.

Silver flashed beneath the imperial banner. Trumpets rang; timbrels sent their clamor up to heaven. The Emperor's cry went up, a deep roar: "Christ conquers!"

And from the ships thundered the reply: "Holy Sepulcher!"

The air thickened with stones and arrows. Near Thea, a man bellowed in pain; his fellow nocked arrow to string and let fly. She swept up a heavy stone and hurled it with all her inhuman strength, well-nigh as far and as true as a catapult; another followed it, and another, and another. Upon the ships, shields bent and shattered; men toppled to the decks.

But the fleet advanced, all the power of the West gathered together, half a league from end to end. The first prow ground to a halt upon the shingle. Armed figures swarmed from it. Ladders swung up against the wall.

A galley ran aground full in front of Thea. From the tower upon its broad deck a bridge unfolded, crashing down over the parapet, bending under the weight of a dozen men.

On either side of Thea, Varangians gripped their axes. With a roar they sprang forward. Half hewed flesh and steel; half struck at the bridge, battling the Franks who would have bound it to the wall.

Thea turned her axe against the bridge. As she smote, she laughed. "The wind fights with us!" she cried. "Ho! There it blows!"

Southward, driving against the ships, thrusting them back. Of them all, but five had reached the walls; and those wavered, losing their precarious grip.

A sword glittered before her eyes. She parried it with a vicious, curving blow that whirled the swordsman about. He staggered upon the bridge and fell. Thea's axe crashed down where he had been. The bridge rocked. Two more axes struck it; three; half a dozen. With a groan of parting timbers it collapsed.

For an instant no one moved. One Latin only had set foot upon the tower. He lay dead, sprawled over the parapet. With a swift contemptuous gesture a Guardsman thrust him off. His body plunged to earth in the midst of a company of his fellows, a missile more deadly than any stone.

The Guardsman turned back to the rest, a feral grin upon his face. "That for the cursed Normans," he said.

"But he was a Fleming."

"Eh?"

Alf stared blankly up at Thomas' round puzzled face. He looked down. His body seemed thin and frail after Thea's robust Varangian-shape. It lay on a pallet in a small bare room, the air sharp-scented with herbs, the air of Saint Basil's. Nikki slept beside him, Anna and Irene guarded by Corinna across the small space. From the angle of the sun, it was full morning.

He rose, careful not to wake Nikki, smoothing his rumpled tunic.

Thomas managed a creditable smile. "Isn't that like a child? Up all night, determined not to miss an instant of the adventure; and sound asleep by sunup."

Alf followed him out and eased the door shut. "It's an adventure," he conceded, "but it frightens them too."

"Of course it does. That's half the pleasure." Thomas looked hard at him. "Were you having a nightmare when I came in?"

"No," Alf said, "not precisely a nightmare. Why did you wake me? Is something wrong?"

"That depends on what you call wrong." Thomas was as grave as he could ever be. "The Franks have attacked."

"I know."

"Know everything, don't you?" Thomas shook his head. "You and the Almighty. And of course, Master Dionysios. He wants you up and working. Just because you have a bed here, I'm to tell you, doesn't mean you're ill."

"Or privileged." Alf shook back his tangled hair. "May I have a bath first?"

"I'll pretend you didn't ask." Thomas grinned up at him. "Don't take too long about it."

From the walls, empty now of enemies, Thea could see the sweep of the battle. Most of the fleet had retreated out of catapult range, driven by the brisk south wind. The shore was thick still with Franks, most afoot, a few mounted on horses that slipped and shied upon the shingle. But she had marked the companies which struggled back to their grounded ships, straining to thrust them out into the open water. More now as the sun sank. Those who fought on, fought against a solid wall of Greeks.

Up on his hill the Emperor sounded his trumpets. Below the wall, the Greeks gathered and charged. The army above them hurled a new volley into the sea, mingled with that horror of the East, the dragon-blasts of Greek fire.

And the Latins crumpled. Some few strove to hold fast; but

their strength had broken. All at once and all as one they gave way. One ship and then another clawed away from the deadly shore.

The enemy had fled. The City had held against them.

"Victory!" roared the Guard. They laughed and whooped and threw their axes up flashing in the sun. "Victory! Victory!"

Jehan stood in the stern of the last ship, leaning on his sword, paying no heed to the few missles which fell spent about him. All along that lofty and impregnable wall, the ranks of Greeks had turned their backs and bared their buttocks to the fleet.

Beside him Henry laughed, a tired, bitter sound. "Now we know what they really think of us."

"Didn't we always know it?" Jehan wiped his blade on his cloak and sheathed it. "I can't believe it's ending this way. After all that's been said and done and promised . . ."

"You put too much faith in soothsayers."

Henry was jesting. Perhaps. Jehan pushed back his mail-coif and let the wind cool his burning brow. "So," he said, "we lost. What now?"

"A council," Henry answered him.

They held it on the northern shore of the Horn beyond the camp, in the empty shell of a church; their table was the broken altar.

Count Baudouin struck it with his fist. "Are we knights or women? We've lost a battle, true enough. We won the last one. Who's to say we won't win the third?"

One of the Frankish lords swept his hand in the direction of the City. "Against that? There are a hundred thousand Greeks inside those walls, and an empire full of them all around us. We lost a hundred men today; they lost none that we know of. How can we hope to face them?"

"How not?" Baudouin's eyes flashed round the assembly. "It's more than our hides we're fighting for. It's our honor. Are we going to let a herd of traitorous Greeks boast that they had the better of us?"

A young lord nodded eagerly. "They tricked us into setting

up an emperor. Then they murdered him and told us all our treaties were worthless. Now they want to trample on our prowess in war. No man will ever be able to say that Thibaut de Langliers was bested by any coward of a Greek."

The younger men murmured, assenting; their elders sat silent. Baudouin faced the latter. "My lords! Does honor mean nothing to you?"

"Not," said a grim graybeard, "when it's so obvious that God is punishing us for our sins. We've pursued this unholy war against Christians, under Christ's cross; we'll die for it in God's wrath."

From among the bishops and the abbots, a man in Benedictine black leaped to his feet. "Not so!" he cried in a voice honed and trained at the pulpit. "God tests us; God tries us to find us strong enough to fight His battle. Have not the Greeks rebelled against our Church? Have they not denied the Lord Pope and twisted the words of our Creed and turned the Mass into a celebration of pagan magnificence? God cries out against them. Woe, woe to my people, that have become even as the Infidel!"

Jehan, seated behind the Cardinal Legate, bit back the words that crowded to his lips. His Eminence sat like a graven image, making no move to suppress such idiocy. They were all in it now, priests and knights, disgustingly eager to set the seal of divine approval upon their folly. A just war, a holy war, a Crusade—God willed it; they had only to obey.

It was a lie. But it gave them strength. Their cheeks lost the pallor of fear; their eyes glittered with newborn courage. Someone began to chant a hymn: " '*Vexilla Regis prodeunt*'—'Forth advance the banners of Heaven's King.' "

He would not sing it. He would not.

"Another attack!" a baron called out as the *Amen* died away. "We failed on the Golden Horn. Why not try the other side? The Bosporus, maybe, or the Sea of Marmora. All the Greek defenses face us here. We can take them from the other side and be in the City before anyone can stop us."

The council had waked to life and to hope. The Doge cut into the excited babble with a quiet word. "No," he said. "We cannot venture upon the Bosporus. Well before we could mount an assault, wind and current together would sweep us away from the walls into the open sea."

"That," someone muttered, "might be all to the good, if only we can be away from here."

Dandolo glowered in the direction of the dissenter. "Our loss today is a disappointment, but far from the disaster it appears to be. We need only to rest, to restore ourselves and our ships, and to prepare a new and stronger assault. Two days, my lords. Only two, and we can return in force to take the City."

"Two days' rest," said Baudouin, "and a new plan of attack. Aye, my lords. I swore I'd hear Mass at Easter in Holy Wisdom; that, I swear anew by God and all His saints, I shall do."

"So shall we all." Thibaut de Langliers sprang up with a cry. "*Deus lo volt!* God wills it!"

They echoed him, all of them, even the grimly smiling Doge.

But Jehan set his lips together and said not a word.

27

"It's *not* a just war!"

The Cardinal Legate regarded his secretary with lifted brow. He was, perhaps, amused. He was certainly not afraid, although Jehan's white fury would have given most men pause. "Certainly," he agreed, "it is far from just."

Jehan struggled to master himself. "Out there," he said in a voice that was almost steady, "priests are saying Mass. They're preaching sermons. They're telling the men that God is with them. The Greeks are traitors, oathbreakers, worse than Infidels."

"I know. I can hear them."

"And you sit here? You read your breviary, say a prayer, meditate on the Infinite? You're the ambassador of the Holy See!"

"So I am." Pietro di Capua brushed a speck of dust from his scarlet sleeve. He was always immaculate, this prince of the Church; his fine white hands had never known greater labor than the raising of the chalice in the Mass. But the eyes which he fixed on the other were clear and sharp. "I know my rank and my station."

"Then use it!" cried Jehan, unabashed by the open rebuke. "You know what His Holiness thinks of all this. He excommunicated the Doge and all his followers with full and formal ritual after they took Zara. But those madmen from Francia have called them back to the sacraments and told them they're forgiven. Is the Pope's will worth nothing at all?"

The Cardinal shook his head slightly. "Have you been preaching that gospel to the army?"

Jehan drew in his breath with a sharp hiss. "I'm outraged, but I'm not insane. One of the bishops tried to get me to preach his lies, flattering me with foolishness about my famous way with words. I escaped before I said anything we'd all regret."

"So," His Eminence said. "As you have so bluntly reminded me, I am the vicar of the Vicar of Christ. Unfortunately I dwell in the midst of Gehenna. The army can escape this trap only by fighting; the priests are in like case. Should they preach what you would have them preach, and die for it, and drive the army in turn to its death?"

"I fight because I swore an oath, and because I can't bear not to. That doesn't mean I have to proclaim a lie from the very altar." Jehan leaned across the Cardinal's worktable. "My lord! Are you going to allow it?"

"I have no choice."

Jehan spun on his heel and stood with his back to the Cardinal, fists clenched at his sides.

"The Pope has no choice," His Eminence continued quietly. "The Church has a head, but that head is far away. The members are here, and strong, and accept no guidance. They will do what they will do, whether His Holiness wills it or no."

"He could condemn them from every pulpit in Christendom."

"Could he? Would you, Father Jehan?"

The title stiffened his shoulders and brought his head up. He swallowed hard. Slowly he turned to face the Cardinal. "My lord, I . . . forgive me. I presumed far too much."

The other did not quite smile. He was a small man, dark and

inclined to plumpness, but in that instant he made Jehan think of Alf. "My son, you are forgiven." He made a quick sign of the cross over the bent head. "Go now. I need to meditate." His eyes glinted. "Upon, of course, the Infinite."

Jehan prowled the camp, restless and ill-tempered. It did his mood no good to see the men, knight and common soldier alike, laboring with new and firm purpose, preparing for the morrow. There were no idlers; the few who were not at work gathered round the priests, deeply and devoutly absorbed in prayer.

A commotion drew him toward the shore. Women's voices, shrieks and sobs, and the occasional sharp cry of a child. Under the hard eyes of a troop of monks, all the whores and camp followers crowded aboard a waiting ship. The army would sail to battle with all stain of sin washed away, all temptation banished as far as wind and oar would carry it. Great temptation, some of it, languishing against the guards, pleading to be left behind. Not one man yielded.

The last buxom harlot flounced onto the deck. Mariners sprang to draw up the plank; others weighed anchor. The ship slid slowly out into the Horn.

He watched it go, scowling so terribly that no one ventured to approach him. Women he could face. They only tempted his body, a hard battle but one he could win; for though he was young and his blood was hot, both his will and his vocation were strong. But there were worse temptations.

He had his sword with him; he had been meaning to try a round or two at the pells to work off his temper. Slowly he drew the bright blade. It was Henry's best, the winnings of his wager, the edges honed to razor keenness, the steel polished until it shone like a mirror. It could cleave a hair or a body with ease, needing only a firm hand upon the hilt. Chanteuse, he had named it, for it sang when he wielded it.

He swung it about his head, rousing its sweet deadly voice. But it would drink no blood this day.

It flashed home to its scabbard and fell silent. He was on his knees, sword upright before him, fists clenched upon the guards. The carbuncle upon the pommel blazed at him like a great fiery eye. Alf's eye set in a rim of silver, piercing him to the soul.

"I swore an oath," he whispered. "I took the cross. I promised . . ."

To slaughter Christians? The voice was like Alf's, remote and clear and not quite human.

"Schismatics," Jehan said. "Heretics. They deny the procession of the Holy Spirit from the Father and the Son, and ignore the supremacy of the Chair of Peter, and—"

Quibbles, said the other.

Jehan's jaw tensed; his mouth set in a thin line. He was closer to handsome when he was smiling, a lady had told him once. When he was angry he was frankly ugly.

Vain youth. The voice sounded both amused and impatient. *Do you intend to join in this final spasm of the war? Swordplay in plenty, great deeds of daring, and a place in a song at the end of it.*

"Aye," muttered Jehan, "the *Requiem aeternam*. Not that I care. I like to fight. It's simple, and it keeps me from thinking."

Yes. One must never think. That one's best-loved friend is there among the enemy; that all one's conscience cries out against this murder of Christian by Christian; that—

"Enough!" Jehan's ears rang with the power of his own cry. He bent his head upon his fists. The sword hilt was cold against his brow. More softly he said, "I've fought till now. I'll see it through to the end. Whatever that end may be."

Valhalla, most likely. You've earned it. All those battles against your soul's protests: Zara, and the conquest of the City before Alf ever came there. You've fought well and valiantly and gained the admiration of even the staunchest priest-haters. There's not a man in the army who can call you a shaveling coward or mock your long skirts. Ah yes; you're a man among these mighty men, and well you've proved it.

Jehan bit his lip until he tasted blood. That was not Alf's firm and gentle guidance. It was more like Thea, who could prick a man into madness with the barbs of her wit.

O bold brave Norman, earl's son, knight of Anglia, the world will marvel that you challenged the power of Byzantium. And perhaps, by God's will, won.

He squeezed his eyes shut. Warm though the sun was, he shivered convulsively; cold sweat trickled down his sides. Fight—he would fight, though it damned him. He was not afraid to die.

Truly he was not. No more than he was afraid of the women on the ship now far down the Golden Horn, riding the current into the open sea.

His trembling stilled. He opened his eyes. It came all at once, as they always said it did. Light; revelation. For a moment he was back in the West with a long anguished day behind him, driving himself to distraction with some complex question of logic or of philosophy, and then, without warning or transition, he knew. So clear and so simple; so beautifully obvious.

He rose slowly, cradling Chanteuse in his arms as if it had been a child or a woman. He was smiling. If his coy lady had seen him then, she would have conceded that indeed he was not ugly at all.

On this last Lord's Day before Palm Sunday, the City kept festival. The enemy was driven back, the Emperor's words echoing from Blachernae to Hagia Sophia and from the Golden Gate to the Golden Horn: "Never have you had so splendid an Emperor. All your enemies shall bow before me, and I shall see them hanged upon the walls they would have taken."

As the day wore toward evening, Alf left his labors and went up to the roof. The air was soft, the garden coming into bloom; birds sang there, piercingly sweet above the manifold sounds of the City.

Nikki had followed him. After a little, Anna came to settle on his other side. He laid an arm about each and held them close. From his vantage he could see the imperial tents on their hill. Thea lay in one of them, stretched out at her ease, half asleep, half watching the dice game in front of the open flap.

That is no place for a woman, Alf said sternly.

She laughed and rolled onto her back. A man's back and a man's body, with no hint in it of the truth.

He shuddered inwardly, unable to help himself. Witchery he was learning to accept, even to take delight in. But this went against nature.

Thea stretched luxuriously. *One day, my saintly love, you must try the shape of a woman. It would teach you a few valuable lessons.*

Thank you, he said, *but no. Do you insist on pursuing this devil's work?*

I'm defending the City. Rather well, I might add. We'll drive the Latins off yet.

He drew a sharp breath. A sudden chill had struck him, like a cloud passing over the sun. But the sky was clear. *Thea, I command you. Come back to Saint Basil's and put an end to this game of yours before it kills you.*

Now you see why I won't marry you. "Wives," intones the great but misguided saint, "obey your husbands." Though, she mused, *I probably wouldn't pay him any heed even if I were decently and lawfully wedded. I never met a man yet who had sense enough to command himself, let alone anyone else. Now a* woman . . .

Eve, having been created in Paradise, can be regarded as infinitely more blessed that Adam who was shaped outside of it. Alf's mind-voice softened although his will did not. *Thea, for once will you listen to this poor lump of clay? It's driving me mad to have you out there so far from me, so perilously close to death.*

I can take care of myself, she snapped.

Then, he said, *I'm coming to join you.*

She sat up appalled. *You are not!*

I can fight. I have a gift for it. I only need gear and weapons. Surely you can arrange that?

No!

Well then, I'll do it myself.

She struck him with a lash of power that staggered him where he sat.

He shook his head to clear it, and confronted her, determined as ever. *I promise I won't shame you, in battle or out of it.*

You never have and you never will. It's not shame I'm thinking of. It's plain good sense. There are enough and to spare of us fighters. We don't need another, not even one whose skill is pure witchery. But true and talented healers are few and far between. You belong where you are. Stop your foolishness and stay there.

She had the right of it, as usual. But the shadow lingered. He cursed his power that granted no clear foreseeing when he needed it most.

You're seeing the general slaughter, she said without the slightest sign of doubt. *That's all. And I don't intend to be part of it. I'm too fond of this handsome hide to let anyone spoil it.*

She would not yield. Nor could he force her, short of entering the camp and carrying her off bodily, a feat which he suspected was somewhat beyond him.

And, she added with a touch of smugness, *being what I am, I'd simply witch myself back again. Be gracious, Alf. Grant me the victory.*

He never knew for certain what he would have done, for a student burst upon him crying, "Master Theo! It's one of the women, the one who's been so ill—she's birthing too soon with too much blood and the child too large, and Master Dionysios says the law be damned, with Mistress Maria gone we need you."

She pursued him with the last of it, finding herself entrusted with the care of the two children. Their rebellion gave her more than enough to think of; she gave up her effort to catch him and settled to the task he had left her.

Night had long since fallen when Alf straightened from his task. The woman was dead. Her daughter lay weak but alive in the arms of a wet-nurse. The woman surrendered her when he asked, with some surprise; he cradled the small body tenderly, looking down into her clouded eyes. "Ah, child," he murmured, "what a place and a time you chose to be born in, and no mother to ease your way for you."

They were staring at him, all the women there, most in

wonder, a few in disapproval. He regarded the last with weary amusement. "Our Lord healed women, did he not? and he himself neither woman nor eunuch. Then why not I?"

He left them to ponder that, walking slowly, weary to the bone. And battle tomorrow, with such darkness in the thought of it that his mind shied away. He had to sleep, or he could not endure what must be.

But there was no mercy in Heaven tonight. Thomas met him at the door of the sleeping-room, his face for once utterly serious. Over his head Alf could see empty beds, and Nikki huddled with Anna. They looked both miserable and furious, their eyes red with crying. There was no sign of Irene or of Corinna.

"Gone," Thomas was saying. "Both of them gone. Irene first, and Corinna went after her."

Anna stood up, breathing hard. "They went home. Irene swore she would. She said one of us should stay with Mother. It was going to be me. It was *supposed* to be me!"

"Corinna will bring her back," said Thomas with confidence he did not feel.

"Corinna *won't!* Corinna thought Irene was right. I could tell. Now they're home and I'm here, and I'll hit you if you try to keep me in."

Alf breathed deep to calm himself, to gather what strength he had left. "I'll go and get them. Anna, if you try to follow me I'll lock you up and set a guard over you."

As he turned, he swayed. Thomas caught him. "You're not going anywhere either, my young friend, except to bed."

He shook his head, resisting. "I have to go. It's deadly for them there."

"It will be worse for you if you fall over before you get there. Now, lad. In with you. In the morning you can fetch them, if the Lady Sophia hasn't already sent them packing."

"Not tomorrow. No time. I must—" Darkness swooped close; he struggled to banish it. It retreated; he was lying down and Thomas bending over him, undressing him with plump deft hands. He resisted, but his body would not heed him.

"Thea," he breathed. "Witch! Let me go. Let me . . ."

His voice faded. The darkness covered him.

28

Once again Jehan beheld the dawn from a crowded deck. Yet it was a new dawn and he had slept well and deeply, without fear or foreboding.

He yawned and stretched. The wide sleeves of his habit slid back to reveal the glint of mail beneath. He turned from his post and picked his way to the cabin.

Henry emerged from the reeking gloom, rumpled with sleep, stifling a yawn. "How goes the morning?"

"Bright and clear and a good wind blowing," Jehan answered, bowing to Count Baudouin, who stepped past his brother to peer at the sky.

The Count turned his narrowed eyes on Jehan, taking him in in the pale light. "What, priest! You're in the wrong uniform this morning."

Jehan smiled. "No, my lord, it's my proper one."

"Mail under it," said Henry, gripping his arm and finding it steel-hard. "No sword, man? What foolishness is this?"

"Not foolishness. A vow."

"To die under the walls of Constantinople?"

Jehan shook his head, still smiling. "I'll be with you in the battle. I promised you that. I didn't promise to carry a weapon."

"You've gone mad." Henry looked a little wild himself, holding hard to Jehan's arm, glaring at his brown habit.

"I'm wearing mail," Jehan said. "I'll carry my shield. I won't burden any man with fear for my safety. But I'll carry no weapon against a Christian in battle."

Baudouin seized him and spun him about, tearing him from Henry's grasp. So like they were, those brothers, and so different. Baudouin was clever, Jehan decided, and ambitious, and reckless when it served his purposes. Henry was wise, which was a far rarer virtue.

The Count's eyes upon Jehan were both cold and burning. "Why?" he demanded. "Why now?"

"I'll help you take the City, my lord," Jehan said, "but I'll kill no Greek doing it."

Baudouin bared his teeth in a mirthless smile. "Ah," he said. "So. What did he say to you, that white-faced witch, when he crept like a thief into our camp?"

"Witch, my lord?" Jehan asked. "Thief? I've had no dealings with any such creature."

"Don't lie to me, priest. What did he say? How much did he give you to betray us?"

In spite of Jehan's control, his lips tightened and his eyes began to glitter. "My lord," he said, cold and still, "I never gave you cause to insult me. If by your words you mean that you saw me with Master Alfred a fortnight past, neither he nor I made any secret of his presence here."

"All the more clever of him to lull our suspicions while he spied on our army."

"If you believe that of Alfred, my lord, nothing I say will make any difference to you."

"My lord!" someone called. "My lord Baudouin!"

The Count paused for a long moment, eyes locked with Jehan's. The priest did not falter. Abruptly Baudouin turned on his heel. "Take him with you," he rapped over his shoulder to his brother, "and mind you watch him. At the first false move, kill him."

Jehan stood still, face to face with Henry. The young lord was pale—with anger, Jehan realized. Even in battle he had never seen Henry angry.

"Pay him no heed," Henry said after a moment, keeping his voice light with a visible effort. "He's never in his best humor before a fight."

Jehan shook his head. "No, my lord. He's right, as far as he goes. It does look suspicious, Alf being where he is and what he is, and now this sudden whim of mine. There'll be no duel of honor fought between us."

Henry's eyes upon him were dark with worry. "You aren't ill, are you?"

Jehan laughed aloud. "Ill? I? Never! Here, the sun's almost up and you're hardly out of bed. Well; they said of Alexander that he slept like a baby before a battle, and had to be shaken awake to get to the field on time. That's a reasonable precedent."

"You're well enough," Henry said, reassured. "But, Jehan, that vow of yours—"

"Is between myself and God, and you'll not trouble yourself with it. Now where's your lazy lout of a squire? You don't even have your surcoat, let alone your sword. Did you even remember to bring your helm?"

Henry laughed and let Jehan herd him into his squire's waiting arms. Even as he moved the trumpets rang, rousing the fleet to battle.

It was the same long line, each of the forty great rounders mounted with a tower. Yet in place of the singlefold assault which had failed so dismally, the Doge had bound the ships together in pairs, two towered ships for each tower of the City which defended the Golden Horn. Behind them on the freshening wind sailed the lesser vessels, bristling with armed men.

The city awaited them with its full might. Every inch of wall and tower seemed rimmed with steel, a wall of men above the walls of wood and stone.

A lone arrow traced its arching path over the water to fall

spent upon the deck of the foremost ship. There was a breathless pause. The Latin archers fitted arrow to string and quarrel to crossbow.

As one, City and fleet let fly.

The City's barrage was terrible, not arrows alone but stones too great for a single man to lift. But Saint Mark's mariners had guarded against them with walls of timber woven with vines. The stones struck with unerring aim, bounded back from the limber shields, fell into the sea.

Steadily the ships advanced. Close under the walls, in a hail of stones and arrows and a searing rain of Greek fire, they dropped anchor. All the shore, like the walls above it, was black with men, that same unyielding army which had driven the Franks already into the sea. They sang and they shouted; their words would have made Jehan's ears burn if he had been a proper pious priest.

One after another the smaller ships beat toward the land. Greek hands and spears thrust them back. Men leaped from them, waist-deep in water. The Greeks surged to meet them.

Jehan kept to his ship. Henry had commanded it, holding his men back with hand and voice and sheer force of will. Yet, command or no command, and in spite of the vow he had sworn, Jehan yearned toward the struggle.

The Greeks fought like demons, yielding not an inch although the sun crawled up the sky and the water reddened with blood. Latin blood, most of it. The City was standing fast. Again, thought Jehan. They were brave after all, those scheming Byzantines.

The sun touched the zenith. Jehan squinted at it. A breeze fingered his hair, freshening as he paused, blowing from the north. The ship bucked underfoot and tugged at its anchor.

Shouts and cries drew his eyes to the wall. One of the great ships lunged against its cable, the bridge swinging loose from its tower. To the very end of it clung a small desperate figure.

It struck the edge of the wall. The single Latin clung for his life, hands locked upon the tower of the City, feet hooked through the bridge. Greek steel flashed down upon him.

Again wind and water surged, thrusting bridge and tower together. A second reckless warrior lunged across the narrowing space, over the hacked and bleeding body of his fellow into the Varangian axes. But he, well armored, sustained their blows and drew his sword. With a shrill yell he fell upon the defenders.

They fell back before him. Latins swarmed behind, binding bridge to tower, overwhelming the Emperor's forces. Full before his eyes they did it as he sat his white stallion on the Hill of the All-seer, raging at the craven weakness of his army.

The wind whipped attacker and defender alike and rocked the great ships upon their moorings. The bridge, fast bound to the tower, groaned under the strain. The tower itself trembled; for it was Mourtzouphlos' second and lesser rampart, built of timber upon the solid stone of the wall.

Far below upon the deck the captain bellowed upward, "Cast off! Cast off, you fools! You'll pull the damned thing down on us!"

The last of the Latins whirled about, hacking at the ropes with their swords, while beneath their feet the tower swayed and groaned. With an audible snap the last line parted. The ship swung free.

But the tower was won. The last Varangian fell at its foot; upon its summit the Franks raised a roar, brandishing their swords. "Holy Sepulcher!" they cried. "Holy Sepulcher!" A banner caught the wind above them, the proud blazon of their lord, the Bishop of Soissons.

"Trust a priest to take the first honors," Henry said, standing beside Jehan.

"The laymen are following," Jehan said. "There! Another's fallen to us. Bracieux, that is, the old war hound. He never could bear to be outfought."

"Come to think of it," mused Henry, "neither can I." His grin flashed round the circle of his knights. "Well, sirs? Is it time?"

"Aye!" they shouted back.

"Then what are you waiting for? Over the side with you!"

The wall of Greeks had broken under the tide from the

West; great gaps lay open within it. Through one such Henry plunged with his men close behind and Jehan at his right hand. The wall loomed above them, poised surely to fall upon them. They stumbled over dead and groaning wounded, advancing in close company.

Jehan thrust an elbow into Henry's mailed ribs and set his helm against the other's. "Look. There. A gate!"

A postern, walled up but plainly visible. The company bolted toward it, unlimbering bars and pickaxes. Quarrels rained down upon them, and stones as huge as hogsheads, and a torrent of pitch searing all it touched.

"Shields!" Jehan roared. "Shield wall!" He flung up his own; others jostled with it, overlapping, shielding the heads of the men who tore at the wall.

It was dim under the laced shields, as clamorous as any smithy Jehan had ever heard, reeking with sweat and pitch and the sulfur stink of Greek fire. His arm rocked under the force of a falling stone; but he grinned within his helm and braced his shield arm with the other to ease the strain.

Mortar flew under the blows of the pickaxes; stones loosened and fell, pried out with daggers and even swords. Light stabbed through a chink. The men pounced upon it, tearing at the stubborn stone, widening the gap.

A young knight tore off his helm and thrust his head into the opening, jerking it back with a cry. "Greeks! Bloody Greeks—thousands of them!"

Jehan laughed, short and sharp. "You laymen! Can't you go anywhere without a priest to lead you?" He tossed down helm and shield and shouldered through the press, bending to thrust himself into the gap.

Henry cried out behind him. "You fool! They'll kill you!"

A pickaxe lay close to his hand. Its haft was warm still from the hand of the man who had held it, a solid and satisfying weight. He crawled forward with it into a rough-hewn shallow tunnel with a mass of yelling faces beyond. A strong hand seized his ankle; he kicked violently, striking something that yielded and groaned in Henry's voice. The fingers snapped open. He scrambled forward, half falling into open air.

Stones hailed about him; Greeks closed in upon him. He roared like a cornered lion and charged, brandishing the pickaxe like a club. The Greeks shrieked and fled.

He stopped, breathing hard. No one menaced him. No one even dared to face him.

"It's clear!" he bellowed through the gap. "All clear!"

Henry was the first to pull himself through with the others hard upon his heels, spreading along the wall in a wary line. One had brought Jehan's shield; he settled it on his arm, letting the pickaxe fall. Now, he thought, the enemy would come and sweep them all away. Now, truly; for as he looked up, he gazed full upon the Emperor's hill rising before him, a long open slope, new green with spring. Near the summit a great force gathered with the Emperor at its head. Trumpets rang the charge; timbrels set its swift pace.

"Stand fast," Henry said, low and clear. "For your honor, my friends, stand fast."

Each man set himself, feet braced, shield raised, sword at the ready.

The Emperor charged.

The thin line held firm.

The white stallion slowed. The Greeks faltered. Mourtzouphlos wheeled about; the trumpets sounded the retreat.

The Latins stared, stunned.

Henry struck his sword upon his shield, rousing them with a shock. "You—you—you. That gate yonder—open it. We're going to take the City!"

They tore apart the iron bars with swords and axes and flung the great gates wide. The wind blew fresh and strong upon their faces.

From the ships a shout went up. The sailors of Saint Mark drove their vessels to the land. Men and horses poured forth through the gate, into Constantinople.

The Greeks had fled from a handful of men on foot within

their city. Knights in full panoply, mounted upon the great chargers of the West, sent them flying in panic. The Emperor himself was swept into the tide of terror and borne away.

The sun hung low over the walls and turrets of the City, casting long shadows upon the streets. In a great square under the cold eyes of old gods and emperors, the Latin army gathered. Weary though they were, spattered with blood, many limping with wounds, they counted scarce a handful of dead. All the blood was Greek blood.

Jehan sat his stallion in grim silence. No Frank within his reach had slain any but the Emperor's soldiers, but his reach was no longer than one man's could be. He had done little good. By far the greatest number of slain were unarmed citizens, old men, women and children.

The Latins drew together now, as the heat of their blood cooled and it sank in upon them that they had dared in their small numbers to violate the greatest of all cities. All about them the labyrinth of streets and passages glittered with hostile eyes. Surely at any moment the enemy would surround them and hew them down.

Their lords gathered in the center of the square, dismounting stiffly, greeting one another with weary courtesy. The Doge stood in the very midst of them, erect and in full armor, with his sword in his hand.

Jehan nudged his stallion closer to halt beside Henry's bay, exchanging a glance of recognition with the squire who held the bridle.

"We have won," the Doge said in his strong old voice, "for the moment. All this quarter of the City is ours. But the rest holds still against us."

"God save us all," muttered one of the barons, crossing himself. "We'll have to fight for every alley. It will take us a month at least of hard work before we can claim the victory."

Count Baudouin spoke clearly and sharply. "What use to count the hours? We hold what we hold. I for one will not let go one inch of it."

"Commendable," said Marquis Boniface, "and better certainly than despair. But we can fight no more tonight."

The Doge sheathed his sword with a firm practiced motion. "No; we cannot press the battle further before morning. Let us mount guards within the City to keep watch against attack. The bulk of the army shall camp by the sea walls to keep open the path of escape. And mark me well, my lords: Let no man of guard or army stray out of the sight of his fellows. Cowards the Greeks may be in open battle, but in the dark and upon their own ground, they are deadly."

"Born thieves and cutthroats." Baudouin turned toward the hill which the Emperor had abandoned, where the tents glowed crimson in the sunset, glinting with gold. "There," he said, "I shall mount my guard."

Marquis Boniface fixed him with a hard stare. "I shall make my camp on the Middle Way, as near to the Forum of the Bull as I may go. For," he said, "one man at least should guard against the greatest massing of the enemy."

Baudouin smiled. "My valiant lord. I'll think of you when I lie in the Emperor's bed."

"Which," said Boniface, "is also a coward's."

Henry stepped swiftly between them, catching Baudouin's hand as it fell to his sword hilt. "My lords! Haven't you exchanged blows enough with the enemy that you have to turn on each other?" Under his steady brown eye they subsided, glaring at one another but saying no word. Henry smiled and bowed to them, and again to the Doge. "I, for my part, am minded to keep watch over the servants and eunuchs barricaded in Blachernae. If my lords will agree to it?"

They all nodded assent. "Go," said the Doge, "do as you will. In the morning we shall renew the battle."

Henry took his charger's bridle from the squire's hand, flashing a smile to Jehan, and swung lightly astride. "Until morning, my lords, God be with you."

Anna had camped all day with Nikki atop the roof of Saint Basil's. She saw the towers taken; she saw the gates flung open and the Emperor routed by the very sight of the knights in their bright armor; and she saw the army's gathering and its swift dispersal.

Alf was with her at the last of it, his day's labor over, his soiled robe laid aside for the only one he had to spare, his best one of pale gray silk embroidered with silver. He looked, Anna observed, as if he were going to a banquet.

They watched in silence as the sun sank and Latin fires kindled before the Emperor's tents. The invaders had pulled down the imperial standard and put up their own, bright and crude as it was, snapping proudly in the wind over the conquered camp.

Anna clenched her fists at her sides. "Why did my people run away? *Why?*"

"They were afraid," Alf answered gently.

She stamped her foot. "They were cowards! Everyone's a coward. Look at all those people down there like an anthill when you kick it, yelling and crying and trying to run in all the wrong directions. *I'm* not running. I'm staying here. And if any of those barbarians tries to break in on me, I'll kill him!"

"I'm one of them," he pointed out.

"You don't count," she said. "You're an adopted Greek. Though maybe you're ashamed to be one, now you've seen what cowards most of us are."

"Your people are civilized. Civilization has never been much good against a determined army of barbarians." Alf shivered slightly, for her benefit. "It's getting cold. Come down to supper and let the City fend for itself for a while."

Saint Basil's was quiet, but not calm. The eyes of healers and sick alike gleamed white, afraid; many prayed softly, a droning murmur.

If there was fear within those guarded walls, there was panic without. As the night deepened, a crimson furnace-glare stained the gathering clouds. For the third time Latins had set fire to the battered and beaten City. Flames raged through the streets along the Golden Horn, a burning wall between the Greeks and the invaders, licking against the foot of the All-seer's hill.

Alf walked slowly down the street which led from Saint Basil's to the Middle Way. In the darkness, lit by the sullen light of the fire, the great thoroughfare was like a road in Hell. People thronged upon it, fleeing the City's center, laden with their children and their belongings, shrieking and weeping and praying in loud voices.

The side ways were quieter, a quiet born of terror. Behind the barred gates men buried or concealed what treasures they had, while their women and children cowered, awaiting the end of the world.

Alf turned aside from the tumult to a street which curved past one of the City's thousand cisterns, a small lake set in a garden and surrounded by high narrow houses. As he passed from stone pavements to the grass of the garden, he paused. The street was full of fleeing figures, but among them advanced a torchlit company. The man at its head glowed in a rich cloak of crimson and gold; armor flashed beneath it and on his head blazed the jewels of a crown. His voice rasped over the cries of panic, harsh yet penetrating. "People of the City! Romans! Why do you flee? The barbarians are within our walls, caught like the fly in the spider's trap. We have but to fall on them and obliterate them." He seized a man who ran wildly past. "You—where are you running? Have you forgotten all the pride of our empire? We have them, I say! We have them where they cannot escape. Come with me and drive them out. Come with your Emperor!"

With an inarticulate cry, the man broke free and fled.

Mourtzouphlos' face was livid in the torchlight, suffused with fury. He pressed forward against the current, shouting, "Are you men or worms? All the world will mock us and call us cowards, who had the enemy within our grasp and let him conquer us."

No one heeded him.

Alf stood motionless upon the grass. His hood had slipped back, his cloak blown away from the silver robe.

Mourtzouphlos drew near to him, silent now, his face a mask of despair. The torch flared in a sudden gust.

The Emperor stopped, staring at the apparition on the hill above him. Slowly he moved closer, motioning to his torch-bearer to raise the brand higher. Alf's form leaped out of the darkness, all white and utterly still.

"A statue," muttered the Emperor.

Torchlight struck Alf's eyes and kindled them.

Mourtzouphlos' breath hissed in the silence. The torch wavered as the bearer recoiled, crossing himself. "Stand, you fool!" the Emperor snarled. Mustering all of his courage, he advanced, stretching out a hand. Marble, it should be. Cold, solid marble. Naught else.

"Your Majesty," Alf said.

The Emperor froze.

"Sire," said the apparition, "I am no graven image."

Mourtzouphlos snatched his hand away, but not before he had felt the warmth of flesh and the smoothness of silk. But he was in no way comforted. "You. Angel, demon—what are you?"

"Neither, Majesty, only one of God's lesser servants. How is it that you walk the City tonight?"

An angel, the Emperor thought. Or as close to one as made no matter. He was of a piece with this terrible night, this shattering of the world that had been Byzantium. It would not rise again. Its people were soft, weakened by centuries of luxury and power, rotted to the core.

Alf shook his head sharply. "Not so, my lord! There's strength in the City still."

"Where?" demanded Mourtzouphlos. "Not in any quarter which we still hold. I've worn my feet to the bone and my voice to a thread, and not one man will follow me. Not one! They flee, all of them, and curse me if I hinder them. Terror is their Emperor tonight, not Alexios Doukas."

"How can they follow you if you yourself despair? You speak brave words, but your heart does not believe them; and your people know it."

"My people are groveling cowards!" Mourtzouphlos tore his crown from his head and cast it on the ground. "Let the filthy Latins rule them. They deserve no better."

The crown lay upon the grass, a splendid glittering thing half hidden in Mourtzouphlos' shadow. "Your Majesty," Alf said quietly, gazing at it, "you know not what you say. You loved your city once. You fought for it when no other man would. Will you surrender now? Remember your own words! The Latins are trapped and cannot escape save past you, for they have set fire to their own path of retreat. If you fall upon them now, you can defeat them. If you do not . . ." Alf raised his eyes. They were terrible. "If you do not, my lord, then this city shall see such horror as she has not seen in all her thousand years of empire. The sack of Rome herself was nothing to what this shall be. For Rome was rich, but Constantinopolis is the richest city in all the world."

"Constantinopolis is dead. She died the day that thrice-damned fleet came within sight of her."

"The Franks have no knowledge of that. They wait in dread for you to smite them. Will you let them conquer out of senseless fear?"

"They have conquered." Mourtzouphlos' voice was flat.

Alf lifted his hands. "Then truly the City is dead, and you have killed her. May your fate be no better than that to which you have sentenced your people."

Mourtzouphlos drew himself up. His eyes glittered; his fingers worked. And yet he laughed, hoarse and wild. "God Himself has damned us all. Tell Him for Mourtzouphlos, angel of the bitter tongue; tell Him that I laughed at Him. He may doom and He may damn, and He may make my empire a sty for Latin pigs to wallow in; but my City was my City. There shall never be another like her." He stooped and snatched up the crown and turned, swirling the splendor of his cloak. That was the last Alf saw of him: a guttering torch and a flare of crimson, and the glitter of the jewels in his crown.

29

Jehan sat up abruptly. It was dark in the tent, but through the flap he could see the gray light of morning. Someone stood there. Henry, he saw, narrowing his sleep-blurred eyes; and another beyond him speaking rapidly in a low voice.

Beneath and about the muttered words, Jehan heard a deep roaring like the sound of the sea: voices shouting and cheering.

He groped for his sword, remembered with a start that he had left it on the other side of the Horn. The others were stirring now, knights and squires of Henry's household, and Jehan's own long-faced Odo, fumbling for their weapons as Jehan had. "An attack?" one mumbled. "Have the Greeks attacked?"

Henry turned quickly. "The Greeks?" He began to laugh softly, and caught himself. "No, sirs, the Greeks have not attacked. The Emperor fled in the night and his army has surrendered to my lord brother on his hill. The City is ours. We rule in Constantinople!"

They all leaped up, shouting, questioning, fouling one another with their weapons. Jehan fought his way through them and confronted his friend. "My lord. It's true?"

Henry gestured to his companion, a sturdy man with a lined intelligent face. "Can I doubt the Marshal of Champagne? He rode through the City with a small escort, and no one molested him. We're masters of the City. We've won the war."

Jehan shook his head in disbelief. Then he raised it, cocking it. "Then those are our men."

The Marshal nodded. "The sack has begun."

"But," Jehan said, "it was decided there was to be no looting."

"Tell that to ten thousand victorious Franks," the Marshal said dryly. "My lords, I'm for the Count's camp again before the army goes quite mad with joy. Have you any messages for me to carry?"

"Only," said Henry, turning his eyes to the loom of the palace wall, "that henceforward he can send his dispatches to me within Blachernae."

The Marshal bowed and took his leave.

Jehan hardly saw either of them. "We've got to stop the sack."

Henry shook him lightly, recalling him to himself. "Breakfast first, and a council. After that, the palace. And then, my dear priest, you may save as many souls as you please."

Well before either meal or council was ended, the gates of the palace swung wide. Henry's troops, restive already with their lords' slowness, drew into rough formation.

But no army descended to sweep the Latins away. A single figure rode forth on a gray mare, escorted by tall guards, each with an empty scabbard and no spear in his hand. They advanced steadily until they met the leveled spears of the foremost rank. The rider dismounted and spoke for a moment, too far and soft to be heard from Henry's tent. At a bark from their sergeant, two Flemings lowered their spears and seized the Greek. He made no effort to resist, even when they searched him, stripping him of all but his silken undertunic.

Henry was on his feet. "Enough!" he called out. "Return the man's belongings to him and bring him to me."

He received his garments, but was given no time to don them; with them bundled in his arms and two stout Flemings flanking him, he came before the young lord.

A fine elegant creature he was, Jehan thought, even in this state; he bowed smoothly, with all courtesy, and said in passable Latin, "Greetings to my lord."

Henry frowned. "Please, sir, dress. And," he added with a swift cold glance at each of the Flemings, "please be certain to reclaim your jewels."

Those hardened faces moved not a muscle; but when the eunuch held out a slender hand, the Flemings emptied their pouches into it. He dressed then, quickly and without embarrassment, and faced Henry with a smile and an inclination of the head. "Michael Doukas gives thanks to my lord."

"No thanks are necessary," Henry said. "You have a message?"

The eunuch sighed just visibly. Ah, his eyes said, these impetuous Latins. Aloud he murmured, "My lord is wise and courteous, after the fashion of his people. I, who was but the poorest of His Sacred Majesty's poor chamberlains, come now to you as a suppliant. His Serene Highness has departed, leaving his palace unguarded and his city in disarray. We of his followers know not where to turn. We have heard my lord's praises, even here where honest praise is rarer than the phoenix. Will my lord please to take us and our palace into his protection?"

Behind Henry, his barons muttered. A sword or two hissed from its sheath. "My lord!" cried a grizzled knight. "Will you trust these slippery Greeks?"

The rest echoed him, some of them in terms which would have sent a Latin flying for his sword. Michael Doukas merely smiled.

Jehan rose, towering over them all. The eunuch's eyes ran over him. "My," he said, "what a great deal of man that is."

"Enough," growled one of the knights, "for both of you."

Jehan schooled his face to stillness. "My lord, I think he can be trusted."

"Why?" demanded Henry.

"He's as treacherous a Byzantine as ever haunted an emperor's court. But now he's in a corner. We'll overrun his palace whether he surrenders or not. This way he has a chance of escaping with his skin intact."

"And perhaps with that of a friend or two into the bargain?"

Michael Doukas looked from lord to priest and smiled. "No, my lord, you think too well of me. The holy Father is quite accurate. And, perhaps, a shade more intelligent than he looks."

"A shade," Henry said dryly. "Very well, we accept your surrender. You'll come with us, of course. Close by me, if you value your life as much as you pretend."

"It is my most precious possession." Michael Doukas bowed low. "I am entirely at my lord's disposal."

"Come then," Henry said, striding toward his horse.

The calm of Saint Basil's broke soon after sunrise. The Latins' rampage had not yet reached that quarter save for a distant and terrifying tumult, but the wounded had begun to make their way there as best they could. Crawling, some of them, or staggering and carrying others worse hurt than they. The gates opened for them and shut again, with the strong company of Master Dionysios' guards at arms within.

"They're beasts," said a boy whose arm had been all but severed by a sword-stroke. "Animals. Demons. My—my mother—they—"

Alf laid a hand on his brow, stroking sleep into him. He was not the worst wounded in body or in mind, and he was only one of the first.

So many already, so sorely hurt, and so few to tend them. Still more of the healers had fled in the night, mastered at last by their fear; those who remained were white and trembling, ready to bolt at a word.

The boy was as comfortable as he might be. Alf left him, crossing over to the women's quarter. There were more women than men, for the pillagers were less eager to kill women this early in their madness. Only to rape them.

Only, Alf thought, bending over the nearest woman. A child truly, little older than Irene, in the tattered remnants of a gown. It was of silk, and rich.

She lay like a dead thing save for the sobbing of her breath. One eye was swollen shut, the other squeezed tight against the world. When he touched her she recoiled violently, gasping and retching.

"Hush," he said to her in his gentlest voice. "Hush, child. I bring you no hurt. Only healing."

She drew into a knot as far from him as she could go. Her mind knew nothing of him. She was in her house as the barbarians battered down the door, and one struck her father when he ran against them, no weapon in his hands; and his head burst open like a melon in the market, and his face still angry and his eyes surprised. One mailed monster came toward her, all steel, stinking the way the gardener stank after his holiday, and laughter rumbling out of him, and hands stretching out to her, bruising, tearing, hurling her down; and that, oh that, the *pain*—

She shrieked and lay rigid on the bed, her good eye wide, roving wildly. It caught on the white blur that was Alf's face. All her mind bent to the task of making clear those features, of drowning memory, of forcing him into focus.

For a long while she simply stared. At last she spoke, soft and childlike. "Are you an angel?"

He shook his head a little sadly.

"Ah." It was a sigh. "I hoped I was dead. I'm not, am I? I hurt. I hurt all over."

Even through his healing; for it was her mind and not her body which tormented her. He did not venture to touch her, but his voice caressed her. "You hurt. But the hurt will go away and you will be well. No one will harm you again."

She did not quite believe him. But she believed enough that she let him summon one of the women to undress and bathe her and cover her with a clean gown, when before she had let no one near her. Nor would she allow him to go until sleep took her; even at the very last she fought it, in terror of the dreams it would bring.

Alf rose from her bedside, gazing down the length of the room. It was not full, not yet, not with bodies. But it was filled to bursting with pain.

An uproar brought him away from a woman who had taken a dagger in the breast, to collide with Thomas in the passage. "Latins!" the small man panted. "They're beating down the door, I can tell by the sound."

Alf shook his head. "Not yet. It's something else. I think . . . ." His eyes went strange; he leaped forward, nearly toppling the other.

The guards had braced themselves against the gate. Heavy fists hammered upon it; a deep voice roared, "Let us in, damn you! We're friends!"

"Let them in," Alf said.

One of the men whipped about. "Have you *seen* them? They're—"

"I know them." With that strength of his which seemed to come from no visible source, Alf set the men aside and shot the heavy bolts.

Half an army tumbled in. Later, when Alf counted, there were only nine, but they were massive, huge tawny men in scarlet, armed with axes. But he had eyes only for the foremost. The Varangian with Thea's eyes was blessedly unhurt, grinning as he stared, sweeping him into a vast embrace. "Little Brother! It took you long enough to open up."

Alf wanted to crush her close, even as she was. But there were eyes upon them. Her companions stood in a circle about them, eyeing him with interest and a touch of contempt.

It amused him, but it angered Thea. "This," she said in Saxon, "is Master Alfred. Any man who says an ill word of him will have my axe to face."

No one argued with her, although her fierce glare challenged them all to try. After a moment she named them for him: "Ulf, Grettir, Sigurd, Wulfmaer; Eirik, Haakon, and Halldor, and the downy chick is Edmund Thurlafing. I, of course, am your own dear brother Aelfric. Can your guards—" her glance at them was scornful "—use reinforcements?"

* * *

Dionysios contemplated the invasion with a total lack of surprise. "Where you are," he said to Alf acidly, "all manner of prodigies follow. If they can feed themselves, you can keep them. They'll billet on the roof."

They had brought all their gear, and food with it, enough for several days. The roof suited them admirably, although young Edmund gnashed his teeth as the enemy rioted below. He would have plunged into the midst of them, even from that height, had not burly Grettir wrestled him down and sat on him. "We guard," the big man rumbled. "Not fight."

"Guard!" The boy spat. "That's all we've ever done. Guarding and no fighting. Look where it's got us."

"Edmund," Thea explained, "still has a few ideals intact."

"That seems to be true of all of you," said Alf.

Haakon shrugged. He was the eldest of them and the only one with a wound, a deep slash in his arm that Alf had bound up over his protests. "Our company has always been the odd one. Heming—that was our decurion—died in the fighting on the walls. We were called back to guard the Emperor. When he bolted, most of the Guard surrendered or bolted after him. We didn't. We swore an oath: We'll hold off the damned Normans or die trying."

"And I knew exactly the place to do it," Thea said.

"This one." Alf touched her arm, the most he could allow himself. "I have duties, and I can't shirk them any longer. You'll be well?"

"Perfectly, little Brother. Go on, work your miracles. When Edmund is ready to be human again, we'll see about coming to terms with the idiots at the gate."

As Alf left her, he heard Grettir's hoarse whisper. "So that's your famous brother." He laughed like a rumbling in the earth. "It's easy to see who's the beauty in your family."

Thea's reply was lower still, the words indistinguishable. But her flare of temper was bright as a beacon. Alf smiled wryly and descended the stair into Saint Basil's.

* * *

The Latins' madness abated not at all with the sun's sinking; rather, it worsened as they drained the City's vast store of liquors. Wine ran in the streets, mingled with beer and ale and Greek blood.

Somewhat after midnight Alf withdrew for a moment to one of the few quiet places in Saint Basil's, a room just beyond Master Dionysios' study, no more than a closet. Books lined its every wall, save where a slit of window looked down on the inner court; he leaned against the frame and closed his eyes.

Strong slender arms circled his waist; Thea kissed the nape of his neck and laid her cheek against his back, between his shoulders.

He turned in her embrace. She was in her own shape, clad in something dark and loose, with her hair free. She smiled up at him.

He kissed her hungrily. "God, how I've missed you!"

"It's only been a few days."

"Years." He kissed her again. She dropped her robe, but he withdrew a little, reaching for it. "Not here. Not like . . . like . . . a soldier and his doxy."

Her hand stopped his. "Certainly not. We're a soldier and her handsome lad."

His answer was a gasp. And, much later: "We're utterly depraved."

"Aren't we?" She raised herself on her elbow, looking down at him, her cat's-eyes flashing green. He lay on his back, knees drawn up in the small space, his robe spread beneath him like a pool of silver. Even as she gazed at him, he drew down his undertunic.

She caught his hand and kissed it. With a sudden movement he drew her to him, holding tightly. "Thea, beloved," he whispered, "don't ever—don't ever—"

She felt his tears hot and wet upon her breast. "There now," she crooned, stroking his hair. "There."

He pulled away sharply. His cheeks were wet, but his eyes glittered diamond-hard. "Promise me, Thea. You won't go out of Saint Basil's for anything."

"Why," she said startled, "you sound like an anxious nursemaid. What's got into you?"

"Promise me," he repeated.

"What for? I won't bind myself just to keep you quiet."

"You won't—" He broke off and rose, pulling on his robe. His eyes were unwontedly angry. "Not even if I tell you that your death is waiting for you?"

She blanched. But she laughed. "You worry too much. Don't you know how hard it is to kill one of us?"

"It's as easy as a dagger in the heart." He tossed his hair out of his face. "As God is my witness, woman, if you get yourself killed, I'll slaughter every Latin thereafter who comes within reach of my hands, and myself at the end of it."

Thea was silent. She knew his gentleness, which was clear to see, and his strength, which was not. She had thought she knew his temper, which could be terrible. But now he frightened her.

He knew it; he softened not at all.

Nor, fear or no fear, would she. "I can't promise," she said. "I can only try my best to do as you ask. Can you accept that?"

For a long moment he said nothing. He looked proud and cold and hard. His cheek, when Thea laid her palm against it, was rigid.

Little by little it softened into flesh. "Why," he asked softly and reasonably, "can you not be like any other woman?"

"If I were, would you want me?"

He regarded her long and steadily, weighing her words. "No," he said at last. "Unfortunately for my sanity, I would not."

"Love me then," she commanded him, "and leave the rest to God."

The hammering began in the early morning; hammering and shouting, with sword hilts and spearshafts and drunken Flemish voices.

Alf, lying flat on the roof beside Thea in her Varangian guise, peered cautiously down. A large company of men-at-arms massed in the narrow street, growing slowly as more of them staggered out of broken doorways. They were strange fantastic figures, burly and whiskered, wrapped in costly silks over their mail, with rings on their thick fingers and gold about their necks and wrists and jewelled brooches fastened to caps and cloaks and boot-tops, swilling ale from glittering cups and singing in raucous voices.

The first rank endeavored to batter down the gate of Saint Basil's. It was of oak strengthened with iron, triply barred within; it yielded not at all to their blows.

On the other side of Thea, Edmund hissed. His mind was full of strategies, stones and arrows, boiling oil, even brimming chamber pots.

Thea dragged him back. Well before it was safe, he leaped to his feet. "Quick," he said, "while they're too fuddled to look up. If we can pick off a few—"

"We'll bring them swarming onto the roof," Thea finished for him. "The longer it takes them to think of that, the better we'll be. Go down now and lend a hand at the gate."

Edmund balked and glowered. "I came here to fight!"

"You'll have your chance," Alf said. "And soon."

Thea nodded. "You can believe him, too; he's Sighted." She took Edmund's arm. "Meanwhile you can exercise that outsize carcass of yours and help us build a barricade."

Come now, Alf said as she dragged Edmund away, *he's but a lad.*

Oh aye, she agreed with a touch of malice. *He looks almost as young as you.*

Alf laughed, undismayed.

Having failed to break down the door with brute force, most of the Latins wandered away in search of easier prey. But a tenacious few remained, one of whom wielded an axe. The heavy oak splintered under his blows but held.

Within, Master Dionysios had built a second gate all of iron, with narrow bars. Beyond this, several of the guards and Varangians heaped up a barricade of timber, breaking up whatever furnishings the Master would spare. Others meanwhile kept watch on the roof and prowled vigilantly along the garden wall.

The walls of Saint Basil's were thick, the rooms of the sick turned inward, so that the uproar was muted even to Alf's ears. With the gate beset, no more of the wounded ventured in; those who had come before tossed uneasily in dread of the enemy without. The air was thick with fear.

As the hours advanced, one of the healers broke. He left his binding up of a man's wounds and fled, weeping in terror.

Alf saw him go. Leaving his own labors, he followed swiftly.

The man made straight for the gate. The outer door was broken through, but the inner barrier of iron defeated the enemy's axes; the wooden barricade caught the arrows which pierced the bars. Alf's quarry tore at the heap of timber, beating off the guards with a makeshift club. Panic lent him strength; even as Alf halted, a blow hurled one of the guards to the ground. It was young Edmund, bolder than the rest but reluctant to draw weapon on one of his own. He crouched on the stones, shaking his head groggily, while the madman attacked the barricade.

"John!" Alf said. At the sound of his name, the man stiffened and paused. Alf leaped.

He spun, whirling his club. It whistled past Alf's ear as he writhed aside, swooping beneath it, catching John's wrist.

The man fought like a cornered beast. His free hand flailed at Alf's face; Alf caught it and held it in a grip no human could break. "John," he said quietly. "John, you have duties. Why are you neglecting them?"

John struggled and bit, and kicked, a foul, futile blow.

An arrow sang between their bodies to lodge quivering in a fragment of the broken barrier. John stared at it in horrified fascination, and suddenly collapsed.

Alf gathered him up as if he had been a child and not a tall, rather portly man. "You had better rebuild your wall," he said to the speechless guards, "and cushion it somehow. Carpets, I think. Or hangings. Ask the Master."

Edmund staggered up. "I'll ask," he said. "Where is he?"

Alf paused, the healer a dead weight in his arms. "In the men's quarters." His eyes took in the other's face. One cheek was swelling and blackening, and the cheekbone had split, sending a trickle of blood through the young beard. "Have someone see to you when you're done."

Edmund grinned, ignoring the pain. "What's a bruise? Here, let me carry the man for you."

Alf was already moving. "I have him. Hurry now, before the Franks bring up a crossbow."

Alf saw John settled in a quiet place, where he would be watched but not troubled. He had fallen from panic into a kind of stupor; his mind was dull, his thoughts lost in a gray fog of despair that neither voice nor power could dispel.

Alf drew back at last, defeated. Edmund was standing near him, watching him. The bruise on his cheek was in full flower; the cut had begun to close.

"Shouldn't you be on guard?" Alf asked.

The Varangian shrugged. "We made a wall of carpets. Your Master was none too pleased, but he came to lend us a hand. To make sure we did it properly, he said. Just when we were done, they started with crossbows. I saw that our wall was holding and left it to the others." His eyes upon Alf were bright and fascinated. "You aren't half the dainty lass you look, are you?"

Alf dipped a sponge in water and began to cleanse the blood from the other's cheek. Edmund tried to evade him, failed, submitted with a growl. Alf set him on a stool and continued, saying, "To each man his own skills."

"In the palace they'd have marked you out for the angels' choir."

"I sing well, they tell me." Alf set down the sponge and reached for a pot of ointment. "Next time you set out to stop a club with your head, put on your helmet first."

The ointment stung. Edmund's eyes watered, but he was too proud to flinch. "Why didn't you go for the Guard? You're fast enough. Strong enough too, though you don't look it."

"Of the two of us," Alf said, "Aelfric is the fighter. He makes wounds. I heal them."

"And keep lunatics from making them."

"That too." Alf straightened, wiping his hands. It struck him then. "Aelfric. I didn't see him with the others. I can't sense—" He caught himself. "Where did he go?"

"I don't know," Edmund said. "He was there till just before you came. Then he muttered something that sounded like a curse and bolted. I haven't seen him since."

He—she—was nowhere in Saint Basil's. Alf cast his mind wide, thrusting it into the roiling horror that was the City, hurling back fear with grim determination. She would not promise. She would not. And she had gone out into that, without a word to him.

"God in heaven!" he cried aloud. He hurtled past the stunned Varangian, making blindly for the rear of Saint Basil's, away from the beleaguered gate. The enemy had resorted to fire; the guards held it off with water and the same carpets which had foiled the arrows.

They could defend themselves. He came to the bolt-hole, a postern in the garden wall. Thea's presence was a beacon before him. He slid lithely round the startled and babbling guard and out into pandemonium.

He paid no heed to it. Later it would come back in snatches, like remnants of a nightmare.

All round the edge of a great square, men in mail struck at the marble gods with hammers, with axes, or with clubs of wood or iron, shattering the stone, grinding the shards underfoot.

A woman lay sprawled in the street, weeping silently, with her skirts above her waist and blood streaming down her thighs. A man-at-arms, running past, stopped and fell upon her like a beast in rut.

Within the broken doors of a church, a mule brayed, laden with spoil; beyond it, men hacked at the altar with their swords.

A sergeant rode down the street upon an ass, with a priest's vestments over his armor and a jewelled crown on his head and in his hand a chalice filled to the brim with ale. He was chanting, with dolorous piety, the responses of the Drunkards' Mass.

Swift as Alf was, and strange, and wild-eyed, few ventured to molest him. Someone snatched at his robe, half tearing it from his body; he pulled free and ran on, circling a troop of Franks clustered about a silent woman and a shrieking, struggling boy. One of those on the edge, glimpsing Alf as he passed, flung out an arm, overbalancing him.

He had a brief and terrible vision of a bearded face over his, and a breath that reeked of wine, and hard hands groping under his torn tunic. The heel of Alf's hand drove into the man's jaw, snapping his head back. He rolled away, convulsed, his soul shrieking into the dark.

They had broken down the gate of House Akestas over the body of the feeble old porter and swarmed into the courtyard, a company of men who shouted and cursed in the accents of Champagne. All the precious things in the house, all those which did not lie hidden in a great chest under the almond tree in the garden, tottered in a great untidy heap in the center of the court. Close by it like a broken doll lay Irene. Her mother crouched beside her; and Sophia's face was terrible.

Beyond them a battle raged. Thea, in full Varangian gear, stood back to back with Corinna, who wielded a bloody sword. But there were over a score of Franks and a rich prize to fight for; and Corinna, for all her formidable strength, was no swordsman. A tall Frank struck past her awkward guard to open a long gash in her forehead; blood streamed from it into her eyes, blinding her. She stumbled; the Frankish blade bit deep. She fell like a tower falling into massive ruin.

No one watched the gate. Alf poised in it, all his world centered on this that had brought him from Saint Basil's. His mind had room only for wrath. He could not flay Thea with it for blinding his power to her escape, for blocking him when he would have come direct to her by witchery, for striving even to fuddle his mind as he ran until he circled back to his starting place; but that, he had conquered. He called to himself all the forces of his power and shaped them to his bidding.

Thea cried out in her man's voice, a great roar of wonder and of challenge. The Latins, looking back, saw all the far end of the courtyard filled with shining warriors, and at their head a figure of white light. He advanced, raising his hands. He bore no weapon, yet such was the terror of him that the Franks shrieked and fled, running wildly, striking at one another in a blind passion of horror.

There was silence. The last man gasped out his life upon his comrade's sword. The warriors melted into the sunlight; Alf stood alone, half naked, pale and tired.

He sank to his knees beside Irene. She was dead, her neck broken, her eyes staring up at him in innocent surprise. Tenderly he closed them.

Sophia sagged against him. "They didn't touch her," she whispered. "They tried, but she fought; one of them struck too hard. That—that one came then." Her eyes found Thea, whom she did not know in that shape. "He fought well. So well, and for nothing. You . . . both of you. Oh, you were wonderful in your power!"

Alf's arm circled her shoulders. She felt thin and cold, trembling in spasms. His mind brushed hers; he gasped.

"Yes," she said, "I offered to trade myself for her. Perfidious, they call us Greeks. And what are they? They . . . accepted . . . and thought to have both of us. And Corinna after. It took three of them to hold her back, till the stranger came and she broke free. But she died. She . . . died. Who will nurse the children now?"

Alf moved as if to lift her. "You will," he answered her, "after I've healed you."

She shook her head. "No. It's too late even for a miracle. I'm all torn. I've lost too much blood already. And there's this." Her hands had been clasped tightly to her belly. She opened her fingers. Blood oozed between them. "One of them had a dagger in his hand. It won't be much longer now."

Alf covered her hands with his own, summoning the last of his power.

She smiled and shook her head, as a mother will whose child persists in some endearing folly. Her lips were white, but her will was indomitable. By it alone she clung to her body. "My beloved enchanter. Tend my children well for me."

He nodded mutely. Her smile softened. She laid her head upon his shoulder; closed her eyes and sighed.

Gently Alf laid her down. Her hands, loosening, bared what she had hidden. He swallowed bile. Behind him he heard Thea's catch of breath.

From the heap of plunder he freed an armful of richness, the carpet which had lain in his room. He spread it over them all, mother and daughter and the body of the servant who had died for them, and knelt for a long while, head bowed. At last he rose.

The courtyard was like a charnel house. All beyond was stripped bare, stained with the blood of its defenders. Even the stable lay open and plundered, the old mare slaughtered in her stall, the mules and the pony gone.

Yet one creature remained alive. Nikki's kitten wove among the bodies, mewing plaintively. Alf gathered it up. It clung to him with needle claws and cried, until he stroked it into calmness.

His eyes met Thea's. They were as bleak as his own, and as implacable. Minutely she nodded.

For a little while the street was quiet, littered with flotsam. In the center of it, Alf turned. House Akestas loomed before him, brooding over its dead.

He called the lightnings down upon it.

30

"They're gone."

The defenders of Saint Basil's stared dully at one another, blinking in the torchlight. The hospital stood intact, its defenses unbreached.

"They're gone," Edmund repeated. "They've given up. We're safe."

"For the night." Thea leaned on her axe and mopped her brow. "Why should they wear themselves out in the dark, and on our territory at that? We should follow their example. Short watches for all of us and plenty of sleep."

One of Dionysios' men frowned. "There are a thousand easier prizes in the City. Maybe they won't come back."

"Don't lay wagers on it," she said. "Edmund, you look lively enough. Relieve the men in the garden and send them to bed. I'll take the first watch on the roof."

In the unwonted quiet, even Master Dionysios succumbed to sleep. Thea walked the dim ways on soft feet, her watch over, her man-shape laid aside.

Alf lay on his pallet with open eyes. Nikki clung to him even in sleep, cheeks damp, eyes swollen with weeping; the kitten crouched like a tiny lion in the curve of his arm, wide-eyed and watchful. In the far corner of her own bed Anna huddled awake, oblivious to all save her own terrible grief.

Softly Thea lay on Alf's free side, stroking his hair away from his face. He shivered under her hand; his wide eyes closed. *I can't weep,* he said silently. *I try and I try, but no tears come. Thea, if I don't weep I'll go mad.*

She kissed his eyelids, his lips, the hollow of his throat. *You grieve. I feel it in you.*

It goes too deep. Irene—I let her go. When I could have fetched her back again, I tarried to play avenging angel before the Emperor; and after, I let myself forget. I could have forced them both to my will, Irene and her mother. Her mother . . . oh, dear God, the agony I let her suffer!

You, Alf? Thea raised her head from his breast. *No. It was God. As well you know.*

Anna hates Him, he said.

But not you. You, she loves.

Alf's breath caught as he drew it in, almost a sob. *I'm all she has left. Her mother is dead. I burned down her house. It was dead and it was a horror, but it was hers. I never asked her what she wanted to do with it.*

You did the only thing you could have done.

He was silent, mind and voice. When at length she slept, he was still awake. Even she could not follow where his mind had gone.

Morning dawned damp and gray: the third day of the sack of Constantinople. As the light grew sluggishly, the guardians of Saint Basil's looked about them and swallowed cries of despair. All about the walls on all sides massed an army of Franks, knights and men-at-arms in full array. And each company bore a ladder cut to the height of the hospital.

A horn sounded, short and sharp. The ladders swung up.

Varangian axes met them. But there were only nine of the old

Guard and a dozen ladders, and sixscore men swarming up them; and on the roof across the way, a company of bowmen rising from concealment behind a parapet.

Edmund thrust back a laden ladder with the haft of his axe, and laughed as it fell. "Ha! Here's a fight at last!" He wheeled, struck aside a Flemish sword, clove helm and head together with a single sweeping blow.

In the garden below, Dionysios' guards fought hand to hand with men who had scaled the wall and strove now to throw open the postern.

Edmund began to sing.

All the sick in Saint Basil's lay in the centermost of its great wards, the women set apart from the men by a curtain. Of the healers who had labored there when the City was whole, only Master Dionysios remained, and Thomas, and Alf; and two frightened but loyal students. All the rest had fled.

"This is ridiculous, you know," said the woman Alf was tending. She had been a tavern keeper until a Frankish sergeant beat her senseless for refusing to serve him in the cup he proffered, a chalice from Holy Apostles. "The devils will set fire to us, and here we'll be like rats in a trap."

A man's voice called through the curtain, as calm as hers. "It won't happen. They must think we've got real treasure here, with the Emperor's axemen guarding us. We're a nut they'll crack before they try to light any fires."

"Maybe they'll take pity on us," said a boy's breaking voice.

"Them?" The man laughed until his breath caught and he choked.

"They don't pity anything," the woman said for him. "They're devils, I say. Devils straight out of Hell."

Another of the women stirred on her cot. "We should surrender. Why are we fighting them? We'll only make them angrier."

"Would you rather be alive now or dead two days since?" Master Dionysios examined the last speaker with a hard eye and gentle hands. "Well, mistress, you'll walk out of here if I have anything to do with it."

"They do admire courage," Alf said softly, as if to himself. He rose from the tavern keeper's side and passed on to her neighbor.

Slowly the Varangians gave way before the enemy. There were but six now, Grettir fallen with Sigurd and Eirik before the Latin swords; and Halldor had dropped his axe to wield his sword awkwardly left-handed, with an arrow in his right shoulder. Edmund sang no longer. He had no breath to spare for it.

A bolt caught Ulf in the throat. He toppled, taking a Latin with him, gripped in a death embrace. Wulfmaer howled in grief and rage and flung himself forward.

Thea hauled Edmund back by the belt. The three who remained, with Edmund, held the door into Saint Basil's.

Halldor reeled and fell.

Thea's arm was leaden; she breathed in gasps. Her body ached and burned under the Varangian armor. Before her she saw not human forms but a thicket of blades.

Haakon loosed a gurgling cry; and her left side, her sword side, was empty. On her right, young Edmund hacked and cursed and wept without knowing what he did.

In the garden, a shout went up. The enemy had broken through.

Thea kicked open the door she guarded and flung Edmund through it. He tumbled headlong down the steep stair. She whirled her axe and sent it flying, mowing down the startled Franks; slammed the door upon them and shot the bolt. It was a full second before the first body crashed against it.

She was already at the stair's foot, dragging Edmund to his feet. He swore and struck at her with his fist, bruised and winded but unharmed. She cuffed him into submission. "The hellhounds have got into the garden. Move, or they'll find the wards before we do!"

Without a word Edmund bolted down the passage. Thea ran fast upon his heels.

Behind them, the enemy hurtled through the door.

Both forces met in the wide passage outside of the inmost ward. No gate or door stood in their way there; but a pair of Varangians held the entry, one armed with his axe, the other with a sword. Beyond them the attackers could see what precious hoard they guarded: a roomful of the maimed and the dying, a child or two, and three weary men in blue.

The Latins gaped. For this, they had forsaken the rich plunder of Byzantium?

With a howl of frustrated rage, one of the captains charged. His pike pierced through Edmund's guard and clove his mail, striking him to the heart.

He fell against Thea, staggering her with his dead weight. Her eyes flared green in the Varangian face; her lips drew back from sharp witch-teeth.

Alf saw the crossbow raised, the finger tensing on its trigger. "Thea!" he cried sharply.

She turned startled. The quarrel, aimed for her heart, plunged deep into her side, piercing the mail, driving her back, sprawling, shifting and changing under the shock of the blow. It was Thea whose body Alf caught, the helm falling from her head, her hair tumbling over his hands to mingle with her blood.

Very gently he laid her down. No one had moved, save by instinct to shape the sign of the cross.

Deep within him something broke. He took up the sword that had fallen from Thea's hand.

In silence more terrible than any cry, he sprang upon the bowman. The man fell with his head half severed from his shoulders. Alf drove deep into the ranks, crowded as they were, hampered by the narrowness of the passage. They closed in about him. He backed to the wall, holding them off with a circle of steel.

Alf. Thea's mind-voice was feeble. *Alf, don't!*

He faltered. A pikestaff swung round and struck him hard on the side of the head. He staggered, but kept his feet and his sword. With a panther-snarl he slipped beneath the pike and hewed its wielder down.

Stop! Thea cried through the haze of her pain. *Stop, you fool! They'll kill you!*

"I want them to," he said aloud, fiercely.

A scarlet figure wavered in his vision with a host of shadows before and behind it. Thea beat her way through the massed Franks, armed only with her fists and the dying flare of her power on which no weapon could bite, and threw herself upon him. The sword dropped from his numbed hand. He saw her face, white as death, and her wild eyes. The ring of steel drew in upon them both.

"That," said Master Dionysios, "will be quite enough."

The Latins could not understand his Greek, but his tone was clear. He made his way through them by the path Thea had opened and glared at them all impartially.

One or two men raised their weapons. But a helmed knight struck the blades down. "No. Enough. He can't fight; he hasn't even a knife."

Alf crouched at the knight's feet, holding Thea close, eyes burning with wrath thwarted but far from quenched. "Murderer," he hissed in the *langue d'oeil.*

The knight's blank helm betrayed no emotion at all. He seemed to be scrutinizing the upturned and hating face, pondering it. "You speak Frankish, do you? Tell the old man we're claiming this house in the name of the Crusade."

Alf bent over Thea's body, probing her side. Mail and the fading remnants of her power had slowed the quarrel, but it had gone deep, nearly to her back. The black bolt stirred slightly with an indrawn breath; the point of it grazed the farther side of her lung.

A mailed foot drove into his hip. He surged upward.

Dionysios seized his arm and clung grimly. "Kill yourself if you like, you young lunatic, but don't drag us into it. Tell the beast he can have what he pleases if he leaves the sick and the medicines alone."

There was a long pause. Alf shuddered and looked about as if he could not remember where he was. Slowly he repeated the Master's words in Frankish.

The knight unfastened his helm and handed it to a man-at-arms, baring a lined ageless face, tired and sweating and somewhat pale. "You'll look after our wounded, then. These—" he indicated Alf, and Thea whom he had gathered into his arms "—we take."

"The woman is mortally hurt," the Master snapped.

"The boy is a doctor. Is he not?" The knight turned away as Alf choked on the Greek, beckoning to one of his men. "Bind them."

Dionysios stood his ground. "The woman will die. I will not have it. Get out of my hospital!"

"Bind them," repeated the knight implacably.

31

House Akestas was a smoking ruin, black and hideous in the rain. It stank of burning and of charred flesh.

Jehan stood in the half-burned garden, cowled against the drizzle. His face was as bleak as the sky. "Sometimes," he said to it, "it's perilously easy to hate my own people."

His escort of Flemings prowled through the rubble, pausing now and then to take up something of interest, skirting the occasional beds of coals. Even in the rain the embers smoldered unabated, as if they disdained to die.

A shout brought him about. Part of the stable stood intact, set apart from the house as it had been. His squire struggled with someone there, a scarecrow figure, very small and very black. Jehan strode toward them.

Odo's captive was a boy, ragged and covered with soot, who struggled and bit and cursed in half a dozen languages. Even the squire's hard blow neither stilled nor silenced him; but when he saw Jehan he froze. To his wide eyes, the priest seemed a giant.

Odo shook him roughly, nursing a bitten hand. "The little beast was rooting in the straw."

"Wet, probably, and cold," Jehan said, speaking Greek—it would not hurt Odo to exercise his brain a little. "Look; his teeth are chattering. He's thin as a lath, too. He was on short commons well before we closed down the markets."

"Please," the child whined. "Please, noble sirs. You don't want me. I'm too thin, no meat on my bones, see. Just skin."

Jehan laughed without mirth. "So we eat little children, do we, lad? What else do we do?"

"Kill," the boy answered with sudden venom. His voice slid back into its whine; he cringed in Odo's hands. "Please, great lord, holy Patriarch, I'm worth nothing, I never was. Don't kill me."

"Why should I want to?"

That, the boy seemed to think, was unanswerable.

Jehan freed him from Odo's grasp and held him lightly but firmly. His arms were no bigger than sticks. "If you can tell me something, I'll let you go. I'll even give you money."

The black eyes narrowed. "Show me."

Jehan took a bit of silver from his pouch. The boy swallowed. It was more money than he had ever dreamed of. His fingers itched to snatch at it. But Jehan's grip was too strong. "Here. This for the truth." He held the coin up in front of the child's eyes. They fixed on it, fascinated. "Did you see what happened to this house?"

The urchin's eyes flickered. Fear, or the effort of inventing a lie?

Fear, Jehan decided. The emaciated body shook with it; the dark cheeks grayed. He tried in vain to break away.

Jehan turned the coin until it glittered. "Tell me."

It took a long while, for the boy was truly terrified, more of the memory than of the man who held him. But greed in the end was stronger than fear. With his gaze riveted on the coin, he said, "It was an angel." Pressed, he went on in fits and starts. "I was hiding. I peeped out. The dev— Your people were all over, killing and stealing and doing things to people.

Some were in the house. Then there was nobody in the street, or nobody much. And he came out. He was an angel, like in church."

Have you ever been in one? Jehan wondered. But he said, "Go on. What was he like?"

"An angel. All white. He—I think he had people with him. I didn't notice them much. He came out of the house. He stood and he shone. And the fire came down."

Jehan gripped the boy till he yelled, then let go. The urchin snatched the coin and bolted. Jehan hardly noticed him. "Fire," he said slowly. "Fire came down."

"A patent lie," Odo declared. "The looters must have torched the place."

"What?" Jehan had forgotten the squire was there. "What? Set fire to it? No. Not they. There are bodies in those ruins. Several bodies, if my nose is any guide. And an . . . angel. He would look like that when his power was on him. He lives then. Thank God. But why destroy House Akestas?"

"Divine vengeance?" Odo suggested, not quite flippantly.

"I hope not," Jehan said. "For his sake and for all our sakes, I hope not."

Jehan almost wept when he saw Saint Basil's. It was beautifully, blessedly intact, save for the splintered outer gate; although Latin guards stood there, the courtyard was whole, untouched.

They let him in readily, with proper respect for his priesthood. Wonder of wonders, he thought, they were both sober and sane. Nor had they plundered within. Part of the hospital was a barracks, but a well-disciplined barracks; the rest kept to its old function. And there bending over a wounded soldier was Master Dionysios, as brusque and grim-faced as ever, tyrannizing over the conquerors as he always had over his own people. Even the Frankish surgeons seemed content to bow to his rule.

As Jehan approached him, a shrill cry echoed through the room. Anna ran down an aisle among the beds, her braids flying, to fling herself into Jehan's arms. She was babbling like a mad thing, too swift and incoherent for him to follow.

He held her for a long while. They were all staring at him. Latins, he noticed, lay beside Greeks, all mingled and apparently amicable.

Anna had fallen silent, weeping; her whole body shook although she made no sound. He sat with her on the side of an empty bed.

She stiffened in his arms. He loosed his hold; she sat on his lap, looking into his face, letting the tears fall where they would. "Mother is dead," she said very calmly. "So is Irene. So is Corinna. The Latins killed them. Alf made our house a pyre for them."

Jehan had known how it must be. But it was the worst of all the past days' horrors to hear it from her in that quiet, child's voice ancient with suffering, all her world destroyed in a handful of days. And no hate; before God, no hate. She had gone past it.

She regarded him with grave concern. Her tears had stopped; his had only begun. She wiped his face with a small warm hand. "Don't cry, Father Jehan. You've won. You should be glad."

"*I* haven't won. No one has, except maybe the Devil. We found the greatest city in the world; we've made it an outpost of Hell."

Anna shook her head. "Hell isn't here. It's underneath us. You know that, Father Jehan."

"And belike I'm going there." He mastered himself with an effort. "You're safe, God be thanked. Is—is—Anna, is Nikki here?"

Her face twisted. "No. N—no."

"Dead?"

"No." She was crying again.

"For God's sake, you great lout, stop tormenting the child."

Jehan met Master Dionysios' cold eye. "I'm tormenting myself," he said levelly. And at last: "Where is Alfred?"

The Master glared. "What is that to you?"

Suddenly Jehan could not bear it. "Everything!" he shouted. "Everything, damn you!"

"We are not deaf." Dionysios' expression had not softened, but his eyes had, a very little. "Nor do we know where he is."

"They took him," Anna said. "He fought. Thea—Thea was somebody else, and then they shot her, and she was herself. He tried to kill everybody. They tied him up and took him away. Thea too. Nikki and his cat went after. Nobody could stop him. They were too busy holding me down."

Dionysios nodded shortly. "That in essence is the truth. The woman had a bolt in her lung below the heart. She could not have survived the hour under such handling as they gave her. But mercy is not a virtue you barbarians are guilty of. Your friend was taken with her; where, no one seems able to tell. Some vile prison, no doubt, reserved for those who had the temerity to defend their city."

If Jehan had not been sitting, he would have fallen. "Alf—wasn't—hurt?"

"Not that any of us could see, though he fought like a madman once the woman had fallen."

"It didn't matter," Anna said, "if he wasn't hurt, if Thea was."

No. It did not. And if Thea was dead—

Jehan rose unsteadily, setting Anna on her feet. She held to the cincture of his habit. "Take me with you," she said.

"Child, I can't. You're safe here. There's the Master, and Thomas, and—"

"Take me!"

"What would I do with you?"

"Take me," she persisted.

He hardened his will. She tightened her grip on his belt.

"It's death out there!" he cried in desperation.

"Not anymore," she said. "The riots are over. Everyone says so. All the Latins are sick and sorry and very, very rich. Besides," she added, "you're big enough to take care of six of me."

But not to withstand the pleadings of even one of her. He

tarried, hoping that she would weary of waiting and abandon him. Vain hope. He questioned every Latin in Saint Basil's, of every rank, and she never took her eyes from him.

No one knew where Alf had been taken. Lord Bertrand had commanded it; Lord Bertrand was gone and his men with him. He could be anywhere in the City.

When Jehan left Saint Basil's, he had a small companion. A boy, it might have been, dressed as a healer's apprentice, with a cap on his head and a small, satisfied smile on his face.

Nikki huddled miserably in a corner with his kitten in his lap. It was dark where they were, and damp, and cold. Things scuttled in the darkness, fleeing when the cat sprang at them, creeping back boldly when it paused to make a meal of one of their kin. Once, when men brought food and water, the light of their torches caught the brown-furred bodies and the pink naked tails and the redly gleaming eyes.

Alf did not notice. Alf noticed nothing except Thea. His robe lay under her body, shielding her from the crawling dampness; for himself he had only his thin undertunic. The men had had things to say of that; Nikki had felt their minds when they came, and seen their faces. Not good faces, but not bad ones either. One had tried to touch Alf where a person was not supposed to touch, but the other had stopped him, angry and a little disgusted, thinking words Nikki was not sure he understood.

Alf had not even known they were there. Thea lay very still on his robe. He had eased the bolt out of her side with hands and power, and stopped the bleeding. Strange bleeding, bubbling like water out of a fountain. It frightened Alf, a fear that made Nikki cower in his corner. She was dying the way Father had died. She would die, and there would be no world left for Alf.

Hour after hour she lay there in the darkness and the cold and the pale glimmer of Alf's power. Close to death, hovering on the very edge of it, yet she held firm against his healing. Her will and her consciousness had no part in it; those were long gone. But her body clung grimly to life, and her power kept doggedly to its resistance: two instincts, each powerful, each implacable, each striving blindly to thwart the other.

Alf drove his power to the farthest limits of its strength and even beyond. His body, abandoned, sprawled beside hers; his mind cupped like a hand about the wound which drained her life away, but could not move to mend it. Her shield was like adamant.

He spun back into his body. For a long while he lay motionless. Her face was white and still and achingly beautiful. Already it had the marble pallor of death. Drop by drop, blood trickled into her lungs, crowding out the precious air. Her heart strained; her limbs grew cold as all her forces gathered at her center.

Slowly Nikki crept from his corner. Alf seemed as close to death as she, willing it, longing for it.

There was a small space between them. Nikki wriggled into it. Thea was hard and cold in her armor, Alf cold and rigid, no warmer or softer than the stones on which he lay. They were gone; they would never come back. They had left him alone. He began to cry, deep racking sobs without help or hope.

Alf's power, all but spent, sent forth a last feeble tendril.

Thea's barrier wavered and melted.

Nikki, between them, wept as if his heart would break. Through the perfection of his grief, Alf's healing flowed.

It was very little. He had no more left to give. Yet Thea's life, balancing upon the edge of dissolution, seized the thread and clung. Inch by tortured inch he drew her back. Cell by cell her body began to mend.

At last, exhausted by his weeping, Nikki slept.

Alf woke by degrees. His mind ached at least as much as his body. There was a grinding pain in his stomach; only after a long while did he recognize it as hunger.

His nose twitched. There was food somewhere within range. Blindly he groped for it. Something warm and furred moved against his hand; he started, half sitting up, to meet the bright eyes of Nikki's kitten.

Thea lay on her side, pale and ill to look on but sleeping peacefully. Nikki coiled in the hollow of her body. All around them was a room of stone, bare of furnishings, with a steep ladder of a stair leading up to a heavy door. Not a prison, Alf thought as his mind began to clear. It had not that aura which prisons have, of hate and fear and pain. This place spoke rather of ancient wine and of long-gone cheeses.

Close by him lay a plate and a bowl and a lidded jar. The plate held bread, dry and rather hard but of decent quality; a stew filled the bowl, now cold and congealed, and in the jar was thin sour wine.

He raised the jar with trembling hands. He was as weak as if he had roused from a fever. He drank a sip, two. The wine burned his parched throat, but it warmed his belly. Carefully he set the jar down and reached for the bread. A little only; a spoonful from the bowl. His stomach growled for more; his mind, trained to fasting, refrained.

With his body's needs attended, he sat clasping his knees, chin upon them, gazing at the two who continued to sleep. Perhaps he prayed. Perhaps he dozed. His mind was empty of thought, utterly serene.

He started awake. The kitten crouched at his feet, every hair erect.

Iron grated on iron. Bolts thudded back; the door swung open. Light stabbed Alf's dark-accustomed eyes. He threw up a hand to shield them.

The stair groaned under the weight of several men. They were armed, he saw from the shape of their shadows; mailed though not helmed, and cloaked over it. One carried the torch that still made Alf's eyes flinch. Two others stood with drawn swords.

The fourth stood over him. The little cat struck fiercely with distended claws; met mail; spat and yowled, defying the intruder to advance.

Alf rose unsteadily with the furious cat in his arms, and bowed as best he might. "My lord," he said, neither surprised nor afraid.

Count Baudouin looked him up and down; folded his arms and cocked his head a little to one side. "So, Master Alfred," he said, "even your familiar will fight for you. Have you anything to say for yourself?"

"You judged me when first you saw me," Alf responded coolly. "What could I say that would change it?"

Baudouin's jaw tensed. "My judgment has proven correct."

"In your eyes, perhaps."

"Four of my men died at your hands."

"How many innocent women and children died at theirs?"

"Greek women and children," said Baudouin. "You, sir, are not a Greek."

"No. I am merely a man who saw half his family cruelly murdered and his lady wounded unto death by men gone mad with wine and plundering."

"You took arms against your own people."

Alf's eyes glittered; his voice was deadly soft. "My people, my lord? The only one of my people in this city lies yonder with the wound of a Flemish quarrel in her side. She lives, and will live, but she owes her life to no act of your army."

Baudouin looked from him to Thea. She was little more than a shadow and a gleam, her slender body lost in the Varangian armor, her face hidden by the fall of her hair. He approached her slowly. Alf, with no appearance of haste, moved to stand in his path.

There was a pause. Baudouin glared; Alf met him with a cold and quiet stare. His eyes dropped.

"My lord," Alf said very gently, "with me you may do as you like. But I advise you not to touch my lady."

Baudouin laughed, high and strained. "That? Your lady? A fine lusty wench she must be, from the tales I've heard. But then," he added with a flash of malice, "you seem to be a man after all, now I see you without your silken skirts. Do you keep her satisfied?"

"What can it matter to you, my lord, whether I do or not?"

Baudouin's hand flashed up. Alf seemed hardly to move; but the heavy gauntlet never touched his skin, only ruffled his hair slightly with the wind of its passing.

The Count clenched his fists and spoke through clenched teeth. "Lord Bertrand would like to make an example of you."

"What sort of example, my lord?"

Baudouin bared his teeth. It was meant to be a smile. "We've hanged a number of our own for keeping back more than their fair share of the plunder. It's quieted the men down, to be sure. But it's time we gave them a genuine criminal or two. What could be better than a Latin witch who has thrown in his lot with the Greeks?"

"What indeed?" Alf asked as quietly as ever. "I ask only one concession."

"I grant you none," said Baudouin. "I gave you enough in coming here at all and in letting you fray my temper with your insolence. Lord Bertrand may let you live; you can pray for that if either God or your black master will listen to you. Or he may rid the world of you."

"That is his right. But let him set my lady free. She is a Greek, and fought loyally for her Emperor; she does not deserve a traitor's fate."

"That's for Lord Bertrand to decide. I wash my hands of you."

"And Pilate spake, and having spoken, turned away."

Thea's voice spun them both about. She lay as she had lain for this long while, but open-eyed, weak yet alert; Nikki's great eyes stared up from the curve of her side.

Carefully, shakily, she raised herself on her elbow. She regarded Baudouin with a bright mocking stare, for he was gaping like a fool. He had not thought to find her beautiful.

"Yes, Count," she said, "you're wise to let someone else do your dirty work. You can't have brother Henry guess what you've done, now can you? He might even begin to suspect the truth, that most of your hatred of Alf is simple, sea-green jealousy."

"Jealousy?" cried Baudouin. "Of *that?*"

"Of a man for whom, on a few moments' acquaintance, your much beloved brother conceived a great and lasting friendship. A friendship which he was rash enough to declare in your presence, with considerable and glowing praise of its object."

"Henry is a trusting fool. He saw a handsome face, heard handsome words, and let himself believe in them."

"And you were like to die of envy. He never praises you, except on rare occasions when he thinks you might deserve it. If you want to be Emperor, lordling, you're going to have to learn to be more like your brother."

Baudouin had begun to recover from the shock of her beauty in the bitterness of her words. He opened his mouth to denounce her.

She laughed, sweet and maddening, with a catch at the end of it. "Oh, certainly! I'm at least as bad as my paramour. You'll have to hang us both, your lordship, or you'll never have peace."

"Thea," Alf began, setting the cat upon the floor, sinking to one knee beside her.

She kissed the finger he laid to her lips, and shook it away. "Go on, my brave lord, my Emperor-to-be. Condemn us both to death. Then you'll have no rival for your brother's affections, and no one to take vengeance on you for murdering her lover."

Baudouin's sword hissed from its sheath. She laughed at it. He gritted out a curse and whirled away, half running up the steep stair. His men scrambled after him.

32

Jehan prowled the room Henry had given him in Blachernae. It was a chaplain's cell, with a chapel close by it; in comparison with the rest of the palace it was very small and sternly ascetic. But by the standards of a priest from Anglia, it was almost sinfully opulent.

Anna sat on the large and comfortable bed and watched him. Here in seclusion, she had taken off her cap; her braids hung down very black and thick on either side of her narrow pointed face. She tugged at one. "Won't you let me cut them off?" she begged.

"No!" he snapped. He stopped in front of the saint painted with jewelled tiles upon the wall, and glared into her huge soulful eyes. " 'Holy Saint Helena,' " he read, " 'finder of the True Cross, pray for us.' . . . If you could find a Cross buried for three hundred years, why in God's name can't you find a handful of prisoners lost for a day?"

"Maybe because you haven't asked her before," Anna said reasonably.

He growled and began to pace again.

Someone knocked softly at the door. Anna stuffed her braids into her cap. Jehan muttered something in Norman; and louder, in Greek: "Who is it?"

"You ordered food, my lord," said a light sexless voice.

Jehan shivered a little. These eunuchs made his skin creep, silent gliding creatures, neither male nor female, serving their new masters with obsequiousness which masked deep and utter contempt.

He found his voice. "Come in then."

The servant entered with bowed head and laid his burden on a table. Anna, with the perfect ease of the Greek aristocrat, stepped round him as if he had not been there and began to investigate the various plates and bowls.

The eunuch made no move to go. He was a young one, overdressed as they all seemed to be, painted and perfumed like a woman; there were jewels in his ears and on his fingers and everywhere between. As he lifted his face, with a shock Jehan knew him. Either the chief steward of the palace had suffered a great reduction in rank, or there was something afoot.

Without conscious thought, Jehan reached for his sword and drew it and set himself between the eunuch and the child.

Michael Doukas looked from the bright blade to the cold eyes behind it and smiled slightly. "I take it, holy Father, that we know one another."

"I think," said Jehan, "that we do. Are you in the habit of running errands for minor clerics when there's nothing of greater import for you to do?"

"On occasion," replied Michael Doukas, "I will stoop to it." He laid a delicate finger on the flat of Jehan's blade, just below the point, and moved it fastidiously aside. "Do you mind, my lord? It's quite vulgar to greet one's guests with steel."

"Barbaric too, of course." Jehan returned Chanteuse to its sheath and relaxed a little, though ready at a word to cut the eunuch down.

Michael Doukas sighed, relieved. "Ah. Now I can breathe again. Father, will you hear my confession?"

That caught Jehan completely off guard. "But you're a Greek!"

"So I am. Will you, Father?"

"You know I can't."

The eunuch shook his head sadly. "Such injustice. And all for a word or two in an ancient prayer. Where can I go with such a burden as my soul carries?"

"This place is swarming with priests of your persuasion." Jehan's eyes narrowed. "All right. Out with it. What did you come here to tell me?"

Michael Doukas inspected him in detail, turning then to examine Anna, who ate hungrily but watchfully. One of Jehan's daggers had found its way into her belt. "Your boy, Father? Or—no." He snatched, too quick even for Anna's quick hands, and brandished her cap, meeting her glare with laughter. He was, Jehan realized, much younger than he looked, hardly more than a boy himself. "Indeed, my lord, you take them up young! and out of hospitals too, it seems."

"Saint Basil's," she snapped. "Who are you?"

"My name is Michael Doukas. And yours, noble lady?"

She chose not to answer him. "Michael Doukas? Did you smuggle Alf out of the palace?"

"Indeed, lady," he replied, "and how do you know of that?"

"He's my brother. We're looking for him." Her eyes glittered with eagerness, her anger forgotten. "Do you know where he is?"

"Your brother?" mused Michael Doukas. "Ah, then you are an Akestas."

"Of course I'm an Akestas! They took him away with Thea, and Nikki too though they didn't know he was following till it was too late. Now we can't find him. Where is he?"

"How strange," Michael Doukas said. "I have a friend, you see. He has a friend who knows a man, who knows a woman who plies a very old trade near the All-seer's hill. She likes to talk while she works, and her clients, it seems, like to talk to her."

"Why?" asked Anna. "What does she do?"

"Never mind," Jehan said quickly, glowering at the eunuch. "Go on. What rumor did she hear?"

Michael Doukas sighed and shook his head sadly. "Business, she asserts, is better than ever before, but the clientele leaves something to be desired. But she has a little Frankish, learned in the trade; and, as I've said, she likes to use her tongue. Last night she had a client of somewhat higher rank than usual, a sergeant-at-arms who served one of the Flemish knights. A very handsome man he was, for a Frank, and very proud of it. Our good dame took due note of this. Ah so, quoth he, but he had a rival in beauty. Indeed? said she. Impossible! And he sighed, languishing, and averred that alas, it was so, but certainly she would never see this paragon, seeing that he lay in prison awaiting the hangman's pleasure."

Jehan's fingers locked about the eunuch's throat. "Where, damn you? *Where?*"

Michael Doukas swallowed painfully. "My lord—might you—?" Jehan relaxed his grip by a degree. "My lord, if I may continue, our keen-witted woman of affairs, having some liking for her trade and a certain desire to improve its quality, continued to question her client. He was pleased to tell her what he knew, for her persuasions were quite irresistible. Yes, he had seen the man he spoke of; yes, it was certain: he was destined for the gallows, for he, Latin-born, had fought as a Greek; and there was a whisper of darker things, witchery perhaps—certainly he had a familiar, a small fierce cat that had followed him into his prison. And truly he had enemies. Not the least of whom was my lord the Count of Flanders."

"Baudouin!" Jehan muttered. "I knew he had a hand in this." His fingers tightened till the eunuch gasped. "If you don't tell me now where Alfred is, I'll choke it out of you."

Michael Doukas licked his dry lips. He was not precisely afraid, but he was very much concerned for the safety of his skin. "Very well, my lord. He lies not in any proper prison but in a guarded chamber, very close indeed to Madame's place of business. She, it seems, knows the place well; it was a tavern once before the fires swept past it. Its cellars are intact, and well and strongly bolted.

Jehan loosed his grip but did not set the eunuch free. "Take me there," he said. But then, abruptly, "No. Not quite yet. Where is my lord Henry?"

The City was deathly quiet under the stars, lying stripped and torn upon her hills, her people cowering still in terror of the conquerors. Yet the Latins were quenched at last, exhausted with their three days' debauch; their lords moved now to rule the realm which they had taken, and to repair the ravages of war and plundering.

Along the shore of the Horn, Saint Mark's fleet rode at anchor. One galley glowed vermilion in the light of its many lamps; the lion banner of the Republic caught the light with a glimmer of gold.

Enrico Dandolo received his late guests in a cabin as rich as any emperor's. Weary though he surely was, no less weary than the young men who faced him, he betrayed no sign of it. He listened quietly to the tale Michael Doukas told, lids lowered over the fierce blind eyes, his face revealing no hint of the thoughts behind. The eunuch, for his part, seemed not at all alarmed to be here, face to face with the man who had ordered the conquest of his city.

"What," asked the Doge when he was done, "have I to do with this market tale?"

"An innocent man is like to die," Henry answered him. "I know better than to confront my brother in one of these moods of his. You on the other hand, my lord, he plainly respects. If you pleaded Master Alfred's case, he would be likely to listen."

"Is he innocent?" asked Dandolo.

Michael Doukas smiled. "As to that, my lord, I know he was no creature of ours. Indeed I would have wagered that he was yours, if anyone's."

Anna shook herself awake in Jehan's lap. "He wasn't anybody's! He worked in Saint Basil's and mended the hurts the fighters made. He only actually hurt anybody when they hurt one of the family. They—they killed Mother, and Irene, and Corinna. And then they shot Thea. He loved Thea better than anything else in the world. If he killed people after that, can you blame him?"

"Of blame," said the Doge, "I can say nothing. He is a Latin. He slew Latins."

"Hasn't there been enough killing?" She was close to tears. "He told you you'd win. I know—he said so."

"So he told the Emperor Isaac," said Michael Doukas.

Anna slid out of Jehan's lap and stood in front of the Doge. "You can save Alf's life if you want to. Why don't you?"

"Child," Dandolo said to her, "I am not all-powerful. Count Baudouin is a great prince, at least as great as I. If he chooses to dispose of a man for whom he has no love to spare, there is nothing I can do."

"You can try!"

It was a strange sight, the small girl in ill-fitting boy's clothes and the ancient and terrible Doge of Saint Mark. He, who could not see, yet felt it; a spark kindled deep in his eye. "Very well then. If I set your Alfred free, what will you give me?"

"My thanks," she answered.

The young men and the eunuch exchanged glances, half in alarm, half in laughter.

The Doge nodded gravely. "A fair price, when all is considered. I suppose you expect prompt service?"

"Immediate, sir."

"So." He raised his voice slightly. "Paolo! My cloak!"

With great care and with Nikki's help, Alf eased Thea out of her armor. The wound in her side seemed a small thing to have brought her so close to death, a circle of scarlet beneath her breast, no wider than her finger. Gently, with water from the jar and a strip torn from his tunic, he washed away the last of the blood.

She sighed a little under his hands. "So much metal," she said. "It weighed on my soul as much as on my body."

"You regret your bravery?"

"Of course not!" She had moved too quickly; she winced. "I regret that I didn't give Edmund a better escort into Hell. He was a fine lad. A fool, but . . . a fine one."

Alf touched her cheek. She blinked fiercely. "I'm *not* crying!" she snapped, although he had not spoken. "I'm giving the dead their due. That's all. It's over; we survive, as usual; life goes on. That, dear pilgrim, is the wisdom you came all this way to find."

He touched his lips to the center of her body's pain. *Let me heal you,* he said silently.

No. Her fingers tangled in his hair. *I want to do my own mending.*

Why?

Because, she said, *I want to.*

Monk that he had been, he understood. But he was a monk no longer, and he loved her. *Let me!*

No, she repeated. Aloud she said, "I don't suppose there's anything to eat in here?"

It distracted him, as she had meant. Yet he paused. She thought hunger at him; he yielded at last, with reluctance in every movement.

Jehan's torch, raised as high as the ceiling would allow, illuminated very little. Other senses than sight told him that the space below was bare of furnishings though not of life.

A pool of scarlet caught the light. For an instant his heart stopped. He all but fell to the stone floor; the torch flared wildly as he fought to keep his feet. The toe of his sandal nudged dry softness.

A cloak the color of blood; and under it, curled together for warmth, three larger bodies and a much smaller one. They opened eyes blurred with sleep; Thea smiled and yawned. "Good—morning, is it?"

"It's just after midnight." Jehan was suddenly and blindingly angry. "Aren't you even surprised to see me?"

"Not surprised," Alf said. "Glad, yes. Very, very glad."

Very carefully Jehan unclenched his fists, then his teeth. "I should have known better. You being what you are, and Thea being what she is . . . you've made a fool of me, do you know that?"

"Of course we haven't," Thea said.

Alf was on his feet, hale and calm, embracing Jehan with a quiet joy which slew all his anger.

Light flooded the cell. Henry stepped away from the stair, and after him what seemed to be a great number of men. Some bore torches; others supported a bent figure in rich vermilion, easing his passage down the steep narrow way. Yet, once upon the level, he stood alone with but his sheathed sword for a prop.

Alf bowed low. He had barely straightened before a small whirlwind overtook him. "Alf! Is Thea all right? Why didn't you witch yourself out as soon as you got here? They said Jehan had to go down first, and not me—I don't know why. I'm angry. *Alf!*"

He gathered her up. She buried her face in his tunic and babbled into silence.

"Thea," said that lady, "is quite well. But not, yet, quite up to any greater magic than the healing of her own body. Jehan, help me up."

He approached her almost fearfully. She looked pale even for one of her kind, and thin, almost transparent; but her eyes were bright. Under the cloak she was all but naked; he draped it around her carefully and helped her to her feet.

She drew a cautious breath. "My lords will have to pardon me if I neither bow nor curtsey. I'm . . . slightly . . . indisposed."

"Please, my lady," the Doge said, "spare your courtesy and lie down again for your body's sake."

She made no objection. By that, Jehan knew truly how ill she was. But she insisted on sitting up and on speaking as clearly as ever. "My thanks for my lords' indulgence. To what do we owe the honor of your presence?"

Jehan eyed her suspiciously. She did not seem to be mocking them. But with Thea, one never knew. "It's just a little thing," he said. "A mere rescue. I don't suppose you either wanted or needed to be rescued?"

"Surely they wanted it," said Michael Doukas, moving out of the shadow by the stair. He met Alf's eyes with a smile and a slight bow. "Indeed, master seer, we meet again at Armageddon."

Alf smiled in response. "And now I owe you my life twice."

"Oh, no," said the eunuch, "you owe nothing. You permit us to flatter ourselves that we can aid you. But I owe you all that I am. Had you not foretold this war's ending, I might not have had the good fortune to serve my new and most noble lord." He bowed low to Henry. "Surely that was worth my telling a friend of yours where to find you."

"Just in time too," Jehan said. "I was going mad. When I found out that, with your usual talent for putting yourself in your enemies' power, you were in Count Baudouin's hands, I was somewhat less than delighted. I went straight to my lord Henry; he took me to the one man who could set you free. And that, Messer Enrico did."

"Easily," the Doge said. "Ridiculously so. My lord would not even see me; informed of my errand, he granted what I asked without a word of protest."

"Not quite, my lord," Jehan said. "We all heard him shouting. 'Take him and be damned! Take them all! Only let me never see or hear of them again!' "

Thea smiled. Jehan scowled. "If I'd known you were alive and conscious, I never would have bothered."

"You would have," she said calmly, "and we owe you thanks for it."

Anna snorted, a small defiant sound. "Thank him? What for? He just did the work. Saint Helena did all the rest of it."

"Then," said Alf, "when we've rendered all proper thanks to her earthly instruments, we'll sing a Mass of Thanksgiving in her honor. Meanwhile, demoiselle, shall we leave this place?"

"The sooner, the better," she said.

33

The altar stood in the garden of Saint Basil's, hung all with white and gold for the great festival of Easter. The Latin wounded had been brought out to hear the Mass; some few of the Greeks, Alf knew, listened but would not show their faces. Save for Thea, seated beside him, and the Akestas children. They had insisted upon being there, for it was Jehan who served upon the altar, moving smoothly and surely through the rite.

And Master Dionysios. The Master had made the best of a great evil, and he had prospered. Many of his people had crept out of hiding after the orgy of plundering and returned to their work; with the Latin surgeons, Saint Basil's boasted a full complement of healers. They would do well, whatever became of the City.

We'll always need doctors, Thea said, laying her hand lightly in his.

He laced his fingers with hers. A week's rest and tending, with her own witch-born strength, had done much to restore her to herself. Only a slight thinning of her cheeks, a hint of transparency under her skin, remained to tell the eye of her wounding; and to the mind a slight but persistent pain and a weakness which would not fade.

You'd be weak too if you'd been tied to your bed for a week. Without, she added with a sidelong glance, *any of the usual compensations.*

Such thoughts, he said, priestly-stern, *are not fitting in this place.* But she had caught the flicker of guilty laughter beneath.

Jehan left his acolytes to clear away the vessels of the Mass and sought the four who sat on one stone bench, basking in the sun. Doctors and servants had taken most of the others away; they were all but alone.

Anna gave him her place on the end of the bench and climbed into his lap. "You sang beautifully, Father Jehan," she said.

"I tried my best." He frowned a very little. "Do you think your mother and Irene would have minded that I sang a Latin Mass for them?"

"Oh, no," she answered. "We had a proper priest sing their Requiem. They're buried with Father now. I'm sure they're happy to know that you remember them."

"How could I ever forget?" Jehan's blue eyes looked gravely into her black ones. "What are you going to do now?"

She shrugged. "We're still rich, you know. Mother put all our best things in a box and buried it; we dug it up yesterday. It's in our room now, with a witchery on it to keep anybody from touching it. Alf wants to take it and us to Grandmother and Uncle Philotas in Nicaea. A lot of our people went there; there's even a man who calls himself our new Emperor. Though everyone says it's Count Baudouin who's got the crown."

"The lords elected him, that's true enough."

"He didn't hang Alf. That proved his clem—clemency. And his troops like him. So they crowned him and gave the other man a palace and a kingdom and one of the old empresses. The most beautiful one, of course. I think the other man came out a lot better than he did."

Jehan laughed. "So do I! But His new Majesty doesn't think so. He's succeeded in hearing Mass today in Hagia Sophia, and from the throne besides, with everyone bowing and calling him Emperor. There's not much more he could wish for."

"Except," Alf murmured, "an empire worthy of the name."

"Prophecies again, little Brother?" asked Thea.

"No. Plain observation."

Anna ignored them. "So with the Count and the Marquis taken care of and the Count on the throne, Alf wants to take us to Nicaea."

And leave us.

Jehan blinked. The voice was silent, but it was not either Alf's or Thea's. It was softer, with an odd, blurred, toneless quality. He looked down at Nikki, who sat upon the ground playing with a handful of pebbles. The child returned his stare. *He wants to take us and leave us there and go away with Thea.*

Jehan swallowed. "He—is he—"

"No," Thea said, "he's as human as you are. Or was. That's a matter Alf is going to have to resolve for himself. For our monk that was, out of purest Christian charity, opened his mind to one doubly sealed by deafness and by humanity. The deafness hasn't changed. The other, it seems, has. Our Nikephoros, through constant proximity to power, has found it in his own mind."

Jehan shivered involuntarily. Alf, he saw, was pale and still, rebuking himself bitterly for what he had done.

Nikki's brows knit. With a shock Jehan realized that the child had read his thoughts. *If you want me to stop, I will. But you'll have to stop thinking so hard at me.*

"I—" Jehan struggled to speak normally. "I'll try."

Most people are worse than you, Nikki said comfortingly. And in a darker tone, *If Alf tries to go away and leave me, I'll follow him. I can do it. He'll never even know I'm there.*

"And I'll help you." Thea's eyes flashed upon Alf. This, it seemed, was an old argument. "You can't go away and leave him as he is now. What would the humans do to him? He needs guidance and teaching from someone who understands him.

Not from people who would call him witch and changeling and cast him out."

"He needs his kin," Alf said. "They both do. Wanderer that I am, without home or family, what kind of life can I give them?"

"You can stop wandering," Anna said. "You're an Akestas. You can take our money and build a house, and we can all live in it together."

"No." Alf was on his feet. "Not in Baudouin's domain. Not anywhere in this sun-haunted East. My pilgrimage is over. I want—I need—to go to my own people. It will be a long journey through lands you call barbarian; it will be hard, and it may be dangerous. How can I take either of you with me? You're Greek; your faith is different, and your language, and all your way of living. And when you come to Rhiyana—if you come to Rhiyana—you'll find yourself among people twice alien. Don't you think you'll be happier in Nicaea with your kin, among properly civilized people?"

"Civilized!" Anna snorted. "I've had enough of civilization. I want to see new places. Different places."

"What would your mother say if she could hear you now?"

"She'd be coming with us," Anna said.

Besides, Nikki said, *you promised. You swore you'd always take care of us.*

Alf's breath hissed through his teeth. "You call it taking care of you? Dragging you off into the savage West, corrupting your pure souls with the heresies of Rome, turning you into rank barbarians?"

"You're clean," said Anna. "You speak Greek. I can learn to put up with the rest of it."

"Wait till you see the inside of a Frankish castle," Alf warned her. "And sleep in a Frankish bed. And contend with Frankish vermin."

I'll think them away, Nikki said serenely.

Thea laughed. "Acknowledge yourself conquered, little Brother! You've won yourself a family and a fortune; and neither of those, once gained, is at all easy to lose."

Alf tried to glare at them all. But none of them was deceived. Anna seized Nikki's hands and whirled him in a mad dance, singing at the top of her lungs.

He sighed deeply. "God will judge me for this," he said. A smile crept into the corner of his mouth. "Or else He already has."

Jehan grinned at him. "To be sure, He has! Who knows what He'll do with you next?" His grin faded; he ran the ends of his cincture through his fingers, suddenly tense. "Have you given any thought to how you'll travel back to Rhiyana?"

"On foot, I suppose, as I came," Alf said. "With a mule for the children."

"And the wealth of House Akestas in your wallet?" Jehan leaned toward him. "Tomorrow morning a ship sails for Saint Mark with news of the victory. I'm to be on it as my lord Cardinal's messenger to the Pope. Will you come with me?"

"On a *ship?*" Anna cried in rapture.

Alf opened his mouth. Jehan broke in quickly. "I've seen the ship. It's splendid, its accommodations are princely, and the Doge has offered passage to all of you for a fraction of the usual price. You'd pay more for a good sumpter mule—provided you could find one, with the City as it is. And," he added, having kept the most telling blow until the last, "Thea won't be up to long walking for some while yet. Why linger here under Baudouin's less than friendly eye, or tax her with too much traveling too soon? You can take your ease on shipboard, she can mend at her own pace—"

And we can have adventures! Nikki tugged peremptorily at Alf's robe. *Say you'll do it.* We *all want to.*

"We're minded to go on our own, whether you will or no," said Thea. "Well? Are you coming?"

Alf raised his hands in surrender. "Have I any choice?"

"None at all," Jehan said laughing, half in amusement and half in sheer, youthful delight.

As often before, Alf stood in Master Dionysios' study and faced the Master's grim unwelcoming stare. His own was as fearless as it had ever been, with even a touch of a smile. "You asked for me?" he asked.

"Yes." There was a box on the table beside Dionysios' hand, small, plain, of red-brown wood carved on the lid with an intricate curving design. As he spoke, his finger traced the lines of it. "Sit down."

Alf obeyed.

Dionysios' finger continued along its path. His brows were knit; his lips were thin and set. After a time he said, "You're abandoning us."

"Tomorrow, sir. It's much sooner than I'd thought or hoped. But—"

"But you let that outsize heretic talk you into it. He's not thinking of you, boy. He's thinking entirely of his own pleasure."

"Doesn't everyone?"

Dionysios' eyes flashed up. "Sometimes I'm moved to curse the fate that made you a barbarian. Then I remember the time before you inflicted yourself on me. I had peace of mind then."

"You'll have it again when I'm gone."

"No," said Dionysios. His gaze held Alf's and hardened. "If I asked you to tell me the truth, would you?"

Alf nodded slowly, but without hesitation.

"Don't," the Master said. "I had you while I had you. It cost me more than I'll ever be able to recover."

"Some of it I'll give you back. If you wish."

"I don't wish!" snapped Dionysios. "I hired you to work in my hospital. My own well-being wasn't part of the bargain. I don't want to know what you did, or what you are, or what that needle-tongued witch of yours was or is or did." Abruptly he thrust the box forward. "This is yours. Take it."

Alf drew it toward him. It was heavy for its size. He opened it and drew a sharp breath. It was full of gold. "Master! I can't—"

"Stop your nonsense. Every coin is yours. Your due and legal salary, with additions for work done above the normal requirements."

With a fingertip Alf touched a coin. The wealth of the

Akestas he kept in trust for the children. But this was his own. He had earned it.

It was only yellow metal. His payment was the passing of pain. Slowly he lowered the lid and fastened it. "I . . . thank you," he said.

"Why? You worked for it." Dionysios opened an account book and reached for a pen. "Take it and go. Don't bother to come back and say good-bye. You'll get enough of weeping and wailing from Thomas and the rest of them. I won't be troubled with it. Now go!"

Alf paused. He glared. Mutely Alf bowed and left him.

For a long while after, he sat unmoving, staring unseeingly at the half-written page.

The ship's name was *Falcon*; and she was as swift as her name, her hull painted the steel-blue of the peregrine her namesake, her prow adorned with a stooping falcon. Alf, remembering the bird which had pointed his way from Saint Ruan's to Jerusalem, felt his heart uplifted by the omen.

The others had embarked already, Thea borne in a chair like a great lady, angry though it made her to be so helpless. He met her glare with a smile that spread to Anna. She looked splendid in a gown that had come to her as a parting gift from the Doge: "For a brave and noble lady," the messenger had said who brought it, "so that she need not face the savage West as she faced the wicked Doge."

She stood very straight under the weight of the honor and of the silk; but her eyes were shining and her body trembling with excitement. "Won't you hurry?" she called to Alf. "It's almost time!"

As he set his foot upon the gangway, a sudden tumult brought him about. A troop of horsemen thundered to a halt at the end of the pier, one already afoot and running. Alf left the gangway and advanced to meet him.

Henry of Flanders came panting to a stop. Somehow, even in his haste, he managed to preserve his dignity. "Master Alfred. God be thanked! I prayed I wouldn't be too late."

"For what, my lord?" Alf asked, although he knew.

"To say good-bye." Henry's eyes were bright with more than exertion. "I wish that you could have stayed."

"To be your prophet?"

Henry shook his head impatiently. "We've gained ourselves an empire," he said, "but we won't find it easy to hold. We need strong men who also have their share of wisdom—men who can speak to the Greeks as to their own countrymen, but who can speak as well for us of the West. There all too few of them. And two are leaving on this ship."

Alf glanced back at Jehan, who stood motionless on the deck, listening. "My lord, we would stay if we could. And yet—"

"And yet." Henry smiled a hard-won smile. "I should know better than to ask for what I can't have. But it's more than your talents I'll be missing, Master Alfred. Will you say good-bye to me as a friend?"

"Gladly," Alf said, coming to his embrace.

He stepped back quickly. "Farewell, my friend, and a fair voyage."

The captain bellowed from the bridge, cursing the laggard. Alf retreated to the gangway. There for an instant he paused. "Farewell, my lord Henry," he said. He smiled his sudden smile. "It will be something to brag of in years to come, that I had the name and the love of a friend from the Emperor of the East."

"But," Henry said, "I'm not—"

"Yet," Alf said in the instant before he turned and sprang lightly into the ship.

They stood at the rail, all of them, even Thea defiantly erect. Alf took his place beside her; Anna's hand slipped into his right and Nikki's into his left, gripping hard. Smoothly *Falcon* slid from her berth and came about, her bright sails swelling with the westward wind.

Slowly, then more swiftly, Henry's figure dwindled behind them, and beyond and about him all the ruined splendors of Byzantium.

"There never was a greater city," Alf said, "nor ever one so beautiful."

"Even in her fall." Jehan shook himself and turned his face toward *Falcon*'s prow. "Well, we're done with her. God help her and everyone in her. I'm for the West and home, and glad I'll be to get there." He left the rail, staggering a little as he found his sea legs, holding out his hands to the children. "Who'll go exploring with me?"

Alf watched them go, smiling slightly as Nikki, running, snatched at his cat. The beast eluded his hands and dove beneath a coil of rope. He wavered, torn, and sprang forward with sudden decision in pursuit of his sister and his friend. Alf's smile widened almost into laughter.

Thea's arms slipped about his waist. "Well, little Brother? Has it been worth it?"

"Every moment of it."

"Even the pain?"

"Even that," he said. "Out of it, and in spite of it, I've gained more joy than I ever dreamed of: wealth and kin and friends, and," he added after a pause, "a lover."

"Last in your reckoning, I see. But I hope not least."

"No. Far from the least." He took her face in his hands. "Will you marry me, Thea?"

She pondered that with every appearance of care. "Maybe," she answered him at last. "Someday. If I'm properly persuaded. Meanwhile everyone is out and about, and we have a cabin fit for a prince, that's cost us no more than an earl's ransom. And in it . . ." Her gaze met his, bright and wicked.

He stared back, all innocence. "Yes, my lady?"

She tossed her bronze-gold braids and laughed. "Yes indeed, my lord!"

He swept her up and kissed her soundly, and bore her away.

Author's Note

The world of *The Golden Horn* is not precisely the world we know. Yet in that world as in this one, between spring and spring, 1203–1204, a Western army advanced upon and eventually conquered the city of Constantinople. Our historians have named this conflict, with its confusion of aims and motives and its devastating outcome, the Fourth Crusade.

I have taken few liberties with the framework of my history or with its major characters. Enrico Dandolo, Doge of Venice, may in fact have been a mere eighty years old at the time of the Crusade. He was certainly blind, and he was almost certainly the motivating force behind the diversion of the Crusade from Egypt and the Holy Land to Byzantium. The rivalry between Count Baudouin (Baldwin) of Flanders and Marquis Boniface of Montferrat simmered throughout the campaign, culminating some weeks after Easter, 1204, with the election of Baudouin as Latin Emperor of Byzantium. He was crowned in Hagia Sophia in May of that year. Boniface, for his part, married the great beauty, Margaret of Hungary, widow of the mad Emperor Isaac; and amid much bitter quarreling with Baudouin, established the vassal kingdom of Thessalonica. Though considerably older than Baudouin, he outlived his rival by two years.

The climactic battles of *The Golden Horn* are based solidly on fact. Henry of Flanders did indeed take the banner of the empire and the icon of the City from the Emperor Mourtzouphlos in a skirmish. It was not he, however, who pierced the walls of the City in the final battle and threw open the gates, but Peter of Amiens, among whose party was an impoverished Picard knight, Robert de Clari—the author in later days of an account of the Crusade and of his own part in it. Robert's brother, the warrior-priest Aleaumes, was first to climb through the gap in the wall, despite Robert's attempt to drag him back by the foot.

Once the Latin army had entered the City, the Greeks despaired, although the Emperor strode all but alone through the streets, striving to rouse them to battle. With his flight and the panic of his people, the enemy found themselves victorious. There followed an orgy of destruction: three days of unrestrained pillage and rapine. Constantinople was stripped bare. Her unparalleled store of sacred relics was scattered throughout the West; her works of art, both pagan and Christian, shattered or stolen (the Greek historian and eyewitness, Nicetas Choniates, bewails the wanton destruction of, for example, the Helen of Phidias; the four great bronze horses of San Marco in Venice stood once in the Hippodrome in Constantinople); her vast riches scattered among the Latins, never to be restored.

The Latin Empire of the East endured a mere sixty years. The Emperor Baudouin, captured in battle against rebel Greeks and their Bulgar allies at Adrianople in April, 1205—a year only since his taking of the City—died a prisoner. Enrico Dandolo, who came to the rescue of Baudouin's shattered army, died a month after, to be buried in Hagia Sophia. It was his great pride and his Republic's boast that he had ruled a quarter and a half of the Roman Empire; such is the inscription upon his portrait in the Doges' Palace in Venice. Certainly, whatever evil he wrought against the Greeks, he insured the hegemony of his city in the East for many years thereafter.

Henry of Flanders succeeded his brother as Emperor; he was, asserts the historian Donald E. Queller, "by far the ablest of the Latin Emperors, moderate, humane, and conciliatory." He died in 1216, still, at forty, a relatively young man, accepted not only by his own people but by the Greeks whom he had helped to conquer.

His successors could not equal his ability. At last, in 1261, Michael Palaeologus of Nicaea restored Greek dominion in Constantinople. He found the City in ruins and stripped of all its treasures. The empire he established would endure for two centuries until its final fall, in 1453, to the Ottoman Turks. But the greatest glory had long since departed. Byzantium would never again be the great power she had been before the coming of the Latin fleet to the shores of the Golden Horn.

My novel owes it background to many sources. I am particularly indebted, however, to the firsthand accounts of Geoffroi de Villehardouin and Robert de Clari; to Sigfús Blöndal's classic text, *The Varangians of Byzantium*, revised and translated by B. Z. Benedikz; and to that excellent, scholarly, vivid and detailed historical study, Donald E. Queller's *The Fourth Crusade: The Conquest of Constantinople, 1201–1204*.